ANGEL
BLOOD

JOHN SINGLETON

PUFFIN

PUFFIN BOOKS

Published by the Penguin Group
Penguin Books Ltd, 80 Strand, London WC2R ORL, England
Penguin Group (USA) Inc., 375 Hudson Street, New York, New York 10014, USA
Penguin Group (Canada), 90 Eglinton Avenue East, Suite 700, Toronto, Ontario, Canada M4P 2Y3
(a division of Pearson Penguin Canada Inc.)
Penguin Ireland, 25 St Stephen's Green, Dublin 2, Ireland (a division of Penguin Books Ltd)
Penguin Group (Australia), 250 Camberwell Road, Camberwell, Victoria 3124, Australia
(a division of Pearson Australia Group Pty Ltd)
Penguin Books India Pvt Ltd, 11 Community Centre, Panchsheel Park, New Delhi – 110 017, India
Penguin Group (NZ), 67 Apollo Drive, Mairangi Bay, Auckland 1310, New Zealand
(a division of Pearson New Zealand Ltd)
Penguin Books (South Africa) (Pty) Ltd, 24 Sturdee Avenue, Rosebank,
Johannesburg 2196, South Africa

Penguin Books Ltd, Registered Offices: 80 Strand, London WC2R ORL, England

penguin.com

First published 2006
Published in this edition 2007
1

Copyright © John Singleton, 2006
All rights reserved

The moral right of the author has been asserted

Set in Sabon
Typeset by Palimpsest Book Production Limited, Grangemouth, Stirlingshire
Made and printed in England by Clays Ltd, St Ives plc

British Library Cataloguing in Publication Data
A CIP catalogue record for this book is available from the British Library

ISBN: 978-0-141-32019-9

For Colette with love

Contents

CHAPTER 1

Hypo for Lights Out

1

Lights Out is squealing and we're all watching and trembling.

Tin Lid, the nurse, is pulling at her. She's dragging something out of her arms.

'Let go, you stupid girl,' she is saying.

Lights Out won't. She is clinging on and screaming: 'Pippi. Pippi. No. No.'

I've never heard Lights Out scream before. None of us have. Not even Chicken Angel.

But Tin Lid is too strong.

By now she has almost dragged Lights Out off the bed. Lights Out clings and clings and screams and screams.

Another nurse comes rushing in.

The two of them tear Pippi away and Tin Lid throws the little baby doll on the floor.

And Lights Out is screaming and screaming and her thin white arms are stretching out for Pippi and the two

1

nurses are pulling her back and holding her down and forcing her face into the pillow.

Then Security arrive – two Hyena Men.
They take over.
Tin Lid rushes out.
I can still hear Lights Out screaming into the pillow.
We are all shaking.
It's like in *The Natural World*. On TV. When the leopard came.
Last time we watched he got one of the little monkeys.
And the whole colony fitted, racing and jabbering and squealing all over.
No one told Lights Out about the baby monkey, limp and blooded out, little head bouncing in the dust.

I look across at Chicken Angel. She's stuffing her mouth with the sheet. She's shaking and staring at Lights Out.
Suddenly the door swings open and Tin Lid runs back in.
She has a hypo.
She's going to give Lights Out trank. She'll give her double dozie. I know it. I know it. They don't like fuss and mess in the Bin. None of the nurses do.
Then Chicken Angel starts screaming. She's seen the hypo too. She knows how much it hurts her friend Lolo.
Why? Why are they taking Pippi?

'No. No,' wails Chicken Angel.
Tin Lid shakes the hypo at her.

Chicken Angel stops her noise but her mouth is still calling out.

For Lolo.

Cough Cough sits hunched. He's wheezing, wheezing hard. Not because of Lights Out but because climbing on to bed is hard for him. He hasn't got the lung for it.

Tin Lid is leaning over Lights Out now. The Hyena Men are holding her down.

Lights Out has started to fit.

Lights Out is jumping and jumping like something is shaking her. The leopard has got Lights Out too.

They pull her tracksuit down, crush her still and jab in the needle.

Chicken Angel screams.

Lights Out squeals and squeals.

Suddenly Lights Out stops.

Her legs shudder for a bit and then go still.

We all wait, swallowing the silence and shivering.

'Lolo. Lolo. Poor Pippi,' sobs Chicken Angel.

Tin Lid waves the hypo at her again but this time it doesn't stop Chicken Angel.

As she leaves Tin Lid picks up Lolo's baby and puts it in a sterilized bag.

She stares at Chicken Angel. Chicken Angel stares back. Chicken Angel is too upset to be scared.

'It's full of germs,' says Tin Lid. 'It's not safe. You know what Doctor Dearly says. Hygiene. Hygiene. Hygiene.'

She leaves.

She's going to take it to the incinerator. When Chicken

3

Angel's hair falls out that's where she has to put the bits.

Tin Lid is going to INCINERATE Pippi.

2

For the rest of the afternoon Cough Cough and I stay on beds. With Tin Lid, bed is where we have to go whenever there's trouble. First sign of her and we run and crouch there like those skinny monkeys.

When it's not her duty we huddle on the same bed. When one of us is cold or sick or has a big squeal we huddle. We wrap arms round and round like in cosy cosy. We've always done it, huddle together. We breathe to each other and our hearts beat together. A huddle is one big heart. Tin Lid doesn't like us huddling. That's why she makes us sit on our own. On our own is cold. Huddling is like having fur all over you, it makes you warm inside and out.

Sometimes we do Jesus Hands like Mrs Murdoe told us. We all put our hands together and make the roof of the Jesus House. This protects us from leopards and trank sometimes. We don't do Jesus Hands so often now because of Cough Cough. He thinks the Jesus House is daftie. But I think it's a bit like huddling, only it makes you warm in your heart.

After a bit Chicken Angel gets up and kneels beside Lolo and holds her hand and strokes her hair and quietly sings to her.

Lolo will be coma-ed till tomorrow now. Moosed out.

Moose is a stuffed head hanging on the wall in the

day-room above the fireplace. He never moves, that's why when we're tranked we say we are moosed because like him we never move after hard shot. Trank is the same as hard shot.

On the fireplace someone has carved words in the stone. They say BIN LINNIE LODGE and just underneath there's a shield with some more words. Mrs Murdoe said it was a shield and the words were Latin but she didn't know what they said but it means the Lodge is very old. Cough Cough didn't know what it said either, which is strange because he knows everything round here. That's because he reads a lot in the library.

The library has wooden panelling like in the dormie here. And it covers the windows here too because the light's not good for us, especially me with my skin.

The nurses call this place the Bin and it's where we live. We have a day-room where we eat and do fizzio and drink from the waterhole. The nurses call it a water dispenser. When they're not around we call it the waterhole. That's OK because the nurses can't see the animals like we do.

The television is on one side of the fireplace and the nurse's office is on the other side right next to Moose. We can only watch *The Natural World*. Doctor Dearly says it's good for us. Which is OK because it's our favourite programme anyway. It's where the animals drink at waterholes and that's why we call the day-room dispenser the waterhole.

Opposite the fireplace there's a double door that leads to the dormie with our four beds and then there's the washes where we shower and pee and pitch. Sometimes we pitch in the bed and the nurses hate that so now we have to strip them ourselves and put the sheets in the soil tub. It's all the dozie they give us that makes us pitch. Peeing is OK. That's why we have the water dispenser. We're supposed to drink a lot so we pee out the dozie and the chemicals and the tox inside us otherwise we'd all be ill and maybe go takeaway.

We don't think the nurses are any good any more. They're not like Mrs Murdoe. She was our best nurse. She used to pull my sheets so smooth I could slide on them. Now I have to do the smoothing myself.

Mrs Murdoe never gave us dozie either. She told us stories instead – about giants and beans and pumpkins. And then we all went to sleep on our magic carpets. One day Mrs Murdoe said she was a big bad wolf but we didn't believe her. Then she turned us into little piggies and that was like being a pippi at first but then we got the wolf stuck in the chimney and we all laughed, Mrs Murdoe too. Cough Cough didn't. He said being a piggie was daftie, but he only said that because he couldn't grunt like Mrs Murdoe said because of his lungs.

She's gone now, Mrs Murdoe, and there are just the four of us left: Chicken Angel, Lights Out, Cough Cough and me. I'm X-Ray.

Some of the nurses, Tin Lid for example, call us 'spooks' but they're not supposed to. Doctor Dearly says they have to use the proper names. I'm G4. Chicken Angel is G2. Lights Out is G3 and Cough Cough is G1. They're our new numbers. I've changed from 19 to 4. It's because we are only four and it makes it easier for

the nurses to remember who we are if w̶
That's what Doctor Dearly says anyway.

Why are we G this and G that?

When we were littles G was for Giraffe but Mrs Murdoe said it didn't stand for that any more. It stood for Gemini, which means twins. Which makes sense because Cough Cough and I share things – I help him and he helps me. And Lights Out and Chicken Angel are close and Chicken Angel does Lolo's hair just like her own. Mirror images of each other Mrs Murdoe used to say. Of course, we only have mirrors in the washes because of Lights Out not having eyes.

I don't know when we got our real names, X-Ray and stuff. I think it was when Mrs Murdoe was here because she taught us our words and things, short words mostly. We don't use our real names with the nurses, especially Tin Lid. We keep them for ourselves. It's our secret. Only Mrs Murdoe really knew who we were. She never called us 'spooks' like Tin Lid does. We are 'spooks' to her and always will be says Tin Lid.

We don't like Tin Lid.

She and Doctor Dearly don't like germs.

So they say.

They make you ill they say. Germs are very dangerous when your immune systems are JEOPARDIZED.

Jeopardized!!

I asked Cough Cough what Doctor Dearly meant by that.

Cough Cough said it meant our bodies weren't strong enough to fight germs.

We're OK I said to him. None of us have been ill for ages.

Cough Cough smiled. But we will. One day germs will pounce. Catch us he said. Pull us down. Remember what happened to the others. They got the lumpies and they went takeaway.

But that wasn't germs. That was . . . I stopped. I'd no idea why the others all went takeaway. If it wasn't germs, what was it?

What did kill them? I asked CC. But he said nothing.

He can be such a MISERY can Cough Cough.

Mrs Murdoe taught us misery. 'You're a wee misery,' she used to say.

Well, I think it was germs I said. I suppose we'll all be leopardized sooner or later.

I think Tin Lid and Doctor D are trying to scare us, put the squeal on us. Yesterday at first tuck-in I found egg on my fork. Old egg, all crusty. We're supposed to have forks and knives sealed in germ-free packs. And that old egg means no one is doing the STERILIZING. And that means germs are getting in. And that means Doctor D is lying – about not liking germs.

3

Cough Cough teaches me and Chicken Angel big words. He gets them from the library. He's the only one allowed there. It's because he's a GENIUS and because he has to sit all the time because of his pulmonaries. They take him there because then he's out of the way and no trouble. They know he can't go far. Three or four steps and he's wheezing.

Before they took away the pencils that was one of the first words he made me write down. PULMONARY. It's to do with your lungs. Cough Cough has very low-grade lungs and reading's good for them because he doesn't have to breathe much with books. While he reads we do fizzio.

Just to show how clever Cough Cough gets, here's some of the words he's taught us: RETINAL, OCCLUSION, LONDON. And the very latest is DEGRADATION. Things are getting degraded round here he says. But that's just an example. He doesn't really mean it. Next he's going to teach me SUBCUTANEOUS and INCONTI-NENCE. These are the biggest words so far.

Chicken Angel says it's daftie learning big words. Why do we need such big words? she says. Because they use them, Tin Lid and Doctor Dearly, and we need to know what they are saying says Cough Cough. Why? says Chicken A. If we are IGNORANT says Cough Cough, they will MANIPULATE us. It will be like people whispering about you behind your back. Cough Cough means Chicken Angel and how she and Lights Out are always having PRIVATE CONVERSATIONS and EXCLUDING everybody else.

Everybody else is just me and him.

The cameras are off so I lean across and whisper to Cough Cough.

'Why did they take Pippi?' I ask him. 'It's not because of germs, is it?'

After all, they could have sterilized baby Pippi and given her back to Lights Out.

Cough Cough half opens his eyes and peers at me like I was nearly too small to see.

'No,' he says. 'Not germs.'

'Then why?'

'Because they want to kill baby Lolo.'

Lolo is our other name for Lights Out. She's the only one with two names.

I stare at Cough Cough. He can't be serious.

'But Lolo is growing properly, apart from her eyes that is. She's not a baby.'

Cough Cough doesn't mean arm and leg growing. He means inside growing, right inside.

'You mean in her pulmonaries?' I say.

He frowns, leans back, looks at me and shakes his head like I'm a bulb that needs fixing.

'In her head she's still a baby,' he says.

I'm staring at him. He's very clever but is he going mad?

'Pippi is Lolo. Lolo is Pippi,' he says. He tells me about Siamese twins and sometimes doctors have to let one die so the other can live.

I begin to think.

At tuck-in Lolo and Pippi always sit together and Lolo feeds Pippi and Pippi feeds Lolo. Even Chicken Angel feeds Pippi. In bed Lolo hugs Pippi and Pippi hugs Lolo. Chicken Angel, Lolo and Pippi do everything together.

Cough Cough could be right.

'If you don't kill the baby, the baby kills you,' says Cough Cough. 'You can't hang on to cosy cosy all your life, huddling and noo nooing forever,' he says.

'But huddling's important,' I say. 'Mrs Murdoe said so. You used to like huddling.'

'Huddling's for noo noos,' said Cough Cough. 'We're not baby monkeys any more!'

Is he right, I wonder?

I shake my head. All this stuff about killing and baby monkeys is just leopard talk.

I look over to Chicken Angel. She's still kneeling next to Lolo's bed and is morsing her arm, tapping her finger-tips gently up and down. I can't see what's she saying.

Morsing is how Lolo talks. She taps out letters with her fingers on your hand or on your face. Sometimes she draws pictures on my back when she massages me with the skin spray. She has very gently hands.

Lights Out can talk with her mouth like us if she wants but Chicken Angel says she's just got used to finger talking. I think she just likes morsing because it keeps her in touch. It's like cosy cosy for her. Mrs Murdoe used to say that hugging and stroking and spooning, cosy cosy as she called it, were very important for us. When we were younger Mrs Murdoe used to let us cosy cosy a lot. Cough Cough said it was good for our EMOTIONAL BALANCE. Without cosy cosy said Mrs Murdoe, we would die. And look at us now. We're still alive, so she must be right. I think it's because cosy cosy kills germs. I don't say this to Cough Cough because he would prob-ably laugh at me.

Chicken Angel's wasting her time. Lights Out will be light out till first tuck-in tomorrow.

'Chicken Angel's going lumpy.'

It's Cough Cough. His voice all breath. It's coming out of his throat not from his mouth. That's why he's Cough Cough. Because he's got these depressed pulmonaries, when he was little the fizzio nurse used to make him cough and cough and blow up balloons.

Since Doctor Dearly came we don't have a fizzio nurse to help make Cough Cough bigger.

Mrs Murdoe said he'd always be little. I suppose it's because he doesn't breathe a lot. You see, according to CC you need OXYGEN to grow. I told this to Chicken Angel. Oxygen gets in your blood and blows you up so you get bigger and bigger like CC's balloons. If they took all the blood out of you you'd go thin, you'd DEFLATE like a wrinkly balloon. Huh said Chicken A, you're forgetting about bones. Bones hold us up. Without bones we'd just be blobs.

Cough Cough takes a dozie from his squirter.

'Did you hear me, X-Ray?' he says.

I nod.

I'm ignoring him. I don't want to think about lumpies. Especially Chicken A going lumpy like I said.

Mrs Murdoe warned us about lumpies. There used to be more of us here in the Bin and some of them got lumpy and went takeaway. That's why there are only four beds left and why there's a big space in the dormie. Every time someone got lumpied they took the bed away with the lumpy in it.

Nobody's gone lumpy for a long time now. I think it's because of the dozies they give us. I don't mean the trank. As CC says, that's not treatment, it's torture. The nurses jab us to stop us jumping about like monkeys and fitting but we don't fit much now. So why do they still do it to us? They could just as easily give us some tabs to make us sleep. Cough Cough says they're always testing some new dozie on us, CHEMICALIZING us. This might be true because sometimes when we are tranked and coma-ed they take us away. Doctor Dearly says we go to a special unit to recover, so we are under constant SUPERVISION and it's for our own good. After all he says, with just the four of us left they'd have to be extra VIGILANT.

Well, if the testing stops us getting lumpies, OK. Even trank's better than having lumpies. It's just that the hypo squeals us all.

And Tin Lid likes doing it. You can tell. It's because she hates us says Cough Cough. When we get hypo from her it's double dozie really because we're getting hate injected as well as trank.

Why does Tin Lid hate us? I asked Cough Cough once. Because we don't fit he said. I said we're always fitting. Don't be daftie he said. We don't fit in. We don't fit together. We spoil the order of things. Some people don't like that. Tin Lid doesn't. But we're full of order I say – the same every day – tuck-in then tidy time then fizzio then tests then puzzles then tuck-in again then TV then napping then tuck-in then washes then dozie then bed. That's timetable order says CC. I mean jigsaw order where things fit together neat and complete. We're the wrong shapes – too little, too thin, too coughy, too blind – we're the last pieces and we stop the picture being perfect.

'What picture?' I ask.

Cough Cough raises his eyes. Like I've suddenly knocked all his pieces on the floor. He thinks it's one of my daftie questions. These are the ones he says have no answers to them. I think there is an answer to my picture question but he doesn't know it. If I ever get up to the library I'll find a book with the answer in it. And then I'll tell Cough Cough and he'll see I'm not such a daftie after all.

I think about my Tin Lid question again. She's just evil I say. CC shrugs. She's possibly got PSYCHOTIC TENDENCIES he says. I'm not going to ask CC what he means by that. It'll make me look double daftie.

So I frown because frowning helps you to think hard. That much I've learnt from CC.

It's certainly working now because I suddenly think, yes, I've not seen any TENDENCIES on Tin Lid. None at all. So they must be hidden like Chicken Angel's wings. And that means Tin Lid's a wrong shape as well. And that means she's no one to talk.

CHAPTER 2

The Bin – Puke and Dozie

1

Cough Cough calls me X-Ray because of my skin. I have to be careful. They tested me and said I was photo-sensitive. That means I'll blackout like a film if I get exposed to too much sun. I have to wear this special tracksuit with a hood and gloves just in case daylight ever gets in here. It never does because of the panelling.

The others wear trackies too but mine's special – especially soft because I split easily and blood out and it gets on the sheets and Tin Lid doesn't like that.

Chicken Angel says she can see through my skin. She says when she screws up her eyes and stares at me in the shower she can see bone shadows in my chest. My ribs look like spook fish she says, suspended inside me.

She can talk.

She's got these little stubby fingers growing out of her shoulders at the back like baby wings. She can wiggle them a bit. They feel spongy and slippery when they get wet.

Now she's got these two little things growing on her chest. That's what Cough Cough thinks are lumpies.

I'm not sure.

I've seen her in the shower and they don't look like lumpies to me.

When you get lumpies it's takeaway all right. Takeaway overnight almost. Well, it's not overnight with Chicken A. She's had these chest things for ages. So they can't be real lumpies like Cough Cough says.

I look across at Chicken Angel.

She's got golden hair and gently skin. If she went takeaway I don't know what I'd do.

Next time we have showers I'll check on Chicken Angel again.

She always smells the strangest even after soaping and showers.

Puke and dozie.

I suppose it's her tabs. I quite like it now.

Cough Cough says I smell of CHEMICALS too.

Don't we all.

But I think CC smells different now. It's not just his breath. It's all over. I think it's pee and pitch. They're making him wear pads on his bottom now. He can't get to the washes very quickly so he has to wear them.

Chicken Angel has gone back to her bed. She is lying under a blanket. I know she's crying.

Lights Out hasn't moved since the trank.

'Listen, X-Ray.' It's Cough Cough again. 'That's real hard trank they've given Lights Out. Double dozie.' He coughs. Takes his squirter from under the pillow. 'Why are they upping the dozie all the time? Why haven't they fixed the heating?'

I frown.

It's true about the heating. That's why we've spent most of today in bed, to keep warm. 'Doctor Dearly says they're working on it,' I say.

Cough Cough squirts his lips and sounds like a hissing cobra, like the one on *The Natural World*.

'Can't be bothered more like,' he says. He turns to me. 'Listen, X-Ray. Ever since Doctor D came things have changed. Haven't they?'

I shrug.

Maybe, I think.

Cough Cough is lying back on his pillow, his eyes closed.

That's just like CC. He puts these bad ideas in your head then leaves you on your own with them. Walks out on you. Just when you could do with a friend.

Chicken Angel is still crying.

She's been crying a lot recently but that's not Doctor Dearly's fault. He took away the pencils because pencils are unnecessary and can be HAZARDOUS with their sharp points. We have to have a safe ENVIRONMENT he says. It's not like we are ordinary he says. We have to be protected.

It's the same with the tests. Since Doctor Dearly came we have tests twice a week and exams every morning after first tuck-in. It's for our own good says Doctor Dearly. 'We need to MONITOR your condition regularly so any DEFICIENCY can be dealt with immediately.'

It is a change but it's a change for our own good. That's what Doctor Dearly says: 'Everything is for your own good.'

2

Chicken Angel doesn't like the tests because Doctor Dearly is always twiddling with her wings. She says he doesn't like her and that's why he's taken away her pencils. You see Chicken Angel keeps a story of what happens, writes it in a book that Cough Cough found for her in the library. Cough Cough says she's still got a pencil left, one they didn't find. I hope she keeps it secret because if they find it she'll get trank double dozie.

I sometimes ask Chicken Angel if I can read her story. She reads it to Lights Out so why can't I read it. She always says no, it's a secret. Cough Cough tells her she shouldn't have secrets, none of us should. It's OK to have secrets from Tin Lid and Doctor Dearly he says, that's different. But secrets between us four is not right.

Yes, I think. Says you, Cough Cough.

I know he's got a secret store-away, under a floorboard, like me. Chicken Angel doesn't know this or she'd give Cough Cough some mouth mouth if she found out. I won't tell her because CC's my friend.

We all have secrets says Chicken Angel, inside our heads. We have secrets secret from ourselves she says. Tell me one of your head secrets says Cough Cough. It wouldn't be a secret then would it says Chicken Angel.

I think Cough Cough has more secrets than any of us. He watches all the time and sees things we don't and he reads strange things up in the library. Books are full of secrets. You only have to open them up. Books are the biggest store-aways you can have anywhere he says.

Then he says I've got a very big secret. It's bigger than anybody else's. And when I'm ready I'm going to tell you. He looks very serious. I don't know whether he's just saying this because Chicken Angel's keeping her story to herself and he's jealous and annoyed or because he really means it. Sometimes you can't tell with Cough Cough.

Has he really got a big secret?

Of course we all hide things.

I think that's why they've started doing searches. I've got a pee bottle. I keep it under the floorboard beneath my bed. The cleaner knows it's there but she never says. She never says because she doesn't like Doctor Dearly. Once she called him a cold fish. When you say 'fish' to Lolo she turns into one, gliding and finning along the floor and mouthing for air. But then she is a daftie is Lolo. She doesn't do floor swimming any more though. I think it hurts her now.

Anyway a mouse ate through the end of my pee bottle so it's no use to anybody.

3

'You don't agree then?' says Cough Cough, wide awake now. It's like he's been listening to me thinking. 'I tell you, X-Ray, since Doctor D came things have gone down-hill.'

19

I shake my head. 'That can't be true,' I say. 'They still keep testing us. We still have our tabs. You've got your squirter. Tuck-in's just as good as before. Routines are the same.'

'So what happened to the fizzio nurse?' he says. 'Soon as Doctor D came she went takeaway. Now they're searching us all the time. Tranking us every five minutes. They've taken away our pencils. I can't draw any more. It's too dangerous Dearly says.'

Cough Cough snorts. He puts on his Doctor D voice.

'After EVALUATING your PROCEDURES we have decided to INSTIGATE a RISK-REDUCTION programme. Sharp INSTRUMENTS such as pencils are to be CONFISCATED.'

Cough Cough's getting worked up and has to take a dozie from his squirter. 'He's mad,' he says. 'Next they'll close the TV, you watch. *The Natural World* will be no more. No more jungles and oceans and deserts and mountains and rivers, no more lions and elephants and eagles and bears and monkeys and parrots.'

I'm stunned.

Cough Cough has never talked like this. We've always been looked after. That's what the nurses are for. Doctor D says that. Why should they take *The Natural World* from us?

I lie back.

Everything they do is for our own good I say to myself. Everything they do is for our own good.

I can hear Cough Cough. 'And how good is a hypo, X-Ray? Tell me that?' he says, coughing.

*

I think about Lights Out. Trank knocks you up. It takes days of fizzio to get back to normal again. They've taken her baby. Pippi's not dangerous. Maybe they want to break her heart, send her takeaway. Maybe Cough Cough's right.

Maybe not.

He always sees the bad side. Miserable, like Moose he is.

Poor Lolo.

She's the real spookie here. Even though she has no eyes she can still see. That's what Cough Cough says: she's light-alert. She's retinal all over. That's what Doctor Dearly says. She's retinal. Which is why she doesn't bump into objects. And she knows when things are moving about and when people are coming or just standing nearby. It's her skin does it says Cough Cough. It listens to the air. Cough Cough told me how it works. When we move, when we breathe, we all make invisible ripples in the air he says. Even our heat moves the air. Lights Out can read the ripples of our breathing, read our heat. According to Cough Cough she can even hear the singing of a midgie's beating wing. All with her skin. Real spookie.

I can't hear anything through my skin. I suppose it's because I haven't got the right sort. Mrs Murdoe said we all have more than one skin. We have about seven, one on top of another like seven vests. Except me. I've only got two skins. Doctor Dearly told me that. My lips are the worst. They're always bleeding.

Sometimes Lights Out feels all over our faces with her fingers. I hate her so close to my mouth, feeling your

21

eyes and nose and lips and hair. It's like something crawling on you. I used to think that she'd cut me open with her nails and all my blood would come out till there was none left and I was white and flat and wrinkled like a wet vest dropped on the floor.

I like her doing the gently on my back though. That's different. Mrs Murdoe taught her to do that, gently my skin. You've got to learn to help each other she used to say.

Cough Cough says we have to pull together. Pull what I say?

When Doctor Dearly came Mrs Murdoe went away. Went takeaway.

CHAPTER 3

X-Ray Tranked

1

For last tuck-in only Chicken Angel and I sit down in the day-room. Cough Cough is too tired he says, to eat.

Chicken Angel's eyes are red with weeping.

'Why did they take Pippi?' she asks. 'It's cruel. It was her baby.'

I nod and finish chewing before answering. Chicken Angel doesn't think I know why because she doesn't give me time to answer but starts on about the heating.

'Pippi is Lolo's mirror,' I say. 'She sees herself in Pippi. Until the mirror breaks Lolo will always look like a Pippi doll, live like a Pippi, never grow up.'

'That's stupid. I suppose Cough Cough told you to say that. That's your trouble. You talk like a Cough Cough. He's your mirror. You just dummy for him.'

We don't say anything for a while.

I thought I was being clever about the mirror.

Just then one of the nurses comes in, gets the remote from the office and turns on the TV. It's *The Natural World*. We watch for a few minutes. It's the leopard again and the monkeys. Chicken Angel gets up and runs back into the dormie.

I watch the leopard crawl closer and closer to the monkeys. Any moment now he's going to charge and grab the little one.

I turn it off.

It's very strange how the hours go in circles. It's the same thing happening over and over again. Monkey, leopard. Monkey, leopard. Dances, dies. Dances, dies.

That's why our clock is round. Like us it goes in circles.

I go back to the dormie.

I take my trackies off and spray my skin. Sometimes the night nurse does my back, sometimes Chicken Angel. But Lights Out is the best. She has the softest fingers, gentle as the touch of a midgie's wing says Cough Cough.

Tonight I use the silky. This is a strip of silk I spray with cream and run over my back like it's a drying towel. I pull on my gloves and get into bed.

Cough Cough's the cleverest of us because he does all that reading. That's why he knows about the midgie's singing wings. Because he has these funny lungs and has to sit a lot he spends his time looking at things like I said. The longer you look the more you learn he says. He stares at walls for ages. I've tried it. Didn't learn much. My eyes just went funny and I kept falling asleep. And that's not allowed during the day hours. We can sleep in the nap time in the afternoon but not any time we like.

CC's measured everything in here. And drawn it. He's got lots of pictures of the table and the beds and the Coke machine and the waterhole and Moose, brilliant pictures. His best was a parrot. It was blue and red and green. Colours so deep and sharp they cut open your eyes. We had it on the wall but Tin Lid took it down. This is a day-room she said, not an art gallery.

And he's very calm and sensible is CC. Of course he has to be. If he ever got excited like Chicken Angel does sometimes he'd stop breathing. His pulmonaries couldn't take it.

Now I'm listening to those pulmonaries struggling. I listen to each wheeze and cough, wheeze and cough till my pulmonaries start to feel the pace and my chest starts rising in time with Cough Cough's.

I'm sure he's getting worse. Chicken Angel doesn't agree. She thinks he's OK, same as always. I say it's taking him longer to get dressed in the morning. I say he's using his squirter more and more. And he's having to wear pee pads. I say words are getting harder for him and he doesn't use big ones so much. Chicken Angel shakes her head. She thinks I'm imagining it. But she doesn't like hurt and fitting and things going wrong. She cried and cried about the little monkey.

If Mrs Murdoe was right about cosy cosy keeping us alive then maybe I should give some to Cough Cough. Make him good again. Put my arms around him. We could all help. Chicken Angel and Lights Out.

Cough Cough is wheezing quietly. He must be asleep.

From his wall, Moose watches over us – when he's awake. Moose is a friend of Lights Out. She babbles to him sometimes. It drives the nurses mad. That's why she gets more dozies than the rest of us. Sometimes she touches them and the nurses don't like that. And they don't like her morsing and they don't like her talking to strange animals. All this gets them mad and they shout at her and then she rolls into a huddle and they use trank to straighten her out. Lights Out is probably more chemicalized than the rest of us. When we were littles she was Mrs Murdoe's special because she was like a doll. Lights Out got a lot of cosy cosy because she was like a doll. But like Cough Cough says, she's not a baby nor a little any more and that means cosy cosy is now a MEDICATION in short supply.

Moose is a wise animal says Lights Out, like all animals. If you stand on your bed after light-out and look over the partition you can just see Moose in the dim blue of the nightlight. He is huge and dangerous and mad and it looks like he's just burst through the wall and got his head stuck. Of course, because he's burst the wall, all the night pours through the hole he's made and that's why Lights Out calls night Moose-time. Night-time in the Outside, Moose-time in the Bin. And we all agree with Lights Out because it's very hard for someone without eyes, and anyway if we didn't she'd fit out and do a Pippi on us.

Underneath Moose is the Big Chair. When we were littles two of us could sit in it. It's not so big now so it's one at a time. We take it in turns. When it's my turn I talk to Moose. Next time I'm going to tell him about Tin Lid, how she tranked Lolo. One day I'll say, I'm really going to mouth mouth her. But I know what Moose will say to that. He'll shake his head. Not a wise thing to do he'll say. One day something's going to happen in here he'll say. What? I'll say. But he won't tell. So I'll talk to Jack the Cat.

Jack's the best story we have. We often hear him whistling outside. That's his sign, his way of telling us he's there and waiting. Jack's as quick as rain, he can get in anywhere. But he's mischief. That's why we like him, because he upsets things and no one can catch him. Imagine Tin Lid trying to trank him with a hypo. He'd run her dizzy. And wouldn't that be a laughing. If Jack were one of us he'd be tranked all the time because he'd be so out of line. He'd be a full-time chemicalized cat. He's the one who ties Chicken Angel's hair in knots while she sleeps. He pees in our beds and we get the blame. He nudges Cough Cough's elbow at tuck-in times and makes him puke his cornflakes. Cough Cough says he's a squeal in the bum and it's only because we encourage him that he behaves like a daftie.

But none of us want Jack to go. He's our secret. He's invisible to Tin Lid and Doctor Dearly. Only we can see him and hear him. And they could never catch him. One day says Jack, you're all going to be free. When Chicken Angel told us what Jack said about being free we all smiled. But when I thought about it afterwards I wasn't smiling so much. It's all right for Jack but he hasn't got funny skin and bad pulmonaries and wings and no eyes.

*

27

Moose doesn't like me talking to Jack. Well, it serves him right for not telling me about the thing that's going to happen in here one day.

3

'You awake, X-Ray?'

It's Cough Cough. He wants some water.

'Press the call button,' I say.

'Tin Lid's on tonight,' he says. 'She'll just give me a tab. I don't want more dozie. Dozie makes me sick after.'

It does too. That's why Cough Cough lies low during the day, keeps quiet like the tender antelope lying in the bush hidden from the leopard.

Suddenly he is coughing like a barking dog.

'I'll get you some,' I say.

The waterhole is in the opposite corner to the nurse's office – the office where they keep the records and the trank and the hypo and the dozie tabs and the monitors and the TV remote and the camera controls. There's always one nurse on night duty except when they're off sick or having a party, and then they just give us trank so we coma out all night and not wake till late next morning.

Once in bed we aren't allowed to leave, not till light-on. Doctor Dearly's orders. 'Always use the call button,' he says. 'That's what the nurses are for, to look after you.'

'Watch out for Tin Lid,' whispers Cough Cough as I slide to the floor. 'And the cameras.'

'I will.'

In the Bin here they use cameras to watch us. They say it's for monitoring purposes, it's for our own safety, it's to see how we are progressing, whether we're following our PREDICTED DEVELOPMENTAL pattern. Mrs Murdoe didn't agree with the cameras. 'You're just kids,' she said. 'Snooping's wrong. While you're still here, living and breathing, they should focus on making it as comfortable as possible.'

Soon after that she went away. Cough Cough suffered the most after because she used to help him with his breathing fizzio. No one does that for him now. Maybe that's why he's in such a bad way.

Cough Cough said Mrs Murdoe didn't just go, she was sent away. Asked to leave. How did he know this? asked Chicken Angel in tears. Because Tin Lid who took Mrs Murdoe's place had told him he had to start growing up, fizzio himself and not expect mothering any more. She was a nurse, a professional, not one of the Mrs Mummy Murdoe brigade. She didn't believe in cosy cosy.

I move towards the curtain that runs down the length of the dormie and separates our side from Chicken Angel and Lights Out. The curtain is another Doctor Dearly thing. To keep us away from the girls.

'Time you were separated,' he said.

'Why?' said Chicken A. 'Why?'

This was before we learnt not to ask Doctor Dearly why.

'Because I say so,' he said.

We are supposed to shower separately now as well, not like when Mrs Murdoe was here. But I still see

Chicken Angel because I let her use my soap spray. She likes it because it's silky because of my skin. Moonskin she calls me sometimes. Angel Wings I say back. I stroke the little fingers on her back, soft and pulpy. And we smile at each other.

Sometimes after last tuck-in I draw on Chicken Angel's back. Once I did a snake going right up her back, its tail just emerging from her bum parting. The best was a red macaw. She loved that. She wouldn't shower for a week because she didn't want it to fly away.

We never draw leopard things like Tin Lid and Hyena Men and hypo. We draw monkey things that make us laugh and make the world beautiful.

Sometimes when the washes get steamed up we draw on the mirrors and watch the pictures disappear. One day we drew lots of elephants because the voice on *The Natural World* said all the elephants were disappearing and we wanted to watch them go.

4

Very, very slowly I open the door to the day-room and peer round. The light in the nurse's office is on but I can see no one through the window.

I check the cameras. No red lights. They're red-off.

With my back against the wall I start to edge towards the waterhole.

Moose's eye glints. 'Don't do it,' he says.

'Can't leave CC coughing,' I say.

I hold up my hand. The glove is a dull blue colour.

I start to feel along the wooden panelling behind me.

Ahead I can see a section caught in the light from the nurse's office. I have to cross it. I could be seen. I get on my hands and knees and start to crawl.

Then I hear a faint whirring.

Camera.

Cough Cough says they're BEAM ACTIVATED. I must have broken a beam.

I look up.

Yes, one is red-on. I can see its lens swinging towards me. I get up, slither along the wall and hide behind the waterhole.

SLITHER means move like a snake.

I am shivering. It's my skin. It can't sweat out the fear. It just shakes me, all over. It always happens this way.

What am I to do? I've got to get Cough Cough his water.

He could choke.

The camera has stopped whirring.

I peer out from behind the waterhole.

No red-on. Just Moose holding his breath. 'Might as well go for it,' he's saying.

I grab a carton, switch on the tap, listen to the water fizzling.

Stop.

Turn.

Glance across at the nurse's office.

Staring at me through her window is Tin Lid.

She raises her hand. She is wearing her white surgical gloves. Between thumb and forefinger I can see the long steel lance of a hypo.

*

31

No!

I rush across to the dormie, stumble round Cough Cough's bed because going quick is hurting my legs and put the water on his table.

'Thanks,' he wheezes.

Then I'm out and hopping and sliding along the curtain to the washes. I know I'm not strong but I'm going to hold out for as long as I can.

I get into the first cubicle, slam the door and press my back against the metal, feet against the toilet pan, jammed.

But I can't stop the shivering. And the door hinges are creaking with me.

Suddenly the light splashes all over and I hear the voice of Tin Lid.

'Come on out, you, G4. Now, immediately.'

I say nothing.

'Out. Or I get Security.'

Security! The Hyena Men! They're worse than trank. They hold you down after you fit. That's why we call them Hyena Men because they hold you down while trank tears you apart like the hyenas do in *The Natural World*. Once they broke Chicken Angel's arm.

You can get terrible fits and the jumps if they over-dozie you. It's the chemicals says Cough Cough. And the ELECTRICKS in the brain. That's when the jumps are worst. They have to coma you then with double trank, real hard shot.

Suddenly Tin Lid charges the door and I'm thrown hard against the cistern. She forces her way in, gets a hold on my neck and forces my face against the wall. The tiles freeze over my cheek.

I shake and shake.

'No. No. Please, no, no.'

It's too late.

She's ripped my bottoms down and jammed in the hypo.

I scream and scream. The needle's gone right through me. I drive my heart wild. The poison surges through me pulsed by my own panic.

I grovel for air, claw the wall.

Someone else is screaming.

It's not me.

I'm falling. I'm dissolving.

I'm out of here.

Tranked.

Coma-ed.

CHAPTER 4

Coddy, Nail and Kenno

1

Breakfast.

Nail stood by the table looking down on the empty cans and crumpled newspaper yellowed and stiff with last night's chip grease.

If it was his kitchen he'd hose the lot down, get rid of the stink of fags and the odour of flat beer. One thing you could say for his mum back home, at least she opened windows first thing. Liked to start fresh.

Not Coddy. Not his cousin Coddy, sad case Coddy.

Nail began dropping the cans into a bin beside the sink.

Kenno was the same. Just like his dad, a lardy waster.

Slugged in his pit all morning, except on market day when Coddy kicked him out early to help on the stall.

Nail stopped. Upstairs someone was coughing and spitting.

Coddy was up.

He cleared the table, got out the cereal, bowls, a couple of spoons and two milk cartons. He sniffed. One smelt sour. He put this carton and a packet of fags next to Coddy's place. The fresh one he emptied into his own bowl.

Then he waited.

Thing was, he needed money. More than that, he needed space. More than that, he needed to get away. Get back home maybe, to London. Except trips cost money and weeks back his mum had bin-linered him, bought him a one-way ticket and told him to take a holiday with cousin Coddy and his son Kenno in Garvie Town, Scotland. Miles away. Why? So she could take off with some Cuban bruiser name of Costa who called her *mia bambino* and bought her brassy earrings big enough to noose a poodle and who wore necklaces the size of anchor chains.

Well, now he needed to do some binning himself. Bin Coddy because his house smelt of oil and rust and stale smoke. Get rid of Kenno because he spent hours in Coddy's lock-up lifting old tyres, trying to beef up his lardy biceps till he stank of rubber tyre and armpit. Bin Scotland because it was rain and old biddies and kilty nerds and wee thisie and wee thatie and Scottie footie and boring, boring, boring.

Yeah, bin Coddy and Kenno for good. If he wanted chimps for family he'd have hired a tea party. When he arrived he told them his dad was in the army. Truth was he had no idea. Could have been an astronaut whizzing round the planet and he couldn't say for certain it wasn't fibbing true.

So, stuff them both.

Maybe he could lift some booty from one of Coddy's lock-ups and sell it on the streets. He'd done bootleg DVDs and made a mint back home but you needed a crowd of punters for that and Garvie Town just wasn't big on punters. Garvie Town was a squeezie pimple on the bum of Scotland.

Coddy barged in, spat in the sink, put a fag in his mouth, lit up, blew a lungful and left without a word.

That's a definite then said Nail to himself. He had to get some serious fivers. And move on. Before he did some serious damage to himself like getting a job at Budgens packing pet shelves with birdseed.

He breathed deeply. And nearly gagged. He was swallowing last night's nicotine cod and phlegmy peas and Coddy's morning dog breath.

2

Once Coddy had gone Nail padded upstairs. First he went into the bathroom. From the window ledge he lifted Coddy's can of shaving foam.

Kenno lay on his back, mouth open, snoring.

Nail watched him for a moment, the fat boy arms, the doughy breast meat. Then he leant over the bed, lifted the can, inserted the nozzle between Kenno's lips, gently pressed the button and squirted a long slow shot of foam into his mouth till it filled and the white came squeezing out and down his cheeks and chin.

Nail stopped and withdrew the nozzle.

And waited.

*

Suddenly Kenno spluttered, heaved, belched foam all over, and sank back on his pillow snoring once more.

Nail couldn't believe it. He ran back to the bathroom, got a tube of toothpaste. Rolled it up till an explosive bulge grew at the top, jammed it in Kenno and squeezed.

And squeezed.

Kenno started dribbling stripy red stuff and then with a heave and a great gulping swallowed the lot, turned over and didn't lift an eyelid.

Nail stared in amazement.

What he really needed now was a fire extinguisher.

No need.

Because –

ten minutes later Kenno was down and shovelling up cereal like gravel in a cement mixer.

He jabbed a spoon at the bin of lager cans. 'That stuff was rough,' he said. 'I've a mouth like a badger's bum this morning.'

Nail snorted.

Kenno started reading the cereal packet. 'I need two more tokens and we get free tickets to the safari park,' he spluttered without looking up.

Nail sat back watching his cousin gobble. The idiot was eating a packet a day. So he could see lions.

'What's the point?' said Nail. 'The park is the other side of Scotland.'

'But it's free tickets, Nail. Free.'

Nail eyed him. That pusie between his eyes was so big it didn't need squeezing. It needed milking.

'Course it's not free. You pay every time you buy one of those boxes.'

Kenno smiled. 'That's where you're wrong, Nail. You see, we don't pay. Coddy's got this special supplier. Know what I mean?'

Nail groaned. Bootleg Cocopops. He grabbed the packet. Checked the best-before date. 'It's twelve months old, you prat. Stuff's probably off, gone mouldy. It's full of bacteria, micro-organisms eating yer insides. They're probably eating away at this very moment. Munch, munch, munch.'

Kenno swallowed.

'You think?'

'I had a packet once a mouse had got into. Droppings looked same as the rest of the stuff.'

Kenno gulped.

'Only they tasted better.'

Kenno stood up. 'I need the bog,' he said.

Nail got the toast.

Eventually Kenno showed again.

He'd changed his clothes. Now he was wearing his Rangers top, combat shorts in camouflage green, black socks and trainers.

'We going out today, Nail?'

'Not with you looking Oxfam. Where did yer get that stuff, car boutique?' Nail laughed.

'Just cos you come from poncy London,' said Kenno. 'This' – he pointed to the blue top – 'is from Glasgie.'

'And that makes it OK?' Nail laughed again. 'If we're going to do some lifting we don't need a sore thumb footie fan in cut-off combats on the job.'

'Lifting?' said Kenno uneasily. He'd seen what Nail could do. Seen him lift a car from outside the police station itself, tailspin the roundabout opposite the baths and park on a tulip bed in Jubilee Gardens.

Nail nodded. 'We need – I need – money. Girls cost cash. Time I had a mobile. My mum's dying for a call.'

'What you mean? You never ring her,' said Kenno.

'And you never ring yours, Kenneth. And she only lives down the road.'

'Yes. I'm always talking to her.'

'Only cos she rings you, yer nerd.'

'And don't call me that.'

'Nerd?'

'Kenneth. Sounds like I'm in the Scouts or something.' He stood up. 'Jimmyjesus I feel sick.'

He rushed out of the room.

When he returned he was in jeans and T-shirt.

'Nice one,' said Nail. 'Cool.'

Kenno shrugged. 'Real genuine Levis.'

'Fell off the back of a cowboy?'

'Maybe.'

'From Wild Bill Coddy, maybe?'

Kenno half smiled. 'Look, Nail. Are you serious about doing some place over? I mean if Coddy finds out . . .'

Nail wasn't really. He just wanted to put the frighteners on Kenno. He wasn't going to get himself banged up in youth custody. In Garvie he had all the custody he needed.

He smiled.

'Tell us, Nail, please.'

'The Post Office. Now get yer stocking hood and yer shotgun and follow me. We're going up Scootie Hill to case the joint.'

Kenno didn't move. Not the PO. Mrs Korder ran the place. She was a nightmare. Step out of line and she'd have yer guts for tartan ribbon.

'No,' said Kenno. 'She'll kill us.'

But Nail was gone.

3

I open my eyes and hear the echo of my breathing.

I know what it is.

They've put me in a mask. Trank gets to your lungs so they put you on oxygen case you fixy out while coma-ed.

I lift my head a bit.

It hurts.

The plastic rim is pressing into my cheek and the strap has caught some hair at the back and it squeals as I move.

I try to remove the mask but my arm is trapped.

I know why.

They've put me in the hugger. I'm here till the duty nurse comes and unties it.

Are they in the day-room, the others?

I listen.

Nothing. Everywhere is silent. Moose is sleeping. Stuffed and tranked for life.

*

I try and squirm round to lie on my side but the hugger hurts my skin so I go still again.

Then I go cold.

What if they've all gone takeaway? Maybe Cough Cough was right about the nurses not caring any more and about germs escaping and radiators left to gurgle and die and the TV going.

None of the cameras are red-on. Don't they care either? What's going to happen to us?

This is trank panic, I know. Cough Cough says it's the after-effects. But I can't stop the questions fluttering about in my head. Things are trapped inside me. They are saying things in my head.

Nasty things.

About Chicken Angel and lumpies. About Cough Cough and his pippi-little pulmonaries. About me and my lips blooding out.

I don't know. I don't know.

More things are getting trapped. It's more trank panic inside my head. What's going to happen to the four of us? says a very loud voice. What are we doing here? shouts another. Why doesn't anyone tell us? How long have we been here?

I clasp my hands over my ears, close my eyes.

Questions fluttering, fluttering. It's Cough Cough's fault. He started it. All those flutters about Doctor Dearly and things going downhill. He's opened the door and let the flutters in.

I do some deep breathing like they say on the wall charts for fizzio.

In, out. In, out.

Each breath leaves with a deep ping sound.

I open my eyes again. The white strip lights are on low. Well within the safety margin says Doctor Dearly. Don't want to SENSITIZE that skin unnecessarily.

I look up at the clock.

Eleven.

4

Opposite, above Chicken Angel's bed, high on the dark wood wall, its eye staring straight at me, is the camera. It's red-on. They're checking, see if I'm coming out of coma. TRANQUILLITY as Cough Cough calls it. That's one of his jokes.

Trank to you, CC.

As I stare at the wall opposite I suddenly notice the Weather Eye is open. It's looking straight at me and it's bright blue.

If Tin Lid sees that she'll fixy out and it'll be trank all round again. Hypo double dozie.

I only have to think hypo and I get the shiver. Always starts in my arms.

I've got to keep calm. Stop the shiver coming, because if the shiver comes in the hugger I'll go onion skin and then I'll have a blood out and Tin Lid will fixy over that.

I take a deep breath like they say in fizzio.

Tin Lid mustn't see the Weather Eye. It's Lolo's fault. It was her turn to keep the Eye shut. Why hasn't she done it?

Then Tin Lid comes in. I take a deep breath.

'What are you wheezing for?' she says.

'The hugger's too tight,' I say.

She says nothing and puts two fingers on my neck. In the Bin this is how they measure your heart echo.

She examines my eyes. It's always the same. Echo then pupil DILATION.

She nods.

I'm OK.

'It's all right. You don't have to breathe so much. You're not drowning.'

She takes off the mask and unstraps the hugger.

I struggle upright.

Tin Lid pulls back the blanket. 'G4,' she says, 'you're smelly. Shower.'

The bed is wet and as I slide on to the floor Tin Lid is already tearing off the sheets and bundling them ready for the san team and the soil tub.

My legs are wobbly.

Tin Lid walks into the day-room.

I slide across to Lolo's bed.

I look underneath. No sign of the bit of wood we use to put out the Eye. The knot. That's what Cough Cough calls it. It's like the eye he says. The hole is like the SOCKET, the knot is the eye. I say the hole is the EYE because you can see things through it. Cough Cough just shakes his head. But I'm right. You can see the weather. That's why we call it the Weather Eye.

I reach under Lolo's pillow.

Nothing.

I turn and look through the door into the day-room. There's no sign of Tin Lid.

Then I reach under the mattress and there it is.

Still no Tin Lid.

I climb on to the bed.

I wait for my heart to slow and then I stand up. My legs are shaking but I can reach the Eye, just.

I put the knot in place and push it right in.

'G4, what do you think you're doing?'

Tin Lid strides over and shocked I fall back on to the bed.

'It's the mouse,' I say. 'The mouse. I saw it run up the wall. It's come to eat us. All of us.'

Tin Lid closes her eyes. She has no time for stupid mice.

I pretend to shake.

She can't decide if it's after-trank DELIRIUM or me having one of my dreams.

'I think it must be one of my dreams,' I say. 'Doctor Dearly gives me tabs for them,' I say. I know if I say *Doctor Dearly* it'll stop Tin Lid. Stop her in her tracks. *Doctor Dearly* is as good as a tab when it comes to stopping Tin Lid.

'We need Jack the Cat to catch this mouse,' I say. 'It was a giant, big as Moose.'

Tin Lid shakes her head. 'Get out. Get washed. Tabs,

huh. What you kids need is a good shaking now and again. Wake you up.'

I slide off the bed and walk slowly into the washes.

I sit down on the pot.

And smile.

I've daftied Tin Lid.

I've saved the Weather Eye.

5

Sometimes when we're sure the cameras are red-off and we're not tranked out Lights Out stands on her bed, takes out the knot and puts her finger through the Eye so she can feel weather.

'What's she doing?' said Cough Cough first time she did it.

'She's touching the sky,' said Chicken Angel. 'She says the sky has soft skin, like X-Ray's.'

When Cough Cough and I do the weather I look out and if it's white cloudy we say it's mashed-potato weather.

If it's raining we say it's pee-pee weather.

If it's grey we say it's sock.

Chicken Angel doesn't like the Weather Eye at all. It lets in the Outside she says. It's only clouds I say, and rain and stars.

I think about the weather. I used to think that Africa was just outside. I used to think when the wind moaned down the chimney under Moose it was hyenas howling in the distance. But it's not. Africa's a long long way from here. Even further away than London.

Outside is Scotland. Mrs Murdoe told us that. It comes right up to the walls of the Bin. That's how near Scotland is. Is Scotland in the Outside or is the Outside in Scotland? Cough Cough once asked me. As if I would know. Does it matter where it is? I said. And he said it matters a lot because if we could find out where we were we might be able to go away. We could get a map he said. The library had maps. Maps showed you how to go away. And I said go away for what? Where? Why? And he said because . . . because . . . and neither of us knew. We just looked at each other. We were both frightened. I started shaking. It felt like something was fluttering inside me. I could see Cough Cough was the same.

Go away? Outside?

It's different now, as CC says, we're not littles any more and the Outside of Scotland looks OK. I'd still prefer to be on the Inside though. Because of the wild animals. Lolo says they're outside all the time. Sometimes when the wind bangs at the shutters she can hear the wolves howl, and the squeal of littles hurting, and the roar and hoot of beasts and the hum of huge wings in the sky. When Lolo says these things I think Inside's best.

If she hears those littles squealing she gets very AGITATED. Chicken Angel has to hold hands over her ears but she still knows. She shivers for ages.

Cough Cough says in the Bin we're like meercats in a burrow, warm, yes, but blind and dark of mind.

And the Weather Eye throws light down among us, I say. It's a burrow-opener, an eye-opener.

If Tin Lid ever finds out about the Eye we'll all fall

down the trank burrow soon enough like the girl Mrs Murdoe told us about who fell down a rabbit hole.

I go to the bidet and wait for the water.

One thing worries me. If we stay here all the time in our burrow will we miss the Sky Boat? Mrs M told us about the Sky Boat. It flies over the main she said. I asked Cough Cough what a MAIN was. It's the earth he said, everywhere. So the Sky Boat flies everywhere. And people get on and it flies away with them. Mrs Murdoe said one day we will all go in the Sky Boat. It's a great ride she said. And when the boat is full, when Chicken Angel and Lights Out and Cough Cough and me are all aboard, we'll sail away over the main and into the starry sky forever. That's what Mrs Murdoe told us a long time ago.

I haven't asked Cough Cough about the Sky Boat recently because I don't think he believes it exists. I think he thinks it's one of those stories they tell littles to stop them being frightened of the night. Maybe it is just a story like Jack the Cat.

Except he's real.

CHAPTER 5

Morsing Mrs Murdoe

1

The bidet's not working so I go into the shower.

Another thing Cough Cough found in the library was Maiden China. He came down with it one day. In the evening when the cameras were off he brought it out. 'Look what I found,' he said.

It was a little cream-coloured clock.

Lights Out touched it. Then she squealed a bit.

'What's wrong with her this time?' said Cough Cough impatiently. He never liked Lolo doing a bit of a fit and moosing his moment.

Lights Out morsed Chicken A.

'She says there's something trapped inside.'

Cough Cough sighed. 'There's always something trapped somewhere with her,' he said.

'No there isn't,' said Chicken A. 'If Lolo says something's inside she's right.'

Suddenly the clock started ringing. Cough Cough fumbled with the knobs on the back and stopped the sound before the duty nurse heard it and came wanting to know what was going on.

Lights Out was whining quietly and morsing.

'There's a bird trapped inside. It was singing to get out she says.'

Lights Out reached forward.

'Let her have a listen, Cough Cough.'

Reluctantly CC handed the clock over and Lights Out put it to her ear.

She morsed again, fast this time.

'It's got a heart. She can hear it beating faintly, like a mouse tapping its paw.'

Cough Cough made a grab for the clock. Lights Out held it close to her chest.

'Oh, let her have it then,' he said. 'It's only a daftie clock.'

It was me called it Maiden China. Since I had the best eyes Chicken Angel asked me later on about the tiny writing on the clock face. What did it say?

'Made in China,' I said.

'Maiden China,' said Chicken A. It sounded like a beautiful princess out of her fairy book.

Lights Out wanted to open the clock and let the princess out but we couldn't get the back off. She was near another fit when she found she couldn't free the little prisoner.

So later on after light-out Chicken Angel told Lolo the story of the princess who been turned into a bird by a wicked witch and locked in a clock. But the witch couldn't silence the princess's beautiful song and stop her calling for help. And if we promise to help her escape and keep her away from the witch's talons said Chicken Angel to

50

Lights Out, she will be our guide and friend alarming us of danger, warning us of enemies.

Lolo promised, took her tab from Chicken Angel and fell deep asleep.

One day Chicken Angel asked Cough Cough why the clock was called China. Cough Cough, who didn't really like secrets and therefore wasn't good at them, said china was stuff you made plates out of and cups.

'That can't be right,' said Chicken Angel. 'Plates are made of plastic.'

'And china.'

'China's a place beyond Scotland,' I said.

'How do you know that?' said Cough Cough sharply. He didn't like it if I knew more than he did.

'Because I saw it on *The Natural World* when they did "The World of the Panda". The panda is a black and white bear and lives on misty mountains.'

'Like Jack the Cat's an elephant,' said Cough Cough.

2

Today, after the shower, I cream my hands and put on my gloves and trackies. Then I check out the day-room. Tin Lid is sorting out the waterhole so I go back and climb on to Lolo's mattress.

I check on Tin Lid again.

No sign.

Lights Out can always tell when Tin Lid is coming. She can hear the crackle of her legs as she walks and the creak of her uniform. Then she warns us by pattering her hands. It's like the flapping of trapped wings, ear-catching. Like the time a bird came down the chimney right under Moose's nose. That flapped everywhere till Tin Lid hit it with a pee bottle.

I look out through the Weather Eye.

I'm astonished.

The very first time all I saw was part of a tree. It was right next to us, growing up the walls outside and hiding everything beyond. It was all green green leaves, green green all over. 'Nothing but trees and sky just like the Amazon,' I said.

But not any longer.

The tree's gone.

Now I can see forests and animals and some houses, and on the nearest hill I can see children running and swinging on things. They run faster than we do. I can see one child swinging on a rope and climbing and swinging. He's like one of the monkeys. He's swinging and swinging. He's loving it. Dancing on the rope because he's just loving it. Now he's climbing higher and he's swinging on one arm and now he's falling. Something thing must have scared him.

He looks just like us. Except he's not wearing trackies and he's much stronger than us. Because none of us could swing like that. They must be giving him supplements. And some of the other children are jumping about too so they must be on supplements as well. Or maybe they're lucky. Maybe they've got good pulmonaries and lots of skin.

I close my eyes.

I've started trembling and shivering.

It's the leopard. He could be lying in the bush, in the scrub, panting and hungry. That monkey boy probably knows. That's why he jumped. That monkey boy better be careful.

I quickly put the Eye back and climb down.

Just in time.

Because Tin Lid and a Hyena Man come in wheelchairing Chicken Angel and Lights Out.

Lights Out and Chicken Angel have been to tests. Had a primary probably.

I stare at them.

Tin Lid helps them into bed. She says they are allowed to stay there till second tuck-in.

Lights Out curls up and puts her head under the pillow.

Chicken Angel stares across at me and half smiles.

Her eyes are bright yellow.

3

Nap time is over.

Lights Out is sitting up. She is cross-legged and her head is bent slightly forwards. She is very still. I wonder if she's had after-trank like me.

Suddenly she swings her legs over the side of the bed and stands up.

She walks across the dormie and stops in front of Mrs Murdoe. You can just see Mrs Murdoe's face, there, smiling, in the wood. It was Cough Cough first noticed her. He told Lights Out that she'd come back. Lights Out told Chicken

Angel, who told me, but I already knew from Cough Cough that the face was there. It's true. You can see her eyes, dark knots in the oak, and her hair in the falling grain. It's amazing. To think she's here keeping eyes on us.

Whenever we've got trouble we talk to Mrs Murdoe. She's listens. We always do what she says. She's always right. I don't know what we'd do without Mrs Murdoe. Once when the tabs they gave Lights Out were making her sick she asked Mrs Murdoe what to do. 'Flush them down the toilet,' she said. And Lights Out disappeared them down the pan like she was told and she was OK after that right away. Then when we first found the Weather Eye we asked Mrs M what if the Outside would get in? 'Don't worry,' she said. 'Jack the Cat will stop anything bad coming through.' She was right. Nothing bad from the Outside has got in. Except sometimes Jack comes through, but he's a friend.

No one else knows about Mrs Murdoe being in the dormie. They can't trank her. Not Tin Lid. Not Doctor Dearly. Not the Hyena Men. Not any of them. Stick hypo in Mrs Murdoe now and she wouldn't feel a thing.

So, Lights Out is morsing Mrs Murdoe.

According to Chicken Angel, who is watching, she is telling Mrs Murdoe about Pippi. And how Tin Lid took Pippi away. Can she help find Pippi? Can Mrs M send the leopard to find Tin Lid?

I can help says Mrs Murdoe.

While Lights Out is talking I go across to Chicken Angel and she tells me that Lights Out wants Pippi back.

I shrug helplessly.

I look at Chicken Angel.

Her eyes are bright and filling with tears.

'Why are your eyes all yellow?' I say.

Lights Out comes back and sits beside us. She takes my hand. She is smiling.

'Pippi's coming back,' she morses, tapping gently on my arm. 'Mrs Murdoe's promised.'

I look at Chicken Angel. This is where Mrs M can make life very difficult.

I think about what Cough Cough said about Pippi being baby Lolo.

'What are we going to do?' says Chicken Angel.

I look at Lights Out.

'Maybe Cough Cough will have an idea,' she says.

'Maybe I'll have an idea,' I say. She thinks Cough Cough's the only one has ideas. Well, he's not.

I try and have an idea.

Nothing happens.

Chicken Angel wrinkles her nose at me.

Then Tin Lid comes in with a pee bottle. It looks like a cardboard sock. She wants a sample from me. This is usual after trank. They want to see how long the chemicals stay inside us.

I go to the washes. Take down my trackies.

Then,

I do have the idea.

I place the bottle behind one of the toilet bowls. I come out of the washes and tell Tin Lid, who is waiting, that the pee bottle had a hole in it and that I've put it in the soil tub and can I have another one.

She goes to the office and I whisper to Chicken Angel that I've found a Pippi.

'Another Pippi?'

I nod. It's a great idea. Except that if Lolo has another Pippi she won't grow up like Cough Cough says.

I frown.

Maybe we should forget about the doll thing.

But then I think – it's really Mrs Murdoe's idea.

So it's OK.

And it'll make Chicken Angel very happy. That's the main thing. And then she'll like me a lot.

Tin Lid gives me the second pee bottle.

In two minutes I've finished.

I watch her leave the dormie.

'Well, where is it?' asks Chicken Angel.

I take her into the washes and get the pee bottle from behind the toilet pan.

Chicken Angel looks at it, frowning.

'We can draw Pippi's face on it,' I say. I hold up the bottle. 'The big end is the head and the rest can be the body.'

'Huh!' says Chicken Angel. 'It's a spookie. You can't give her that. It's nothing like Pippi.' She turns and starts pinning up her hair in front of the mirror. I watch her wings wiggle under the T-shirt as she reaches up.

Oh!

Then I wonder.

Maybe Chicken Angel doesn't like me making a Pippi for Lights Out because she wants to be the one who looks after her. Does things for her. I think of what Cough

56

Cough would say. 'She treats Lolo like a little girl.' That's what he'd say. And she does. She's like a nurse with Lolo, feeding her and doing her hair and cleaning her up at night when she pitches her bed.

Cough Cough's right.

She gets jealous if he or I step in. Lolo's a baby for Chicken Angel, same as Pippi is for Lolo. Noo nooing Lolo gives Chicken Angel something to do. She's doing helping, that's what she's doing.

It's OK helping each other. That's how we keep going. But you can have too much helping. It's like dozie. You get fixed on it.

'We could draw eyes on it and hair and a mouth.'

'Don't be daftie,' says Chicken Angel turning round. 'What's the point of eyes if you can't see?'

Of course.

Daftie me.

Lights Out is Lights Out because her lights are out.

4

Chicken Angel looks at her pee-yellow eyes in one of the mirrors. 'Lolo had the scan again. I had the eye test,' she says. 'They've put eyes on primary. For you and me and Cough Cough. You didn't get it because you had trank. Cough Cough told us about that. It was Tin Lid, wasn't it?' She strokes her fingers down my face. 'Poor X-Ray, did it really squeal you?'

I like it when Chicken Angel strokes me, does the gently on my face.

I nod.

I push my trackies down a bit to show her the bruise from the hypo. Because of my skin I bruise a lot. Cough Cough says my skin goes jungly, all greens and parrot blue and red. Sometimes when Lights Out does the gently on my back at bedtime and leaves pictures they turn pink all over, especially if she presses a bit too hard. It's because the skin's like paper says Cough Cough, you can write on it.

You could send messages on me.

Chicken Angel looks in the mirror again. She pulls her lower eyelid down. 'They squirt this stuff in and shine lights inside you. It didn't work for Cough Cough. They're waiting for his eyes to clear so they can do it again. One of the test nurses said. Now eyes are on primary I suppose we'll look yellow all the time.'

I start thinking.

Why are eyes on primary now? We've been tested lots. We have the function test, the primary, every day: pee, heart and blood, lungs (respiratory function), fat tissue (subcutaneous and intra-organic) and general motor co-ordination. Once a week we have the secondary: weight, chests, feet, critical joints, spines, neural responses, tongues, skins, scalps, ears.

'They'll test us to DESTRUCTION,' Cough Cough says sometimes. That's because he often gets bronchial occlusion on the pulmonary test and they have to give him a relaxant to open the tubes again. They hypo it direct into the blood. It really squeals. I've heard him crying when they do it.

'What Lights Out wants,' Chicken Angel is saying, 'is something to cosy cosy. Something softly. We'll all have to think of a way to make another Pippi,' she says.

I know what that means. She wants to ask Cough Cough.

And why not me?

But she doesn't know Cough Cough won't help. She doesn't know he thinks Pippies are OK for babies not girls.

And what's more, he doesn't know anything about making Pippies, does he!

I do though.

Back in the dormie Lights Out is asleep. This is OK. 'We are allowed to sleep today because of our eyes and the scans,' says Chicken Angel.

Eyes!

Then I remember.

'Oh, and another thing,' I whisper. 'The Weather Eye was open. And, guess what, the tree's gone and you can see the Outside. I saw a monkey boy swinging and jumping.'

'Outside?' says Chicken Angel. Her eyes widen. 'Oh, that's terrible.'

Suddenly the doors swing open and two of the nurses enter pushing a wheelchair. Sitting in it, tranked out, his head lolled to one side, his eyes closed, is Cough Cough.

He looks small and crumpled.

Chicken Angel and I watch as the two nurses lift him on to his bed, fold his blanket over him and leave.

I look at Chicken Angel.

She looks at me.

Her eyes are full of yellow gold.

She is biting her lip.

Under the bedclothes the little mound of Cough Cough lies motionless.

CHAPTER 6

Doctor D

1

Nail was sitting on the grass breathing hard. He'd just lathered Kenno up the Scootie and was waiting for him to move. But Kenno was having none of it. His lungs were bursting and he was staying put, lying on his back panting at the sky like a dog.

Nail eyed him. No puff in him. For a lumpo that did weights that was some puzzle.

Nail looked down the hill and over a clump of trees to where a street of houses curved round a small green. All their frontages were full in the sun, and hanging outside one of them was a bright red sign. It was Garvie Post Office.

Beyond the houses and up on the far side of the valley stood a large white-fronted building, an old mansion with outhouses and some low-lying modern prefabricated units. It was surrounded by a high wall.

Nail raised the binoculars and scanned the place. There was just the one entrance, and that was blocked by a check-point with hut and barrier. He could see a guard standing staring straight ahead like he was staring straight at him.

*

'Give us a peepie,' wheezed Kenno, settling himself down.

'What's that place? The big white palace over there?' said Nail handing him the binocs.

'Bin Linnie Lodge. Round here it's called the Bin.'

Nail nodded.

'It's where they keep the spooks.'

'Spooks?'

'Dafties. Sick kids. You know. Ones with two heads and things, mouths in their stomachs.'

'Yeah?' said Nail.

'Yeah. Everyone says,' Kenno protested. 'My mum included. She works there. They get sent there from all over the country. It's true. Coddy used to work there as well. In the gardens. He says they're freaks. My mum says they're a menace.'

Nail stopped and looked hard at Kenno. 'Freaks? Maybe we should pay them a visit.'

'They got security, lots of security,' said Kenno. 'I don't like freaks. They should put them down at birth.'

Nail lay back. He was suddenly remembering. He had a brother, once. A baby. He only saw him the one time in hospital. His mum took him. The baby had looked purple. Soon after he died and for a year or so they used to visit the grave, he and his mum, and then they missed a few visits and when they came back it was all over-grown and they weren't sure where the grave was any more and so they stopped going. Then his dad left and his mum moved and he forgot the purple baby.

Till now. Till this minute sitting on Scootie Hill with his lumpo cousin looking at a freak factory. Suddenly it was so clear – the white hospital and the Rupert Bear curtains and the cloche thing they kept over his brother. The poor kid. He didn't know he only had a few days left.

His chest felt tight. He swallowed hard. 'Sod it!' He slammed his heel into the grass.

Sodding Kenneth.

He turned, clenched his fist and swung at Kenno.

But Kenno had caught the sudden anger in Nail's voice and was half ready for something.

The punch missed and he rolled away and sat up on his knees staring at Nail and still holding the binocs.

'What's up?' he said, trembling. He knew Nail had a temper. He'd seen him smack some kid once for giving him the finger.

Nail didn't answer. He didn't know.

Kenno stood up. 'I'm going home,' he said.

Nail shook his head. 'No. No. Sorry. Sorry mate. Just bad dreams,' he said. 'Bad dreams. Come on, sit yer pusie bum down and tell me what yer see.'

Slowly Kenno sat himself down like he had thistles up his jeans.

He raised the glasses and for a long time scanned the street.

'See anything?' said Nail, the past now fading from his mind.

Kenno shook his head.

Nail worked up a smile. 'Coast clear?'

Kenno nodded. 'Does that mean we got to go?'

'Rest yer beating heart,' said Nail. 'We'll wait till the kids come out of school.'

'So we'll be lost in the crowd.'

'Good one, Kenneth. Observation and timing, that's the secret. Knowing when to strike.'

Suddenly he grabbed the glasses. 'Jeez! Look at that.'

Both of them stared at the Post Office.

A girl in jeans and a striped blue tank top was lifting up the fallen ice-cream board. 'Just look at that,' said Nail. 'Work of art.'

'Dunno,' said Kenno. 'Can't read it.'

What a right Kenneth thought Nail, looking at his cousin squinting into the distance.

From where they were it was difficult to tell how old the girl was but the way she tossed her hair as she stood up and the way she slipped on her sunglasses and the way she looked up and down the street and the way she sauntered back into the shop suggested to Nail that here was some tasty stuff.

'Let's go,' he said. 'Change of plan.'

2

A hundred metres or so from the PO Nail called a halt. 'Leave the talk to me,' he said. 'I'll cover for you.'

'Cover?' said Kenno. 'Cover for what?'

'For the five-finger discount, what else?'

Kenno looked at his fingers, puzzled. Then at Nail, alarm in his eyes.

'Nick something,' said Nail reaching out and closing his fingers over some invisible choc bar.

'Nick?'

Nail nodded.

'What if they see me? What if I get caught?'

'OK. OK,' said Nail. 'Forget it. Just forget it.'

Kenno took a deep breath. 'No, Nail,' he said. 'No. I'll give it a try.' He wiggled his fingers. 'I gotta learn sometime.'

'That's my boy,' said Nail. 'Now let's play.'

3

Suddenly the voice-over crackles.

A message from Doctor Dearly.

We'd just finished in the showers. I'd swapped soap with Chicken Angel so I could see her chest about those lumpies. They definitely weren't real lumpies. The real ones were hard and INFLAMED. Chicken Angel's were soft and more like swellings than lumps, like her wings in fact. And another thing, lumpies spread all over you, Chicken A's didn't. She just had the two.

So, they're not spreading.

I think she's going to be all right.

For voice-overs, as we call them, we all have to sit on our beds and listen. We often get voice-overs like: 'Clear your own beds, no san team today' and 'Line up at the food hatch' and 'Remember your toilet, light-out five minutes.' Of course these are tapes not real people and, like Cough Cough, their voices are getting worn out. Some messages don't make sense any more. We get one that used to say: 'Keep the Day Area waste free.' Now it sounds like: 'Eat the diarrhoea pastry.'

That used to make us laugh. We could pitch in our

pants over it. Except we didn't because that got you black points and you had to clear up your own messes. We used to get extra Coke from the machine if we got no black points but we don't play the points game much, not since Doctor Dearly arrived.

When Lights Out messes at night Chicken Angel always cleans her up. She never calls the nurse, not at night. They don't like that.

I think it's something they put in her dozies that makes her mess in the night.

Anyway we all sit waiting.

First we hear the music and then Doctor Dearly's voice comes on.

'G1 to 4 listen carefully. This is a health alert. Your recent tests have shown that there is a higher than acceptable level of retinal damage in your eyes. Factors involved in this receptor deterioration may be physiological, may be environmental. Your doctors are not sure. To prevent further degradation your care team has decided after much consultation to adopt an intensive monitoring and elimination strategy. Eye examination will now be on the primary testing schedule and because screen radiation is a known environmental factor in retinal degeneration we have decided, for the time being, to terminate television viewing. Should eliminating this factor result in some improvement to eyesight then we will have to consider a permanent termination. No *Natural World* till further notice. Remember: your welfare is our first concern. Any questions address them to the day nurse or talk to your primary examiner. Message over.'

*

Silence.

We just look at each other.

No more TV!

No more *Natural World*!

What does it mean? What'll we do?

For Lights Out no TV was OK because when the telly was on she said it made the air crinkly and it itched her. But she always wanted to know what was happening. It was a squeal having to tell her. She was always asking what the animals looked like. Chicken Angel usually told but she left out the squeal bits like the leopard and the baby monkey.

Cough Cough and I look at each other.

'I told you they'd close the channel,' he says. 'If our eyes get better they'll ban *The Natural World* permanently. We won't ever see it again. If our eyes get worse it'll make no difference because we won't be able to see anyway.'

I wasn't really listening. I was thinking of sunrise over the Ngorongoro Crater.

'It's Africa I like best,' I said. 'Then the jungles and the butterflies, the blizzards of butterflies, and the parrots, squawky and blue and green and red.'

'Next they'll close us down,' said Cough Cough.

'It's only a precaution. A temporary thing. Stop us getting worse. Anyway we're having more tests,' I say.

'You're a daftie, X-Ray,' says Cough Cough quietly.

'Tests don't cure you. It's just an excuse for them. Don't you see? Don't any of you see? It's what I've been saying all along. Everything's going bit by bit. Like in *The Natural World*. First you have the green grass and the lakes and the trees. Then they take away the trees, then the water dries up, then the grass disappears, then the animals die, then winds blow the dust all over the land and nothing's left but desert.' He looks at us sitting staring at him, mouths open. 'Sand! Which is what you've got your heads stuck in.'

'Well, I think you're being too pess . . . pess . . .' says Chicken Angel.

'PESSIMISTIC?' says Cough Cough. 'Just wait and see. Wait and see what they do next. And don't say I didn't warn you.'

Lights Out morses. She doesn't mind the television going takeaway because Pippi will be back soon, back off her holiday. She's gone away to the seaside with Mrs Murdoe.

'What she saying?' says Cough Cough.

'She said nothing's going to happen to us. That Doctor Dearly will be good to us like always.'

'Then she's a noo noo brain,' says Cough Cough. 'Like the rest of you.'

5

That night it's busy. The Outside is fitting and howling. We can hear the wind in the chimney in the day-room. It sounds as though it is mooing through Moose.

I lie there in bed thinking about what Cough Cough

has said about us going away and disappearing like the summer grass.

Well, CC, in the Ngorongoro the grass does go, but then it comes back. It only hides. It always comes back.

So you're wrong.

6

First tuck-in next day.

We've given samples, got washed, got dressed. The cameras are red-on and the strip lights are slowly coming up to full.

The nurse gives me my supplement tabs.

Ever since my first primary when they examined my eyes and did the fat test they've put me on special dozie. Doctor Dearly said it was to help my eyes stay healthy, keep them the best in the unit. I was short on a special chemical, an ENZYME I needed to boost my count.

Doctor Dearly has cold hands. They feel like rubber when he touches you.

During my primary after he's done my eyes he holds up a pair of CALLIPERS and takes a pinch of my skin beside the ribs. 'Subcutaneous tissue zero point two mill,' he says to the nurse.

'What's that mean?' I say.

'It means, G4, you're losing fat and there's some muscle wastage.'

'Why?' I say. 'I eat lots.'

Doctor Dearly looks me one. 'You can't be doing your exercises. Check the board. You should be level 3 by now.'

'I try,' I say, 'but I get tired.'

Doctor Dearly frowns. 'Put him on vitamin supplements too,' he says to the nurse. 'He needs building up.'

When I tell CC about building up he looks at me like
I'm goo goo.

'Building you up for what?' he says.

'Building me up so I can get to level 3 in fizzio,' I say.

Next primary they put CC on supplements too. Not for
his eyes but for general body conditioning, for bulking
him up. 'We need to put some gloss in your coat,' said
Doctor Dearly. We'd never heard him talk like that. Like
Cough Cough was a fox or a rabbit. 'Before you get
DEBILITATED,' he said.

'What's that?' I ask CC afterwards.

'It means when you lose your shine.'

I'm glad Doctor Dearly was going to help Cough
Cough keep his shine.

'What about your enzymes?' I say. 'How are they?'

He looks at me frowning. 'Enzymes?'

'You need them for healthy eyes,' I explain.

'I know what enzymes are,' he says sharply.

I don't think he does but I don't say anything. Maybe
he's a bit jealous because Doctor Dearly didn't give him
as many supplements as me. They're small dark-red
capsules like the beads on Lolo's necklace before they
took it away. It was the one Mrs Murdoe gave her just
before she left. They took it off her when she was asleep.
She cried and cried but they told her she'd lost it and it
was her fault and anyway beads were dangerous. They
could make you ill if you swallowed them.

'Tabs can make you ill,' said Chicken Angel, 'but we have to take them.'

We're sitting round the table eating toast, all of us except Cough Cough. He has to wait for the nurses to wheel-chair him and they are late. The wheelchair is because he still can't walk too well after the trank. It is the chemical pooling in his legs. Cough Cough tells us that afterwards.

Next to Lights Out is Pippi's empty chair.

I take one of my tabs and Chicken Angel says my face is getting fat because of the supplements. I tell her that's what they do, build you up. Stop you being skinny. So she wants to know why she hasn't had any because she's on the skinny side. I think, yes, she is skinny, skinny like those mop sticks the san team use in the washes. And no, I don't know why Doctor Dearly hasn't given her some.

Then she asks can I div with her. I don't really need them any more she says, because it looks like I've got my fat levels right up.

I'm not sure about doing a div on tabs. What if Doctor Dearly found out?

'I don't think it's fair,' Chicken Angel was saying. 'Why do you two get dozie to make you fat and Lolo and I don't?'

Maybe because Chicken A already has fat bits like her bum, and the things on her chest, and her wings.

Later on she asks me to watch out for nurses so she can write her story.

'If I do can I read it?' I say.

'Maybe,' she says, 'one day.'

One day?

'Hum,' says Cough Cough. 'One day? It's a sweetie to keep you in line. I don't know why you want to read daftie stuff about pippies and princesses. Anyway she better watch out. If Tin Lid finds it there'll be no more stories.'

'They can't stop you telling stories,' I say.

Cough Cough gives me one of his how-daftie looks. 'It's not them stopping Chicken Angel telling stories that worries me,' he says. 'It's the stories they tell.'

'They don't tell stories,' I say.

Cough Cough pats my hand. 'Dearly tells us the Bin is beautiful. It's for our own good. That's the doziest story out, X-Ray. It dozies us all.' He pauses. 'If you let it,' he adds.

Later I ask CA if she has any Doctor Dearly stories in her notebook. She nods. Only one that she dreamed – where he turned into a giant hypo and tranked everyone, nurses, Tin Lid, san team, Hyena Men, kids.

Well, if all she writes about is dreams she can keep her storybook. It doesn't sound very interesting to me. I'd rather take a tab.

8

I'm much stronger today. I bet I could make level 4 fizzio. Top of the chart. I think Chicken Angel knows this. She's always been best at fizzio. So maybe she's thinking I'll catch her up and get better than her soon.

'Do they make you sick?' she asks.

'No.'

'Give you a head squeal? Do you really feel stronger?' she says.

I nod.

She takes a pill and swallows.

'But they make you pitch in your pants.'

Chicken Angel freezes.

I laugh.

Chicken A scowls. She doesn't like being joked.

'And we'll ask Doctor Dearly to give Jack the Cat some. He's a whisker-thin fatless FELINE.'

We go quiet because the carer comes over with the porridge. We haven't seen her before. We eat quickly because we are all hungry and not slowly like Tin Lid keeps telling us. Because she's not here we can eat how we like.

After the carer brings back toast and jam and butter wrapped in gold paper.

We all stare at the gold butter. We've never had butter like this before, wrapped up and shiny. We only get butter once a week because fat isn't good for us.

CHAPTER 7

Yellow Tears

1

'It's got writing on,' says Chicken Angel, looking at me.

'It says Best Before 2004,' I say.

'What's that mean?' says Chicken Angel.

'It means the year 2004,' says the carer as she leaves.

Chicken Angel and I look at each other. The year? We know about Saturdays and Sundays because those are the dozie days, when we get extra dozie to keep us quiet when there aren't enough nurses. It happens every week. No one ever says about years though. Hours, yes, because of the medicines, tabs and dozie and because of tuck-in time. Yes, we know about tuck-in time but not long time.

2004!

We are like those travellers in *The Natural World* trekking for months across the empty desert and then seeing a signpost – to somewhere we've never heard of.

I can see Chicken Angel doesn't like it being 2004.

'But we know where we are now,' I say.

Suddenly Lights Out begins morsing her.

Chicken Angel turns to me.

'She says why is it Best Before 2004? Is there no Best After 2004?'

Just then the dormie doors open and one of the nurses appears pushing Cough Cough.

We tell him about the gold butter.

'Tell her it doesn't mean Best like Best Things in Life. It means things get used up and go bad after a certain time,' says Cough Cough.

'Like us you mean?' says Chicken Angel.

Cough Cough shrugs. I can see his eyes are still cloudy and faintly yellow. '2004,' he says. 'Now we know where we are.'

'That's what I said,' I say.

'It's our history,' says Cough Cough, ignoring me. 'We ought to have a history. It's good for us.'

'I don't want a history,' says Chicken Angel. 'It's all a blur so far. What's so wrong with a blur?'

Lights Out is morsing again.

'She says it wasn't Best Before when the princess went takeaway,' says Chicken Angel.

'That was . . . that was . . .' she stops.

'Years ago,' I say. We'd all forgotten. Except Lights Out. The princess was the day nurse's fault. He used the remote on the wrong TV channel and we saw pictures from somewhere called Paris instead of *The Natural World* with the wild animals. Paris was near London said Cough Cough. It was the first time we'd ever seen news with houses as well. It only lasted a few minutes. Chicken Angel explained it to Lights Out. 'It's a story about a princess,' she said, 'who's gone takeaway. A big cat car dragged her down to his underground den and ate her up.'

Lights Out squealed. Paris sounded beautiful and soft she said. And why should anyone want to takeaway a princess.

No one had an answer.

'It just happens,' said Chicken Angel.

'If we know what year it is,' says Cough Cough, 'we can connect up things. Otherwise it's like Outside, all noise and storms and things. And blur.'

'Well, I still like blur,' says Chicken Angel. Her lower lip is trembling and I wonder if she is going to cry.

'Cough Cough,' says Lights Out, 'Pippi. Pippi is coming back. She's gone to the sea with Mrs Murdoe. Mrs Murdoe is Best Before everything.'

It's the first time for ages she's used proper words.

They come out of her mouth like beautiful birds flying in through the Weather Eye.

Cough Cough stops and stares at her.

I look at his plate.

The daftie.

He's buttered his toast – with a fork.

'Cough Cough,' I whisper, 'you've buttered your toast with the fork.'

Cough Cough lets out a spitty sound. 'It's the stuff they gave me in the tests,' he says wheezily. 'Leads to PERCEPTUAL MISALIGNMENT. Just a temporary thing. Pass me a knife, please.'

I pass him a spoon. He dips it in the marmalade and uses it to spread the toast.

Chicken Angel and I exchange looks.

This isn't good. What's happening to Cough Cough?

'Cough Cough, that's a spoon you're using.'

He holds it up and runs his finger up its length. Then he squeezes it in his fist and holds it up to his mouth.

He nods slowly, his eyes wide like he knows he has just swallowed a terrible secret.

What can we say?

Chicken Angel leans across the table and gently takes the spoon. Cough Cough's hand drops to his lap.

'They put something in my eyes,' he says in a low whisper.

'Maybe they'll get better,' says Chicken Angel.

I smile for CC's sake but I'm not sure.

Something sticks in my mind. This isn't the first time Cough Cough's done something odd recently.

But before I can remember anything Lights Out starts whining. It's her alarm call. Her face is turned to Cough Cough. Suddenly she stretches across the table and does the gently on his eyes.

Then she starts mewing as if she's in a squeal.

She begins morsing Chicken Angel. But it's too fast to understand.

'What's wrong?' I say.

Chicken Angel shakes her head. 'She's upset at Cough Cough, I think.' She morses this on my wrist so CC can't hear.

'Yes,' I mouth. 'Me too.'

'Go for a pee,' says Chicken Angel out loud to Lights Out. 'Then you'll feel better.'

Lights Out isn't sure.

'Go on.'

Lights Out leaves holding her hands in front of her while she passes Cough Cough as if she is pushing away something bad.

I'm just thinking about Chicken Angel not wanting a history. I don't want a blur like she does. I want a dawn beginning, a bright sun rising like in Africa.

'Where did we come from?' I ask Cough Cough.

Chicken Angel says, 'Yes, did some daftie make us?'

Cough Cough sneezes.

Silence.

Make us? Who?

Chicken Angel bites her lip.

No one says anything.

Doctor Dearly? Make us?

It's a big question. It growls in our heads.

Suddenly the walls of the day-room vanish and we are all out in the open, on the plains where the wild animals are waiting.

The leopard has stepped into our midst.

We don't know who. We don't know how.

Questions. Questions.

Quick, quick, find an answer before they eat us up.

Then we remember Mrs Murdoe. Mrs Murdoe rescues us. She said we were all seeds once, like little beans. And we just grew and grew. Some seeds become flowers and some seeds become babies.

Cough Cough used to say you got beans from beans not babies and children like us.

Then I remember the picture Mrs Murdoe kept in her pocket. It showed all of us in little boxes, bean heads showing and growing. This proves she must be right and Cough Cough must be wrong.

And that's no surprise because Mrs Murdoe is always right.

Then I hear Chicken Angel cry out.

She is staring at Cough Cough.

2

The PO door rattled and rang behind them. Nail and Kenno stopped dead.

The girl was standing on some ladders behind the counter, back to them, filling in the ciggy bank from a box sitting on the counter.

Tight bum thought Nail.

Nail shushed Kenno, finger on lips, and then nudged him forward. 'Five-finger us a bar of Choconut,' he whispered.

Kenno hesitated. Nail pushed him and slipped behind a stand of cards and soft drinks.

At the counter Kenno scanned the sweet packs and the liquorice laces, the mint bags and the lollies. Then he reached up and his shaky fingers crept over the edge of the counter and started to slowly crawl towards a shiny green wrapped choc bar.

Suddenly a hand grabbed his arm, twisted it up his back and slammed him face down among the soft gums and the toffee bags.

Kenno felt someone reaching into his jacket pocket.

'Hey,' he gargled.

'Caught him lifting yer ciggies, sweetie.'

Was Kenno hearing it right? Wasn't that Nail's voice? Nail. He had him slammed down and snorting jelly babies.

'Wha–'

Nail pushed harder. Kenno's voice jammed in his throat.

'Caught him nicking yer ciggies, sweetie. Look.'

Kenno felt fingers in his pocket.

Nail, brought out a packet of Lamberts. Held them up.

The girl reached down and took them. She slotted the packet back on to the shelf and turned round to face Nail, looking down at him.

Lot of shape there he thought.

'I said he was nicking yer ciggies. Didn't yer hear me?'

Kenno gargled. He sounded like a Scottie terrier.

'No dogs, no barking, no swearing,' said Nail. 'Says on the door.'

'Let him go,' said the girl. 'You're hurting him.'

'Your call, lassie,' said Nail. 'Who phones the police, you or me?'

Kenno was rubbing his neck and staring at Nail. He could hear the crackle of a distant voice ringing in his brain saying this is a Nail wind-up, say nothing.

'Nail, what are yer playing at?'

The girl stepped down and asked Kenno if he was all right.

'He's a thief,' said Nail, wondering why she was going soft on his fat cousin.

Then the girl reached below the counter and brought out a phone. 'It's our policy to prosecute shoplifters.'

She started dialling.

'Hang on there,' said Nail. 'This is Kenno the Klepto. He can't help it. I mind him. He just has pockets to fill. He's a nutter and you have to crack him to be kind. Get the picture? He doesn't know he's thieving. It's like magic to him. He makes things disappear. He just has to touch something and it's gone. That's how he gets his kicks!'

The girl looked unimpressed.

'I tell him and tell him and tell him,' said Nail. 'But it does no good. Next time my back's turned he's off lifting again like it's apple-picking time.'

Kenno just stared at Nail, his mouth all orifice and empty.

The girl had her arms crossed, the handset tapping her lips.

'Look,' said Nail. 'You keep this quiet, OK. Anything to do with the police, with authority of any kind, will put him back months. You know, he's under treatment. This is confidential, just between you and me.'

'And him.' The girl nodded at Kenno.

'And him,' said Nail. 'I'm just telling you so you'll understand, right. We've just got him off the drugs. I mean, you're bound to have relapses. Stands to reason.' Nail paused like he was undecided. He was doing a lot of frowning as if he was thinking hard. 'I'll tell you what,' he said at last. 'He'll buy the fags. Buy them.' Nail nodded at Kenno, who was still catching up. 'We need to re-inforce positive behaviour here, sweetie. The more often he pays for things the more he'll get a sense of value, a sense of give and not take.'

Nail nodded at Kenno.

Kenno dipped into his back pocket and pulled out a crumpled fiver. He handed it over like he was in a coma for the day.

'Change,' said the girl. 'And don't call me sweetie. Sherbert's for kids. Suck on that.'

'Well, don't call me slow or I won't be around tomorrow,' said Nail. 'What do we call you?'

'Natalie.'

'Natalie's good,' said Nail.

'And Nail's a funny one,' said Natalie.

'It's because I'm hard as.'

'Hard as?'

'Hard as a nail. Get it?'

'Oh, and there was I thinking it was because you were hammered all the time.'

Nail shrugged. The girl was a rubber mouth but she had a torso you could talk about.

'Look,' he said. 'You around tomorrow? We could do something together.'

'Just what had you got in mind?'

'A ride. Swim in the loch.'

Natalie frowned. 'You got a car?'

Nail nodded. 'Can always lift one.' He grinned. 'Only joking.'

Natalie thought for a minute. 'OK,' she said, 'tomorrow. Two o'clock. Both of you.'

'Both?'

Kenno smiled.

Forget it Kenneth thought Nail. Somewhere on the way you're going to get lost.

Chicken Angel just stares and stares.

Tears are streaming down Cough Cough's cheeks.

Yellow tears.

Chicken Angel puts a fist in her mouth.

'Nurse,' I shout. 'Nurse.'

I take Cough Cough's hand and hold it. 'It's OK, CC,' I say. 'It's OK.' He squeezes me back. It's like he's saying not to worry, I'm all right.

But I am worried. Cough Cough's my friend. We help each other. Cough Cough never cries, never. Something's squealing him and it's squealing me too. And Chicken Angel. Only not so much her. She's got Lights Out to look after. If Cough Cough goes I'll have no one.

'It's G1,' I say as the nurse hurries across the day-room from the office. 'He's not well.'

By now Cough Cough has slumped in his chair. He looks just like the Cough Cough who came back from the tests all dozied out.

Suddenly his hand slips limply from mine.

I look up.

Lights Out is standing in the doorway to the dormie a hand across her face.

'It's those chemicals and all the tox,' Chicken Angel is saying to the nurse.

'Stay here till I tell you to leave,' he says, giving her a Tin-Lid stare.

The nurse then wheels CC back to bed.

*

'He's going takeaway, isn't he?' says Chicken Angel. She bites her lip. 'Cough Cough. Not Cough Cough.'

I get up and put my arm round her slumped shoulders. The little wings are fluttering.

Suddenly she looks up. 'But he's not got any lumpies, has he?'

I shake my head. Cough Cough has no lumpies.

'I didn't think it would be so soon,' she says. She paused. 'It was you said he was getting worse.'

I nodded. 'It's probably the dozie or whatever they gave him in the tests toxing his blood like you said.'

'We should have done something.'

'Done something?'

Chicken Angel doesn't understand. Not like Cough Cough and I understand. There is nothing you can do! Against trank and tox and Doctor Dearly and primaries and lumpies and funny skin and no eyes and finger wings. That's the Bin. That's us, spooks, four walls and leopards clawing at the door.

CHAPTER 8

Killing the Soul

1

That evening I ask the nurse if we can have showers and he says yes.

I watch Chicken Angel in the splashing water. I watch her wings and her bottom and all over. She's no lumpies on her back and legs and arms. She turns round and I can see the two on her chest.

I know they're not like real lumpies at all.

She sees me looking.

'You're staring,' she says.

I nod.

'I don't like it,' she says.

'It's just looking,' I say.

'Looking's different,' she says, turning her back and talking over her shoulder. 'It's like doing gently. Staring's when you look right inside someone. It's like tranking you. It's like Tin Lid. She stares and makes you feel like you've got tox.'

I turn away.

'Leopards stare when they hunt,' she says, 'in *The*

87

Natural World when they've got killing in their heads.'

Then she turns round again. 'It's OK. Just look.'

She's all soapy and shiny.

'Come on,' she says. 'I'll gently your back.'

We stand together, she behind me, under the hot hissing water.

She holds up the soap spray. 'They're not lumpies,' she says in my ear. 'They're mammaries. Doctor Dearly says so. He says I'm a mammal, that's why. The nurse said they're like buds.'

I nod. Like buds! Not lumpies, buddies.

'All angels grow them,' she says.

'Oh!'

That means I won't get them.

Chicken Angel is drying me and doing gently on my back. Suddenly she stops.

'Hear that?' she asks.

I listen.

It's a fast tapping sound. It's coming from the dormie.

'Lights Out,' says Chicken Angel. 'Something's squealing in her.'

We struggle into trackies and leave as quickly as we can.

Lights Out is standing next to the wooden panel and her fingers are drumming drumming. She's morsing Mrs Murdoe.

'What's she saying?' I ask Chicken Angel.

Chicken Angel is shaking her head. She's staring at Lights Out. No, no, no she is mouthing.

Cough Cough hasn't moved.

'What is it?' I say again.

Chicken Angel starts to cry.

'What? What?'

She turns and puts her arms round me.

Squeezes.

I know then it's about Cough Cough.

Chicken Angel whispers.

'Lights Out is saying Cough Cough has gone blind.'

2

We are sitting on beds cross-legged, listening. Lights Out has her head bent back and is sniffing the air for Tin Lid, for the tremble of her, for the bleachy smell of her.

She leans forward again.

No Tin Lid yet.

Chicken Angel is staring at the new voice-over speaker hung high in the corner of ceiling and wall. It looks like a wasp nest.

Cough Cough is lying on his side, back to me, his shoulders rising and falling with each suck of breath.

Lights Out knows Chicken Angel is staring and waiting and worrying. She can hear when a heart hurries and lungs quicken. When a voice blips.

She puts her hands over her ears.

Any moment and the voice-over will start.

'It'll be about the tests, you watch,' Cough Cough had wheezed when Tin Lid warned us about the voice-over coming today.

Suddenly Doctor Dearly's voice crackles from the speaker.

Lights Out shudders.

We look up. Stare at the nest in the corner, waiting for it to burst open and pour out a swarm of buzz and stings.

'Geminis 1, 2, 3 and 4, this is an important announcement. Sit still. The second stage in your ocular test programme has now been evaluated. It has revealed some disturbing results. In every case there has been further significant deterioration in eye function. G1 is particularly problematic in this regard. Your lab team think this loss of functionality is due to a combination of muscle wastage and retinal degradation. The team have recorded growing levels of occlusion and nebulization of the vitreous humour. Because high-intensity optical activities like reading are known environmental factors impacting on retinal degeneration we have decided, for the time being, to ban books from this unit.

'Books over-demand. They damage already vulnerable eyes. An average sentence requires over ten thousand micro adjustments or saccades at the rate of ten per millisecond. This level of activity cannot be sustained without jeopardizing the viability of the whole organ when that organ is already trauma-conditioned.

'Should eliminating this factor result in some improvement to your eyesight then we will have to consider a permanent banning.

'There will be no reading until further notice.

'Remember: your welfare is our first concern. Any questions address them to the day nurse or talk to your primary examiner. Message over.'

The voice-over clicks like a door closing. We stare at the speaker as if it might snarl into life again.

No more books!!

We're trauma-conditioned, leopardized.

Slowly Cough Cough sits up.

He turns my way, his eyes still yellow. He seems to be looking over my shoulder.

'I told you, X-Ray. Now you know. It's their solution. Permanent TERMINATION.'

'That's just books,' I say. But I know what CC really means.

CC shakes his head.

'Books now, us later,' I whisper.

CC nods slowly, drops his head and falls back on his pillow.

I start to wonder about my eyes. Up to now I've had the best eyes here. I look across at Chicken Angel. Focus on her face. Her lips are half open, her eyes wide but her face is slow with shock. It's like on *The Natural World* when they stopped the action before the leopard sprang, before the little wide-eyed monkey looked up too late.

Chicken Angel's face is on hold.

I get out of bed and hurry into the day-room.

The bookshelf is empty already. My *Fairy Tales* have disappeared.

Tin Lid is standing in the doorway of the nurse's office.

'No more book trolley?' I say.

She shakes her head slowly like she's communicating with some simple-minded child. That's Tin Lid though; she can't get it that we are just OKs. She thinks we're

91

deletes already. But we're not. We're just as different as everybody else.

No more book trolley.

I can't believe it.

No one says anything when I get back. Any commotion and we know we'll get a hypo from Tin Lid – hard shot.

I go and sit next to Chicken Angel. 'Why?' she says quietly.

I shrug.

'The books are always the same,' I say. 'They just rearrange them on the trolley.'

'So what!' says Chicken Angel. 'It's having them around that counts. They make a place feel friendly.' She sighs. 'It'll be all empty now.'

She sniffs. I put an arm round her shoulder.

'We really will be blind,' she says sadly. 'Without books we're all Lights Out.'

Lights Out is standing beside Chicken Angel. She starts tapping on her arm.

'What's she saying?'

'She says not to worry. Books live in our heads. They talk inside us.'

'That's just goo goo,' says Cough Cough suddenly.

Lights Out whimpers. Chicken Angel looks him one. She hates it when CC mouth mouths Lights Out.

'They want to kill the soul in us,' she says dramatically.

We all fall silent.

Kill the soul? Only Chicken Angel would think of that.

Lights Out morses again.

I look at Chicken A. 'She is saying books are magic

carpets. She wants to fly on them, away, away over the Bin and out, out into the high skies.' Here Chicken Angel does bird flying with her hands stroking the air and her fingers spread out like wing feathers. 'She wants to be feathered like a bird and skim across oceans and then plunge into the blind and soundless depths and . . . and . . . never come back.'

'If all her magic carpets have been stolen how can she fly on them?' asks Cough Cough.

Lights Out now weaves her hands, dances her fingers through the air.

Chicken Angel smiles too.

'She is saying they've not taken all the books. She's still got one. It's hidden away.'

'Where?' I say.

'Which one?' says Cough Cough.

Lights Out morses Chicken Angel.

'Under the Big Chair cushion she says. It's *The Golden Treasury of Scottish Songs and Ballades*.'

Cough Cough nods. It was the one he borrowed from the library because it had a bird on the front. He said it was EMBOSSED, which meant that Lights Out could feel it. He said that's where Mrs Murdoe got the Sky Boat story from, *The Golden Treasury*.

CHAPTER 9

Sherbert's for Kids

1

I have to know for certain, about Cough Cough.

He's gone to bed and wants me to give him some of my tabs. They're for the bad dreams I get, the shakers. They stop the shakers but I've not got many left. I'll have to ask Doctor Dearly for some more next time I have a primary. Maybe they'll ban tabs like they've banned books and terminated *The Natural World*.

We've had second tuck-in. We decide to leave *The Golden Treasury* where it is until we can find a better hiding place. This we will have to do soon because when the san team come and do the sanitary in the unit they'll find it and then they'll trank us double hard shot.

In the day-room Chicken Angel is finger-combing Lolo's hair. Lolo has crinkly hair that looks like scribble. Every so often Chicken A goes to the soil tub, lifts the flap and drops in a fist of black strands.

Turn to fur, turn to Jack.
Jippity, jippity, bring our sunshine back,

she chants.

Turn to feathers, turn to Jack.
Whippity, whippity, whippity wack.

I tiptoe into the dormie.

Cough Cough is lying on his back, his eyes half closed. His lips are glossy with lick and at the corner of his mouth is a fleck of custard.

I sit on my bed.

Suddenly he speaks. 'X-Ray, is that you?' he says. 'I'm so tired.'

I nod.

I swing my legs round and sit on the edge of the bed.

'CC, you know the clock on the wall over there. What time does it say?'

I feel bad asking because this is going to show him something he doesn't want to see. It's going to squeal him, in the soul, as Chicken Angel would say.

The clock is opposite our beds. I have my back to it. I want to watch Cough Cough's face, his eyes.

For a long time he stares ahead.

His whites look oily and yellow still.

At last he whispers, 'I don't know.' He waits. 'I can't see any more.' He says this in a voice so small and crumpled and tired I have to bend over him to catch what he is saying. His hands cover his face like he is trying to hide some shameful BLEMISH. 'They've shut up my eyes,' he sobs.

His wet fingers reach for my face and morse over my mouth and forehead.

My heart sinks. I draw back.

I can't look at him.

'Don't go, X-Ray. D . . . d . . . don't . . . don't leave me,' he cries, panic drowning his voice. 'It's so dark.' He is gulping.

I turn away and look at the wall.

The clock has gone.

The wall is empty.

For a moment I forget Cough Cough and Doctor Dearly.

I can't believe it.

What's happened to the clock? Our clock?

It's always been there. It winds up each day, ticks us to bed. It's the pulse of our lives. It promises tuck-in, teaches us patience, keeps us in order. It tows us along. It counts us in and it will count us out. Lights Out says it beats with the hearts of mice. Chicken Angel says it looks like Jack the Cat. Cough Cough says they're both daftie. 'But sometimes it purrs,' says Chicken Angel. 'You must have heard it. Lolo can hear it purring at night. And the hands are like whiskers,' she adds. 'Can't you see?'

Cough Cough couldn't. 'It's an instrument for CALIBRATING day and night,' he said.

'Cats are great calibrators,' said Chicken Angel.

None of us knew what she meant by that so no one said anything.

I turn back to Cough Cough. He isn't crying any more but I can see it is still a squeal for him, trank in his soul.

I stop.

I'm talking like Chicken Angel.

Cough Cough has pulled at his thin hair and strands lie scattered over his pillow.

Gently I take hold of his arms and press them across his chest. I hold them down with one hand while with the other I start to stroke his face.

'They've taken the clock,' I say quietly.

'No time for us,' says CC. And his lips part in a brief smile. 'Can I have those tabs now?'

I go and get some water from the washes.

I check the cameras before slipping the tabs to CC.

He swallows two.

His eyes close.

I talk to him quietly. I tell him about Jack the Cat because Jack is in my head now. Jack has a magic tail I say. It can turn him into anything. Into a little bird or even a mouse. That's how he gets to visit us. How he squeezes through the Weather Eye and hides under Lolo's bed. He comes in whenever there's a storm outside. He doesn't like lightning. He doesn't like thunder. Outside is dangerous for cats. Their biggest enemy is cars. They pounce on little cats and eat them whole.

Cough Cough speaks.

'That's pitchie nonsense,' he says. 'Those two are dafties.'

That's more like the old Cough Cough.

He means Chicken Angel and Lights Out.

Of course there's no such thing as Jack the Cat, like he says. We talk about him, he hears us, his ears prick up and before we know it he's right there inside our heads. Doing tricks. The Great Calibrator. He throws eggs up in the air, six at once, and catches them. Of course he turns into a hen beforehand and lays the eggs. Otherwise where would he get them from in the first place? Then he vanishes, jumps into a top hat and disappears in a puff of gone, not a wink too quick. Like he was never there. Vis one min, invis the next.

I stop.

I'm thinking like Lolo. I am.

I can see her sitting in the Sky Boat as it SKIMS over the water.

One day, Lights Out, one day.

2

CC says she's a primitive. A genesis child. Still in the Garden of Beginning.

Maybe, CC. But you with your calculations, you who know the heights and the widths of everything don't always know the depths. Hey, CC, there's stuff inside your head been stuck there for years. Stuff you don't know about. CC, you need a friend to show you the way through all this. CC, you need to clear a little space, a corner somewhere for you-know-who, for Jack that snap-cracker cat. He'll do it. He'll show you.

By now Cough Cough is asleep.

Chicken Angel and Lights Out come in for their afternoon nap. We all need the naps these days.

Chicken Angel points to Cough Cough.

I nod he's OK.

*

Lights Out is morsing Mrs Murdoe. Her hands are moving fast. The two of us watch her.

'Woo woo rubbish,' I hear Cough Cough whisper. Soon he's snoring gently again.

Chicken A comes next to me. 'Lights Out says something bad is coming. She's asking for Mrs Murdoe to help again.'

Suddenly Lights Out darts past us and jumps on her bed. How does she do it without eyes?

Later when all the others are dozing I think again about what Doctor Dearly said. About the tests and about our retinas going off and wearing out. I think about CC and the toast and the fork and the butter. And I wonder if Cough Cough is right about his eyesight coming back and about how it's just the stuff they give you in the tests turns you temporarily blind.

Then I begin to remember other things. How a few days back before the tests he put his nicks on back to front. How they move him in a wheelchair all the time now, how he sleeps more and more, how he hadn't been reading for ages, way before the banning. This is something I've not thought of till now, the reading. No, I can't remember the last time I saw CC with a book. Over the last few days he's just shuffled about from washes to tuck-in, from tuck-in to bed. As I watched his stubby fingers morsing his route I just thought he was still dozied out after the tests and stuff. But now I'm not so sure. He's scared Lights Out. She's knows something.

Will we really go all out blind? Surely Doctor D could stop it if he wanted to. He could give us drops. Lenses.

Do CORRECTIVE SURGERY. After all our welfare is his primary concern.

Poor CC.

I get out of bed and tiptoe to Mrs Murdoe. I put my hand on her face. It has a few wrinkles but it's smooth. I check Cough Cough is still asleep. Then I close my eyes. 'Please, please, Mrs Murdoe, help us. Help Cough Cough's eyes get better. Help his wheeze if you've got time. And if you've any ideas about why they've banned the books let me know. Because I don't believe it's because of all that retina stuff. Hope you're OK. Don't forget us. Love, me and Cough Cough and Lights Out and Chicken Angel. Bye.'

I take my hand away and turn for bed.

Cough Cough is on his elbow and looking straight at me.

'Who's there?' he says.

Tears start to roll down my cheeks.

CHAPTER 10

The Purple Baby

1

Next morning Nail was up the Scootie on his own. He was sitting on a kiddie swing and fixing himself a roll-up.

And smiling.

No Kenno. Coddy had dragged the zombie out early. He needed his muscle lifting half a dozen wrecked radiators being stripped out of some hotel or other. He had till midday to complete the job. 'Thirty-fin Victorian rads,' said Coddy. 'Weigh a ton each.' Nail grinned. Kenno would be so creased he'd slump back to bed all afternoon.

So, he had the sweetie at the PO all to himself.

He lit the roll-up.

For a sweetie she had some mouth on her. But he liked that in girls. A bit of resistance. The easy ones weren't worth the sweat. Yeah, she was right for him. Right size, not too much shape. Yeah, fit for the job. But nothing too heavy, he didn't plan on being around for long. He just needed someone to tie him over till he got back to London where there was some serious choice on the street.

He took a drag and thought of Coddy. Bin-breath Coddy!

He spat out the roll-up and squashed it with his trainer.

The girl wouldn't want minging mouth all over her face.

Suddenly he was in the hospital again on his tiptoes looking through the screen at the incubators and at the tiny purple baby staring back at him through the perspex. Maybe losing a kid had frozen the heart out of his mum, driven his dad into exile. Maybe that's why she'd never bothered with him much. She went through the motions. Said he had to go to school, made sure he had decent trainers most of the time.

He couldn't remember when she started going missing and how often he'd had to help her to bed, cover her with the duvet, fully dressed, and open the window to let out the stink of pub. Then she met Costa, the man with skin the colour of ketchup. And that was it – goodbye Camberwell, hello Havana.

Nail stood up and looked across at the PO but he wasn't really seeing it.

Maybe his mum blamed him. But you can't blame a six-year-old with asthma for his baby brother's death. Can you? And he was bad with asthma for a long time till he grew out of it middle of primary. Maybe in her heart of hearts his mum felt bitter at fate delivering her not one but two sick kids. He was the only one left to point the finger at after his dad upped and offed. Maybe looking after a toddler gasping and heaving at the oxygen mask shot her chances of having healthy babies ever again.

So it was his fault.

He picked up a rock and hurled it at the trees below. It smashed through the canopy of leaves and branches like a bomb through a roof and blew out an explosion of pigeons.

I could have had a brother now he said to himself. A little bro.

And he could have been a Kenno said another voice. Nail nodded.

Can't change yesterday he thought. Let's see if today's doing any deals.

And he started walking down towards Garvie Post Office.

2

Suddenly someone is shaking me. It's one of the day nurses. I look for the clock and then remember the buzzer isn't working.

'Doctor Dearly wants to see you. Go to the washes.'

The others are asleep and the lights are still dim.

As I stumble across the cold dormie floor and past the curtain he says after me: 'It's about the tests. A follow-up.'

The shower's warm but my skin is pimpled with fear and I'm cold inside. I spray soap and gently all over. I look at my hands. The palms are covered in fine strands of hair.

I'm going bald like Cough Cough.

*

Doctor Dearly is sitting waiting. The room is dark except there's a desk lamp lighting lots of dials and screens.

I have to sit down on a wind-up wind-down stool. I can feel my heart rib-butting.

For a long time Doctor Dearly sits examining some cards and occasionally looking at his monitor.

On the screen is the picture of an eyeball. It is slowly revolving in a sea of blue jelly. As I watch it drifts towards me and stares from its strange out-of-space aquarium. It looks like a giant one-spot puff puff fish like we used to see on *The Natural World*. It examines me then drifts away trailing a seaweedy tangle of nerves and blood vessels.

Then Doctor Dearly turns to me, eyes me over his half glasses. It's not just a look. Doctor Dearly never looks at you, he examines you – like the fish eye.

Then he gets up, stands in front of me.

'Look up. Straight into the light.' He has a fat torch with a bright eye.

'Uhhm.'

'You still having dreams, G4?'

I nod. I don't really dream now but if I say I do I'll get more tabs and these I can give to Cough Cough. Help him sleep.

'What do you dream about?' says Doctor Dearly.

'Sky Boats,' I say.

He frowns. 'Sky boats! Why sky boats?'

'To be free. To go on the Outside. To get a cure for my friend Cough Cough.'

Doctor Dearly frowns. 'And what's wrong with G1?'

Suddenly the question's a precipice and I try and stop at the edge but then I'm falling right over it, falling headlong, and I'm terrified. CC's blindness and his hair and his yellow eyes and his wheezing and his crying comes hurtling at me.

'He's dying,' I say. 'And he's my friend. And it's not fair.'

'Yes . . . er . . . well,' says Doctor Dearly. 'Maybe you need a little help here. I'll prescribe something to the nurse. Now let's leave this story about sky boats and people supposedly dying and get back to the task in hand. I want to see that other eye.'

He looks through his torch.

'Ah,' he breathes and I can smell sweeties on his breath, like the mints Mrs Murdoe used to give us. 'As I suspected. There's incipient nebulization in the right eye. Uhhm. We're going to have to do something.'

NEBULIZATION. I can feel a chill sliding down my back. 'Is that bad?' I say.

Doctor Dearly looks down his glasses at me.

Did I dare ask a question!

'Bad if we leave it,' he says. He leans back and studies my face. 'Yes, I think we'll get another doctor in. Have a closer look. Do a preliminary investigation.'

He starts to ask me about the supplements. Am I taking them regularly?

I nod without really thinking what he is asking.

And I am doing the fizzio? He repeats the question like he wants to be sure my life is all-day, non-stop fizzio.

I nod again.

What I am thinking about is what Cough Cough said:

107

'They've shut up my eyes.' Those were his very words.

I look at Doctor Dearly. Out of a plastic packet he's taking a pipette. I can see the blue plastic plunger.

I am fixed by the sharp needle, by the leopard look of Doctor Dearly.

I can feel my legs shaking.

He's going to kill my eyes. Cough cough me.

He turns round.

He approaches.

I've got the shakes.

He raises the pipette.

And I vomit.

I stand up and vomit all over him. All last night's tuck-in, all my terror. I vomit out of me Cough Cough and his weary lungs and Lights Out and her squealing and all the silent screams of Chicken Angel's gently soul.

And most of all, Doctor Dearly, I vomit you, with your bleachy hands and your thin face and your dozie dozie and your needles and your terminations.

Suddenly I'm cold and shivery.

'Sorry. Sorry. Sorry. Sorry. Sorry,' I gabble.

Doctor Dearly hasn't moved. He just stands there, his trousers dripping, hands up in surprise.

'Nurse,' he shouts.

She comes running, stands in the doorway, catches her breath. 'Don't gawp, nurse, get me a lab coat,' says Doctor Dearly. 'And take this vomiter back to the unit. Shower him and give him a shot for his stomach. He's gone hyper. A dose of immo will slow him down. The usual milligrams. And bring me a towel.'

3

Hours and hours later I wake.

The night light is on. Lights Out and Chicken Angel are asleep. Cough Cough is lying on his back. That means he's awake.

'You OK, X-Ray?' he whispers. His voice is more husky than wheezy.

'Yeah,' I say.

But I'm not. My head is fluffy as Lights Out would say and I'm not seeing too clearly. I put this down to the stomach jab and its after-effects.

Suddenly I sit up.

What if . . . what if . . . it wasn't immo? I grab the metal side of the bed to steady myself because I can feel the shakes coming. Sometimes I fit after stomach jabs.

Then I think some more. Immo doesn't put you out, not for hours and hours. No, they must have tranked me.

Why?

I hold on to a few floating thoughts as the trank swirls me round.

I'd sicked Doctor Dearly and made him smell. He wanted his own back. He doesn't like smell and he doesn't like us. His face floats in the water next to me. It's like skin peel. And he hates mess like pitch in a bed. It sicks him, the rubber mats and stuff, especially Lights Out because she pees all the time, because when he comes into the unit he always wears a mask and stretchy gloves, whitish like my skin when it comes off.

*

Now I'm grabbing the bed again because something even worse has just fluttered in my head. Suppose . . . suppose . . . suppose while I've been coma-ed he's come and put that stuff in my eyes.

Doctor D!

I slide out of bed and stumble into the washes.

I stand in front of the mirror but there's no mirror any more. I look around. There are no mirrors anywhere. Just holes in the wall where the screws were. They've taken all the mirrors!

What's happening?

I splash my face with water.

I wait for my head to clear then I drag myself back to the dormie and stand beside Cough Cough's bed. 'Check my eyes, check my eyes,' I cry.

He turns his face towards me.

I gasp.

His right eye is patched.

How could I?

How could I forget?

'Oh, CC,' I whisper. 'Sorry. Sorry. Sorry. Sorry.' I stroke his face, gently gently. 'What's happened?'

'More tests, this morning,' he says. His voice is strong and he's not wheezing. 'They measured you up too,' he says. 'While you were coma-ed.'

'Measured? Why? My eyes are OK, aren't they?'

Cough Cough is silent.

'Yours are good,' he says quietly.

Then I remember Doctor Dearly telling me I was nebulized. I tell Cough Cough about it and me sicking Doctor Dearly.

'Sicking Dearly,' he murmurs. 'It's for his own good.'
He says this in his Doctor Dearly voice.

We both smile.

'And forget about that nebulize stuff. That's just noo noo,
X-Ray. Nebulized means your eyes are going misty. Mine
are nebulized. In deep fog. Yours are OK, aren't they?'

'Yes, yes.' And I blink and blink. Then I stand up,
climb on the bed and look over the partition to where
Moose chews his sullen cud. In the glow of the night
light I can see his eye clear and deep sea blue.

I clamber down and kneel next to CC.

I tell him about the mirrors.

He shakes his head. He doesn't know why they've
taken them down.

'They're up to something,' he says.

'We won't be able to see ourselves now.'

Cough Cough is looking hard ahead almost like he's
talking to himself. 'That's it. They're going to do something to us and they don't want us to see ourselves. That's
why they were measuring you up. That's why Dearly's
lying about your eyes.' He grabs my arm but is still
looking ahead. It's as if he's seeing the truth shining on
the wall above the curtain and beyond Lights Out and
Chicken Angel. 'I think they're going to *experiment* on
us,' he whispers. 'I think they're trying out something.
That's why . . .' He pauses like something's just fired in
his brain. 'Of course! That's why they've been giving us
supplements, building us up.' He turns to face me. Then
he takes my hand. His fingers wrap round mine. 'X-Ray,'
he says, 'I think we're being set up.'

'For what?' I say uneasily.

CHAPTER 11

An Eye for an Eye

1

I can feel Cough Cough's hand shaking. He grips my arm tighter to steady himself.

'What exactly happened with Dearly?' he says. He's wheezing all the time and taking shots from his squirter.

I start to tell him again about sicking and being jabbed with immo but he doesn't want to hear about it. 'What did Dearly say before that? Anything?'

I tell him about the nebulizing and the pipette and the eye on the computer and about the Sky Boat. Then I tell him about another doctor coming and doing a prelim.

'Ah,' Cough Cough lets out a long wheezy breath. 'An OPERATOR then.'

'Operator?'

'They coma you and open you up. That's what operators do.'

I stare at CC in disbelief.

'That's a prelim? They open you? What happens to the blood?'

Cough Cough ignores me.

'Why are they going to open me, CC? Why?'

'It's part of the experiment,' he says.

'But Doctor Dearly says it's to stop my eyes getting worse.'

Cough Cough lets go my arm. 'X-Ray, you are a goo goo brain. There's nothing wrong with you. They want to persuade you there is so they can mess about with you, just like they have with me. Don't believe them. We're their guinea pigs.'

I'd seen those little furry piggies on *The Natural World*. They always seemed OK chewing grass and keeping a lookout for eagles. I could see how we were guinea pigs. The Bin was our hutch. We sleep and eat and pee. And we're warm and we're alive. So I can see what CC is saying.

'Look, X-Ray, listen to me.'

And suddenly I feel him stiffen like he's fitting. I jump up and lean over him, pressing his shoulders down to steady him. Eventually the fit passes. He stares up. At me or beyond me, I don't know.

'You're OK now, CC,' I say. 'I've saved my tab. Do you want one?'

He shakes his head. He's wearied out, moosed.

'X-Ray, just get out while you can,' he whispers. 'Just get out of here.'

'Get out?' I say. 'But that's impossible. You can't get out of the Bin. No one can.'

'Look, I've been telling you for ages, they're trying to break us down. Tranking us with harder and harder shot, degrading the environment – pencils, mirrors, television, books, heating – and fattening us for the knife, you and me. Can't you see it now?'

His voice trails off. I bend down closer so I can hear

the faint words and I smell his breath – dozie and sick.

'Get out, get out, X-Ray,' he says again. 'Dearly's mad. I wish he was dead. We've got to fight them, X-Ray. We can't just sit back like dozied monkeys and give in. It's an eye for an eye, tooth for a tooth.'

He bangs his chest with his fist.

I've never heard CC talk like this. Is it the chemicals? Gradually he calms.

'I dream about him. In my dream we've drowned him, you and I. We're in *The Natural World* and Dearly is floating down a river and on his back is one of those birds.'

'That pick insects off hippos?'

'No, that eat dead people. Vultures.'

He seizes some air.

'He's evil,' he wheezes. 'Evil.'

I sit back. I don't like what CC is saying. I don't think he should be saying such things. I don't like Doctor Dearly but he's not that bad, not evil anyway.

I don't think.

'Well, I'm getting out, X-Ray. I am.'

I stare at him in amazement. 'How?'

But his eyes are closed.

2

I slip back into bed.

It's not fair to call your friend a goo goo brain. The more I think about it the more I see it's not me who's the goo goo, it's Cough Cough.

How does he think he's going to get out of the Bin? Jump through the Weather Eye like Jack the Cat?

Be sensible, CC. You're getting daftie like Moose. Better be a little piggie than a daftie.

I watch the camera's red eye. Cough Cough once said rats have red eyes. That's how they see in the dark. Of course it is. Anyone knows that, otherwise why would our cameras have red eyes? They can easily see us in the dark. One-eyed rats they are.

I think Cough Cough's got Doctor Dearly on the brain. I think the dozie they've been giving him has dizzied his head. I bet the stuff in his squirter goo goos him too. Anyway, Doctor Dearly once said we were valuable scientific specimens. CC's forgotten that.

Cough Cough is snoring.

I'm going to ask Chicken Angel about Doctor Dearly. Just taking away the books and *The Natural World* doesn't mean they're trying to bin us. And no one's given me extra dozie. And the heating's off because Outside's got warm again. It gets warm and then it gets cold. That's how it is. Some Outsides on *The Natural World* are warm all the time like jungles, they have warm Outsides. That's because they have sun. We have radiators. Lolo thinks fish live in radiators. She says she can hear them talking, syllabubbling Moose-time.

I mean, just imagine Lights Out on the Outside. She'd have no dozie, no fizzio, no tuck-in. Who'd do her hair? Cough Cough says she's a genius. But you have to be more than a genius to survive in the Outside.

I think Cough Cough is a genius but he's degrading. He's degraded a lot recently. I think he degraded tonight as we talked. He's degrading before my very eyes. That's why he says these things about Doctor Dearly. But Doctor Dearly looks after our WELFARE, he's says our good is his chief concern. He even said it on the voice-over.

Then I hear Moose moaning.

It's the wind in the chimney Cough Cough always says. Nothing more.

But I'm not sure, CC, I say to myself. Moose may look like a daftie but he still knows a thing or two. He's not just a stuffed animal. He's got eyes that follow you. He's been in the Bin longer than any of us. You can't just ignore him.

Lights Out knows what I mean. She says Moose is her friend. But all animals are her friends, even snakes.

Tell me about the Outside I say to Moose.

Outside goes on and on right up to the stars says Moose. To reach the stars you have to cross the sea he says. Which means you've got to be a fish or a bird or a cloud I say. Or a boat.

Moose looks down his large nose. He is doubtful. Better stay Inside he says. Outside makes you very small. Outside makes you so small an ant could eat you all up.

Moose is tired.

He's going to sleep he says. Sweet dreams he yawns. He sounds just like Mrs Murdoe.

3

At first tuck-in I wait for Lights Out to go to the washes before I tell Chicken Angel about Cough Cough.

First I tell her about me sicking all over Doctor Dearly.

117

'What did he do to you?' she says.

'I thought he was going to cough cough my eyes,' I say. 'And an operator is coming to look at me. From Edinburgh. Cough Cough says that's a London in Scotland.'

Chicken Angel is puzzled.

'What's an operator?'

'Cough Cough says it's someone who cuts you open and lets out the blood so they can look inside you.'

Chicken Angel is horrified. 'That's a leopard,' she says. 'Why do they want to leopard you?'

'I don't know.'

'It'll kill you.'

Her eyes widen. Chicken Angel has beautiful eyes. They glisten. They are green and blue and look like under the sea. Inside each globe there are fish trembling and coral flowers gently waving their long silken fins.

Chicken Angel is very AGITATED. She runs her fingers over her face, pushes them into her mouth. Strokes my hair, gentles my cheeks, wipes blood from my lips.

'You are so beautiful, X-Ray. Your skin shines.'

I smile.

I lean forward and say very quietly, 'Cough Cough says Doctor Dearly wants to get rid of us all. That's why.'

'Yes,' says Chicken A. 'He's always saying that.'

'And everything is being degraded.'

'Yes. He says that too.'

We sit there in silence. We're trying to add it all up. She too is thinking about the television and the books and

118

the pencils. It's all fluttering in my head. Nothing stays still long enough to get a clear picture.

Neither of us wants to admit CC is right. Because where would that leave us?

I look round the day-room. Moose is there, a big cobweb hanging between his antlers, the fur round his nose patched and dusty. The waterhole hiccups at us and under the cushion of the Big Chair I can just see the shiny edge of *The Golden Treasury*.

I get up and tuck the book out of sight.

That's what I want to do with Cough Cough and his warnings and worries and his mouth mouthing of Doctor Dearly.

'He could be right,' I say, returning to the table and hoping Chicken Angel will tell me I'm wrong.

But she is nodding slowly and tears are edging down her cheeks.

'We are going to go takeaway, X-Ray, aren't we?' she whimpers. 'What can we do?'

'Get out. Leave. Escape,' I say, surprised at the words leaping out of my mouth.

She wipes her eyes and looks at me like I've got after-trank.

'Cough Cough says he's going away, getting out,' I say quickly.

She snorts. 'Poor Cough Cough,' she says. 'He has gone goo goo then. That's dozie talk. Surely you don't believe a word. He can't even get out of a wheelchair now. He can't even see.'

'But we can,' I say. 'We could escape if we worked out a way.'

Chicken Angel frowns. 'Tell that to the leopard,' she says.

Just then the door of the day-room opens and Doctor Dearly's nurse comes in and beckons to me. 'The Doctor,' she says, 'wants to see you. You've got a visitor.'

I look at Chicken Angel.

Her eyes are alarm all over. Monkey face.

She reaches across the table and gentles my hand. Then I realize she's morsing me.

Be brave she says.

4

On the screen in Doctor Dearly's office is another eye cut in half. All the blood has gone and there's just the eye left with pink muscles and the lens and the CORNEA and the retina and in between a large CAVITY.

At the desk is a man in a white lab coat. He looks like Cough Cough, chubby and balding.

'Sit here,' he says, pointing to a large black chair.

He pumps the chair with his foot and I am tilted back.

I begin to struggle, try to sit up. He presses me down.

'What are you going to do?' I say.

'Just look at the light. Up. Down. Left. Right.'

He turns to Doctor Dearly. 'I think we can proceed. It's good.'

He steps back and goes to the screen.

Doctor Dearly stands in front of me. 'G4, you want to help your friend, don't you?'

I nod.

'We've reached the end of the line with our present treatment. For G1 something more radical is needed.'

'Your friend,' interrupts the man at the desk, 'suffers from accelerated PREMATURE MACULA DEGENERATION. We cannot save the eyes but we can –'

'Do something else,' says Doctor Dearly taking over. 'But we need you. Now you're on level 4 fizzio so I think we can assume you are strong enough to take the operation.'

'Operation?'

'Yes.'

'Will I lose all my blood?'

Doctor Dearly frowns. 'Who's been putting such rubbish in your head? No, G4, you will not lose all your blood. We are only operating in the eye.'

'Ohh,' I squeak as if a Hyena Man is squeezing my throat.

'Do not worry, G4. We have Mr Shahabi here who is a specialist in OPTHALMIC surgery. You will be safe in his hands.'

'You're not going to kill me, get rid of me?'

'No, whatever gave you that idea? Would we be doing a transplant to save your friend's sight if we had such an idea? What irresponsible nonsense.'

'What's a TRANSPLANT?' I say, beginning to tremble. I can feel my skin tightening. I'm onioning.

The Shahabi man speaks. 'It's where we replace a bad organ like a heart or lung with a good heart or lung.'

'Or eye,' says Doctor Dearly.

I look up at him. His eyes are cold and unblinking.

'You're going to take my eye and give it to C . . .

121

C . . . Cough Cough,' I stutter. I can feel shakers in my arms and the skin of my face pulling tighter.

'G1. Yes, that's the plan.'

'But you said I was nebulized.'

The Shahabi man looks at Doctor Dearly.

'That was a blind,' he says. 'So as not to alarm you. Your eye is a very good eye.'

I sit in the chair trembling. I lick my lips. They are salty with blood.

Mine for Cough Cough's.

An eye for an eye.

CHAPTER 12

Booty

1

When I get back it feels middle of the morning. The lights are full on and there's no sign of Cough Cough. His bed's fresh on as Mrs Murdoe would say.

Mine too.

The others must be in the day-room.

I lie down, still trembling inside. I put my fingers over my eyes. I can feel them, little spongy balls.

Next thing I know Chicken Angel is whispering in my ear and doing gently on my cheek.

'Tell us what's happened?'

I can smell dozie on her tracksuit. Sick and soap.

Lights Out has her head on my middle. She is stroking my knee.

'They're going to operate, Doctor Dearly and the other man.'

I tell them about the other man. I tell them about transplants. I tell them about the eyes.

Lights Out mews and mews.

I stroke her crinkly hair.

Then Chicken Angel squeezes me to her. She is crying. We do Jesus Hands.

Then she whispers: 'I'll write it in my story.'

I know she thinks it will help. But who will it help? Chicken Angel. For her the words will carry the hurt away like those scapegoats Mrs Murdoe told us about.

'It's terrible,' wails Chicken Angel.

'But it means Cough Cough will be able to see,' I say. 'He's my friend. What can I do?'

'But what if it doesn't work?'

'Doctor Dearly says it's routine.'

'Is that what they do on the Outside?' says Chicken Angel. 'Swap eyes?'

I shrug. I can feel her little wing fingers stirring.

'It's terrible,' she says again. 'You mustn't let them. It'll squeal so much. You mustn't.'

'It's for Cough Cough,' I say simply.

What else can I say? I can't say no.

We sit there on my bed, hugging. The nurse walks past but doesn't say anything. She's carrying a towel. Is it for Cough Cough? He's probably in the Recovery Room.

I think they've been told not to disturb us.

When Cough Cough comes back he looks dozied out. The nurses lie him down and cover him with his blanket.

'We've got to talk to him,' whispers Chicken Angel after they've gone.

'Where's he been?' I say.

Chicken Angel shrugs. 'He didn't have first tuck-in,' she says. 'Tests probably. More tests.'

Then Lights Out gets up and goes to Mrs Murdoe.

She doesn't morse. She stands there stroking the face in the wood and shaking her head.

Chicken Angel and I watch her.

This is too much even for Mrs M.

Then Lights Out starts tap tapping the forehead.

Cough Cough has a plan she is saying.

Talk to Cough Cough.

2

Down at the Garvie PO all was quiet. The ice-cream board was out and slapped with a SOLD OUT sign.

Nail walked up to the door and grabbed the handle.

Time for Mister Fox to check out the hen house.

Door stuck?

No. Door locked!

Nail swore.

He checked the opening hours.

Half-day closing.

The sign swung inside the glass of the door. Ha ha it said.

Nail kicked the waste bin next to him. It rattled with empties. He couldn't even get a tin of McEwan's. Garvie – morgue town.

He pressed his face to the glass and tried looking inside.

A light spot-lit the counter and a camera eye peered at him.

He gave it the finger and rattled the door.

No Natalie. No go.

So what was she doing saying she was up for it and available then shutting shop and disappearing? Was it a wind up? She was the sort. A bit stuck-up now he remembered. One of those posh accents. The sort that comes with money.

Well, two can play at that game, Natalie tight-bum with yer doodah glasses.

Well, hang about. He wasn't feeding her meter while he waited.

Give it a couple of days. Don't be seen, keep 'em keen.

He sauntered off like it was no big deal, like he had places to go, people to see.

But Garvie didn't have places to go and by the middle of the afternoon Nail found himself walking down the road to Coddy's. To his surprise he could see him in the front drive standing at the back of his van and looking up and down the road like he was expecting trouble.

As Nail approached he killed his fag and motioned him over.

'Wanna earn a fiver?'

'Doing what?' said Nail. For a fiver Coddy would want blood.

'You deliver these tonight when you pick her up.' He thumbed at the van. Nail looked through the back window. He could see half a dozen white cardboard boxes stashed up against the partition behind the front seats.

Nail had told Coddy he'd passed his driving test so he had occasionally let him have the van.

'Her?'

'Kenneth's mother. She wants a lift tonight and tomorrow.'

Oh that 'her'. Coddy's wife. Separated from Coddy like you'd separate from a crocodile. They kept well apart even though she only lived two miles away on the other side of Garvie. And that was too near for Coddy. Only a 12-bore elephant gun would take him within shooting distance of her.

'Her car's done a sickie. It's in the garage for two days. The last bus leaves before her shift ends. So she needs a lift. She works at Bin Linnie. The nut house. You know that, don't you?'

Nail nodded. So he had to go the Bin.

'And I'm delivering this stuff?' Nail pointed to the van.

'Yeah, and you watch out. I don't want any cock-ups. Go to the Bin a bit early. You deliver to Naz in Maintenance there. Knock twice on the green door and wait. Kenno knows the routine. He's going with you. After, you pick her up, remember. She finishes at eight.'

'What's the booty?'

Coddy said nothing for a second. 'It's legit. Body stockings.'

'For a house of freaks. Come on!'

Coddy scowled. 'Just deliver.'

'Will do,' said Nail.

He grinned. He was going to the Bin to see the monkey heads.

3

Talk to Cough Cough? How? He was dozied out.

'What do you think he'll say when you tell him about swapping eyes?' asks Chicken Angel.

127

'It's not swapping,' I say. 'It's giving.'

'Taking,' says Chicken Angel.

I think about this.

It'll prove to CC he's wrong about Doctor Dearly, about him wanting to experiment on us. This isn't for Doctor Dearly's benefit, CC. He can see OK. It's for yours. So you can see again.

'But what if it doesn't work?' Chicken Angel is saying.

I don't say anything. I've told her what I think. That Doctor Dearly says it's going to be OK. Run of the mill the operator said.

But will it be OK? What if the eyes are different sizes and mine doesn't fit? How do they keep them in? Cough Cough says they have blood vessels. What happens to them? What if the eye dies?

I can feel the shakers again.

Chicken Angel puts her arm round me. 'Take one of your tabs,' she says.

Lights Out joins us.

We do Jesus Hands.

We huddle.

4

And all morning we huddle right up to second tuck-in. No one takes any notice of us. But we know later it will be different. Tin Lid is on the afternoon and evening watch and she hates hugging.

'You look like stupid monkeys,' she'd say. 'It's not normal at your age. Get back to your beds.'

So we'd sit on our own and wonder about our ages.

Chicken Angel liked twos and said she was going to be twenty years. Cough Cough said she was daftie because by twenty all your ORGANS are fully developed and hers weren't even half developed from what he could see. I asked him about Chicken Angel's organs developing but all he said was wait and see. I don't think he knows really. I'm not sure she'll ever develop her organs properly. We've all got some organs fallen behind. I've not developed many skins and not much hair, and Lights Out has eyes that haven't even started. So it's likely somewhere Chicken Angel has some still waiting.

Anyway what difference does it make whether we are twenty or thirty or even a hundred years like Mrs Murdoe?

According to CC we're not going to be here much longer.

5

Chicken Angel and I have decided to wait till after light-out before we talk to him. If Lolo is right about what Mrs Murdoe says then we'll soon find out about his plan.

How can Mrs Murdoe know about Cough Cough's plan? Is Lights Out just making it up? She makes all the animal stories up about bears and thunder and lightning and birds and things. What if there is no plan? And anyway how could we take CC with us? I won't be able to go if I lose an eye. Because if you've no hair and funny skin and you lose an eye on top of that it's the last nail in the coffin as Mrs Murdoe used to say.

After third tuck-in we wash and I put on my silk bed suit. It's the last one I've got and it smells. Then we play snakes and ladders and Chicken Angel says we could do with some ladders so we could climb out of the Bin.

And I say we could do with some snakes to bite Tin Lid.

All the time we watch out for her and sometimes we forget to slide down a snake. But Tin Lid doesn't come round much. Instead she stays in the nurse's office working on her desk and shouting at her mobile. The mobile means Tin Lid can hear the Outside. Whenever she's on the phone we listen in and try and see who it is and what's going on. When she shouts we go to the water-hole where we can hear better. This evening she is mouth mouthing someone called Kenny.

During snakes and ladders we do a lot of yawning. This is so Tin Lid will think we're too far gone to be trouble and she won't turn the cameras on later and she may even leave out the tabs.

But no. We still get tabs. She watches as I take mine. I take the water, tuck the tab under my tongue and pretend to swallow. She makes me open my mouth. But she can't see the tab. She never does. She thinks we're too stupid to daftie her. She only makes us open mouth to warn us just in case, to show us no one dafties her.

Then she goes to Chicken Angel.

I lean over and tap CC on the shoulder. His hand comes out from under the sheet. His fingers waggle and disappear.

I slide the tab out and put it under my pillow to give him later.

Then the light dims and ghosts the dormie bluish.

CHAPTER 13

Cough Cough's Secret

1

'Twenty bleedin' rads,' moaned Kenno.

'*Bleedin*' all right,' grinned Nail, revving the engine.

Kenno flexed his stiff fingers. They were stained reddy brown from radiator gunge.

'Five quid. The tight old git. A fiver for lumping scrap all day. I tell you, Nail, he can go swing if he tries that one again.'

Nail said nothing. The van ground round a corner.

Kenno frowned. 'What did you do today?'

Nail shrugged. 'Bit of this, bit of that.'

'You didn't go and see that girl then?'

Nail ignored him. Ahead the Bin came into view.

'Thought you fancied her?' said Kenno, bit suspicious. 'I bet you did. You'd do that behind my back, you would.'

'You don't know anything do you, Kenno. Let them wait. No rush. You don't want to look like a pushover. Harder you play, harder they fall.'

Kenno grunted. With lassies you just never knew.

'But what if they go off the boil?'

131

'Turn up the heat,' said Nail.

He slipped into third.

Across the road ahead was a security gate. They were entering Bin Linnie.

Nail braked gently as a figure stepped out from a small portahut.

'They got us on camera back there,' explained Kenno. 'Looks like it's Dougie on tonight.'

Nail eased the van down and rolled it slowly slowly till it was almost touching Dougie's trousers.

'That's prat driving,' hissed Kenno. 'He'll have us for that.'

Nail wound down the window.

Dougie walked round slowly. He bent down.

'And who do you think you are?'

Nail turned to Kenno.

'He's my cousin and a police training cadet,' said Kenno.

Dougie frowned.

'Coddy's got a bad back,' Kenno added, explaining why Nail was driving.

'Police, eh!' said Dougie. 'Sorry about that, Kenny. Police in the Coddy family, eh! Now there's a 999 story. Mind, about time something dropped in his beer. He'll have to watch his back now.' Dougie couldn't get over Coddy's bad luck. 'Police, eh!' he repeated. 'He'll be doing community service next.'

And with that he waved them through, a grin all over his face.

'Dougie's a prat,' said Kenno. 'One of Coddy's drinking mates down the Lobbie.'

'Like this Naz bloke?' said Nail swinging the van left through an archway and into a small parking area.

'No. He's as bent as a plumber's elbow. He and Coddy were at school together, occasionally. They were always out pulling a trick or two together, even then.'

Nail circled the car park till they saw signs to Maintenance and Stores.

Naz was waiting by the green door.

The three of them had the van emptied and doors shut in seconds.

'Coddy said yer bringing more stuff tomorrow night.'

Kenno nodded.

First Nail had heard. Still, smuggling NHS surplus was better than doing the five-fingers in the local Post Office.

Naz lowered his voice. 'Only come if Dougie Brown's on the gate. If he's in the office he thinks he's Steven Spielberg with those bleedin' cameras, he has them jumping everywhere.'

Ten minutes later, in the van and Kenno's ma was giving it some.

'The spookies are getting more and more spooky,' she said. 'It's the doctor's fault for cutting off the television. It makes them restless. And anyway they're starting to run down, sleeping longer and longer, eating less, losing weight. They're getting high maintenance and it's either more nurses or more sedation. It's just getting too much. You can't get staff. Who wants to work with things like that? It's a nightmare.'

Nail was uneasy but curious.

'So why work with spookies?' he said.

'Because that's all there is in Garvie, spooks and wasters like yer cousin.'

'Why spooks? What's up with them?' said Nail.

'They're retards,' said Kenno from the back. 'One of them's got wings, hasn't she.'

'Wings?' said Nail. 'An angel then?'

'One had two heads.'

Nail swallowed. It made him feel sick.

'But he died. And another didn't have any –'

'Shut it, Kenno. Shut it,' he snapped.

He remembered the purple baby.

'Ohhh!' said Kenno.

'Why are they kept in there?'

'Because who wants retards,' said Kenno.

'But why lock them away? You see funny kids in wheelchairs in parks and everywhere nowadays.'

'But you've not seen this lot, Nail. I mean think of it,' said Kenno. 'Two heads. You don't see that in Garvie, do you? You wouldn't want to see them either. They're retards, honest, mate, they are.'

'In the office they call them deletes,' said his ma. She turned to Nail. 'It's because something went wrong, and nobody wanted them so we have to look after them.'

They drew up outside her flat.

She rummaged inside her bag. 'I'm all fingers and thumbs,' she said. 'It's being in that place all day.' She turned round to Kenno. 'Same time tomorrow night,' she said.

Kenno nodded.

Nail turned the van and headed towards the Golden Fry.

'It's double mushy peas for me,' said Kenno.

Suddenly he leant forward. 'It's her,' he said pointing through the windscreen.

Nail squinted.

Natalie. Carrying a bag of chips.

They just had time to see her slide into the front seat of a small red car. The door slammed and she was gone.

'We could get a portion of that tomorrow,' said Kenno.

Nail said nothing.

2

We wait.

'She's asleep.' Lights Out is asleep.

Chicken Angel slides into my bed. We cosy cosy for a minute. In our heads things are fluttering and flying into each other. Can we really get out of the Bin? What happens when Tin Lid and Doctor Dearly catch us and bring us back? How much trank will we get then?

I can feel Chicken Angel's little wings flutter. They're only POLYPS says Cough Cough. An organ. When we lived in the sea everyone had them.

Lived in the sea? That's one for Lights Out, CC. But Cough Cough insisted. We all came out of the sea. Changed our life form. Like from tadpole to frog to prince said Lights Out like on *The Natural World*. No said CC, there are no princes out there. No, like from fish to monkey he said. He'd read about it in the library.

*

The cameras are red-off.

'Cough Cough,' I whispered. 'You awake?'

He grunts.

Chicken Angel and I get out and help him up. She sits one side of the bed, I sit on the other.

'I've got something to tell you,' I say. 'It's very important.'

He's wheezing heavily and I can feel the damp from under his arms as we hold him steady against the pillow.

'I need a drink,' he says. His voice is croaky.

Chicken Angel goes to get her drink for him and I tiptoe to the washes and find a paper towel.

When I get back the top drawer of CC's bedside cabinet is out and Chicken Angel is reaching inside feeling under the top of the unit.

I wipe CC's forehead.

Meanwhile I can hear a tearing sound from where Chicken Angel is pulling at something.

'Shhshh,' says Cough Cough.

Slowly she brings out a small packet which she holds out for CC.

He shakes his head and nods at me.

Suddenly I'm in charge.

Chicken Angel gives me the packet. Thrusts it at me like you do in Pass-the-Pippi, the game we used to play with Mrs Murdoe, where no one wanted the pippi.

I take it.

It's flat, big enough to hold a knife and fork and is wrapped in lint and bound by sticking plaster.

Cough Cough wants me to open it. He seems to be in a hurry.

I peel the plaster off one end, and out of the lint sleeve slides a white plastic box.

'Open it,' wheezes CC.

I open it.

'Oh!' I lean back astonished.

'Is that all you can say?' says Cough Cough.

'What is it?' says Chicken Angel.

I hold the box up for her.

A look of horror spreads over her face. 'Where did you get that from?' she whispers.

3

We both stare at it, at the white plastic cylinder and the thin steel lance and the two capsules neatly bedded in soft pink foam.

'It's only a hypo,' says Cough Cough. 'You've seen lots of these. What's so bad bad about it?'

'What's it for? I mean what are we going to do with it?' I ask.

'Stick it in someone,' says Cough Cough. 'Now take it out. Feel it in your hand. Come on, it won't bite. Not you anyway.'

I ease the hypo out of the foam and hold it up. It hardly weighs a cotton ball. Over the point there's a plastic cap.

'You take this off,' whispers Cough Cough. He reaches out and I place the hypo in his hand. 'Then you push the needle into the capsule . . . pull out the plunger . . .

so it sucks the trank out and into the delivery . . . cylinder of the hypo.' He says all this halting every few words for a good breath.

I nod.

I know how hypos work. We all do.

'But where did you get it from?' says Chicken Angel, staring at the thing but not wanting to touch it.

I'm wondering who Cough Cough thinks we're going to trank.

Cough Cough gasps and looks at Chicken Angel. 'Tin Lid. Remember when they tranked Lolo because of her Pippi? They all had trank sets. In the chaos this must have got dropped because I found it under the bed.'

Chicken Angel shivers at the memory.

'Cough Cough, I've got to tell you something. It's about your eyes. And mine.'

CC turns his head towards me. He is slowly nodding. 'So you've found out,' he says.

'Found out?'

'About the experiment.'

'You know?' I say uneasily.

'Yes. They want to do an eye transplant.'

'If you knew why didn't you say?'

'Because it's not for us, it's for them. It'll be a break-through. A scientific first. Dearly wants the credit. Doctor D the father of the new optics, the eye popper.' Cough Cough snorts. 'And anyway I was hoping it wouldn't happen, hoping I was wrong. I didn't want to tell you because I knew it would scare and squeal you.'

I squeeze Cough Cough's hand.

'But it's not an experiment, CC. It's for you,' I say. 'I know it's for real but I'm not scared because I'm doing it for you.'

'It's for them,' says Cough Cough fiercely. 'You'll be doing it for them. That's why you've got to get out. They can't do it if you've gone.' He paused for breath. 'I guessed something was up when I saw them measuring you while you were coma-ed that time you got the immo.'

'But we can't leave,' says Chicken Angel. 'Not without you and how can we get you out like this?'

'I stay,' says Cough Cough. 'I've got my own surprise. Something they won't expect. You'll see.'

'What are you going to do, CC?' I say.

'Wait and see. You'll find out soon enough. Now listen. There's something else you'll need. This.'

Cough Cough points to the drawer that Chicken Angel has left on the floor. She picks it up and places it in front of him. CC takes out a tube of toothpaste. He unrolls the flat end and pulls out a small object. He rolls up the tube. 'It's a key card. Opens the fire escape door in the library. I've been waiting years to use it. Now it's time.' He turns to me again.

'X-Ray, you take these, the hypo and the key. You've got to do it, before it's too late. Get out now. Tomorrow. Soon. Trank the nurse with this, go to the library up the stairs outside the day-room, go down the fire escape and –' He stopped. 'After that you have to work out the rest for yourselves. I've done my bit.'

He lies back on the pillow exhausted. I wipe his forehead again. The skin is clammy cold.

'Trank the nurse!' says Chicken Angel, hands half

covering her face. 'Trank a nurse! How could we do that?'

'It looks like it's Tin Lid on duty,' says Cough Cough, his voice very feeble all of a sudden. 'Wait till it's nearly dark on the Outside. Keep the Weather Eye open. Then give it her, in the buttock, up to the hilt.'

'But how?' I say.

Cough Cough splutters and flaps his hands on the bed. 'How daftie are you, X-Ray? Use your imagination. One of you plays sick. Ram it in while she bends over the bed. Just do it.'

4

I look across at Chicken Angel sitting on the other side of the bed. Her eyes are wide with the idea of tranking Tin Lid.

Suddenly CC starts coughing.

'Give him water,' I hiss at Chicken Angel, 'before the night nurse hears him.'

She puts the beaker to his lips. CC splutters and calms a little. I reach under my pillow for the tab I'd hidden earlier.

CC starts shaking again and I can see he's going to blow his lungs any moment. One tab won't do it. I hurry round the bed while Chicken A tries to get more water into his mouth. I pull out the second drawer of the cabinet. I'm looking for another tab, like the one from yesterday he never took.

The drawer slips and as I grab it I feel something underneath.

I turn the drawer over. Taped on to the wood is an envelope. I peel away the tape and open it.

I give it a shake and one, two, three packets of tabs fall out into my hand. Enough to dozie the lot of us for a month.

'Where did you get these from?' I ask in amazement.

Cough Cough waves my question aside.

I break one open.

Tape the envelope back.

Cough Cough grabs my wrist. He's smiling and wheezing. 'They're for putting in her tea.' The words are squeezed out. 'Knock her out for good.' He giggles and wheezes and his chest heaves. He points shakily at the two drawers. We slide them back in place.

Just in time.

Because then Cough Cough blows. His whole body shakes with coughing.

Chicken Angel runs to her bed before Tin Lid appears.

I shove the key card and hypo and wrappings under my pillow, climb up, pull the sheet tight against my neck and close my eyes.

Cough Cough is shaking to bits.

The nurse runs in. I hear her rush to the bedside. I can smell her – dozie and sweat.

I open my eyes a fraction.

She is bent over CC. I can see she's holding a hypo.

Cough Cough is pulling in great moans of air but he's stopped coughing.

Tin Lid is waiting. Another cough and she'll trank him.

If I stretch out my arm I could touch her easily.

I slide my hand under the pillow.
I can feel my hypo.
My fingers close round it.
Cough Cough knows.
Slowly his breaths quieten.
I can hear him no more.
Silence.
The waterhole gulps.
Tin Lid walks away.

CHAPTER 14

Gone Takeaway

1

Next morning Nail watched Coddy leave.

He had to deactivate Kenno. He didn't want him turning up at the PO eager to make up for lost time and get his 'portion' as he called it.

So as soon as the van was out of sight he went into the kitchen. He found what he wanted under the sink behind the bucket.

The water stop tap.

He turned it off.

Then he went into the front room and unscrewed the bleeder valve on the main radiator till black water started to dribble out.

Back on the kitchen table he wrote out a note. 'Kenneth,' it read. 'Rad leak. Mains off. Wait in for plumber. Dad.'

Upstairs in the bathroom he pulled down the toilet seat and stuck the note on it with a squirt of toothpaste. Kenno wouldn't need eyes in his bum to read that. Then he tiptoed into Kenno's squat. The lardy lad was giving it some grunt.

In the front room a dark patch of wet carpet had spread two or three feet up to the edge of the fireplace. He tightened the bleeder valve on the radiator and watched the dribble stop. Then he slipped out, along the hallway, into the kitchen and quietly out through the back door.

'PO time,' he said stepping into the bright sunshine.

2

There was no sign of the girl.

Just some old biddy behind the counter.

'Is Natalie around?'

The woman gave him a look to freeze.

'Who's asking?'

'Name's Nail. Hard as.'

'Well, she's out.' The woman put on glasses and turned to her forms.

'When will she be back?'

'None of your business,' she said without looking up.

Nail didn't move.

The woman ignored him.

'Up your bum,' he said.

'Up yours,' said the woman.

Nail laughed and left.

He thought about getting a bus back to town but he needed to move not sit in some shelter waiting for a shuttle full of prams and kids and shopping bags and crinkly biddies on the charity-shop run.

He started walking.

*

He'd not gone far when he heard someone calling him.

He turned and saw Natalie standing in the middle of the road and waving him back.

He stood his ground.

'Where you going?' she shouted.

He raised his arms. Armpit Garvie. End of the line he thought.

Beyond Natalie he could see a series of hills, stacked higher and higher, the lower ones pinked with heather, tapestried with dark green, the farther ones blued in the mist of distance.

'Glen Nowhere,' he shouted back.

'Same here,' she called.

Nail began walking slowly towards her. She had jeans on and a short pink wrap-around top tied at the waist.

Natalie watched his stroll. He had his hands in his pockets and looked Mister Top Shop.

She waited, head on one side like she was trying to get a different angle on him. He seemed taller than she remembered. He was smiling this time but as he got nearer she sensed it was a camera smile being shot at her. A smile that had an eye behind it watching and calculating. Well, she could deal with that. All boys wanted you in the frame, nicely posed. This one looked no different.

'You were dead rude in there just now,' she said once he'd stopped in front of her.

Nail raised his hands.

'Well, try that again and you're dead.'

'Nail in my coffin, eh!'

'Ha ha. Too right, it'll be bye bye. End of story. You won't see me again.'

'I've seen what I want already.'

'Well, what you want and what you get are two different things.'

He grinned. 'I'm sorry. Next time I'll kiss her backside.'

'There won't be a next time.'

'There's always a next time whether we like it or not.' She frowned at him. 'I thought you were coming yesterday, you and your mate?'

'Waited, did yer?'

'Long enough to check m'watch.'

'Then what?'

'Then I put you back of the queue.'

'Then what?'

'Then I had a good day.'

Nail nodded slowly.

'But you did wait.'

'But you did come.'

'Nah.'

'So what kept you?'

'Had things to do.'

'Like get up.'

Nail ignored that. 'And before you ask, Kenno, my mate as you call him, is all-day closed after a night on the juice. He's somewhere else.'

'Oh!' Natalie sounded disappointed. 'He's sort of chunky and pobby at the same time. Safe to be with. Maybe he can come tomorrow and we'll all go for a picnic.'

Picnickers to you thought Nail.

'I'll try and persuade him,' he said aloud, 'but I doubt

146

he'll want to come. He's always on the Internet.'

'Oh!' said Natalie.

'Burning tunes he shouldn't.'

'That's so boy,' she said and started to walk back towards the PO. 'We can go to the pub later,' she said over her shoulder. 'Coming?'

'Later?' said Nail smiling to himself. 'What comes before later?'

'Helping me clean out the caravan.'

Caravan! Nail swore quietly.

'That's so girl.'

Natalie eyed him. 'And next time you try kicking our waste bin, do it quietly. Aunty doesn't like her nap interrupted.'

Nail groaned. 'Right,' he muttered. 'Got you.'

3

I'm suddenly wide awake and scratching. This happens sometimes when I get hot. It's because I don't have good sweat glands and I itch and then I scratch and then I blood out. And that's another reason they get the cleaners or the san team in first thing to clear the beds.

I throw off the sheets and breathe slowly like our fizzio teacher used to say. Best way to chill he said.

Next door I can hear the waterhole gurgling and across the room the faint sound of Chicken Angel breezing in her sleep.

Through the glass windows at the top of the wall dividing us from the day-room filters the pale blue of the night light.

I look across at Cough Cough. He's huddled on his side as usual and all I can see is the back of his head, a dark pod nestled in the white of his pillow. He is neither wheezing nor snoring. Dozied out I think.

I decide to go for a pee. I've just finished when I hear the slap of Chicken Angel's slippers. She never puts them on right.

'I heard you,' she whispers.

She puts her arm round me.

I hug her.

'I'm scared, X-Ray,' she says in my ear. 'I've had this bad dream. We're in the Outside and the wind is blowing and blowing. It gets stronger and stronger and bits of us blow off, fingers and arms and nails and hair and ears even. And then we go looking for our lost parts. And I'm looking for my wings and I can't find them and I think someone has found them and stolen them and it means I can't get back in.'

'In what?' I say.

She pulls away. 'In here. Whenever we find a keyhole we can't turn the key because we have no arms and fingers left.'

'It's only a dream,' I say.

'It's because of Cough Cough,' she says. 'And his daftie ideas.' From across her face she pulls aside a hanging tress of hair and looks at me frowning and with her eyes squinting. 'I don't think we should try and escape,' she whispers. 'Not if it means we finish up in bits and pieces.'

I nod.

'And anyway in the Outside you would just have blood

148

outs all the time. And Lolo . . . well!' She sighs and shrugs. 'She'd get eaten up by the first leopard we bumped into.'

And with that we go back to bed and sleep till the buzzer wakes us.

The day nurse is on and she's new and as I walk towards the washes she stops me.

'Girls first,' she says.

'Girls?'

'The blonde one – G . . . G . . . whatever – and the little blind one.'

'But we all go together. No one's stopped us before. It's OK.'

'Not any more, Doctor Dearly says. You're getting too old for that sort of thing. Sexes are always segregated. You're ignoring the rules.'

I wonder if being SEGREGATED squeals like having trank or your eyes squirted.

'But I do her back,' I protest, 'and wash her wings and she does my back because of my skin and we look to see if any of us have lumpies growing.'

She looks at me as if I'm all over daftie and shakes her head.

'Orders. There's to be no more monkeying around like that. You're going to be segregated and that means being cut off, separated. Got it? Now just wait.'

As I'm dressing I decide to ask CC how they SEG-REGATE sex.

I'm about to tap him on the shoulder when the new

nurse barks at me. 'No. Leave him. He's sedated and needs to wake in his own time.'

I back off.

4

Opposite, Lights Out is sitting on the edge of her bed and sniffing. She's working out what we're having for first tuck-in. She picks up two pretend spoons and does porridge eating, each hand dipping into an invisible bowl and feeding the hot grainy slop into her mouth.

'Have you checked Cough Cough?' says Chicken Angel.

I say no because of the new nurse saying he needs to be left and I tell her about no more washes together. 'It's because of the sex,' I explain. 'We've got to be SEGREGATED.'

'What's segregated?' asks Chicken Angel.

'It's where you're cut off,' I say.

Chicken Angel goes pale. 'Like in my dream,' she says. 'I'm going to lose some bits, am I?'

Suddenly I'm not sure.

'When Cough Cough wakes we'll ask him,' I say. 'He'll know. He knows lots.'

Chicken Angel and I and Lights Out are sitting at the table eating porridge. Well, Chicken Angel and Lights Out are eating. I'm waiting for my supplements. I have to take them before I eat.

Chicken Angel's almost finished.

'Just eat it,' she says. 'It's going cold.'

Lights Out nods and nods.

'I need the supplements first or they don't build me up,' I say.

Chicken Angel is silent. She has red eyes because she hasn't slept much. She's been wondering what to do, I can tell.

It's so big, everything's so big. What Cough Cough says is so big. Outside is so big.

I'm beginning to feel angry at Cough Cough for making everything so big. It means we've got to be big. And choose. We've never had to choose before. It's Cough Cough making us choose. Choose between tranking a nurse and having an eye out. Choose between going on the Outside and degrading on the Inside. It's so big. And another thing just as big. We have to choose between two Cough Coughs. One Cough Cough is my friend, someone who needs cosy cosy a lot. And the other Cough Cough is a goo goo brain who's having HALLUCIN-ATIONS because of the dozie he's getting now. He's so dozied he can't see Doctor Dearly is only trying to help. All this is very very big and I don't know which big is the right big to follow.

I'm thinking this and watching the porridge. My spoon is resting on the top hardly sinking in because of the skin.

I pick up that daftie spoon and my hand is shaking. I dip it in the porridge and just as I'm about to put it in my mouth someone screams.

It comes from the dormie.

We all go on hold.

We are staring at the dormie door, which is only just open.

Someone is moving inside.

'It's that new day nurse,' I whisper. 'She's still in there.'

I try and take a deep breath. No need to panic Doctor Dearly is always saying. If the alarm sounds stay calm, stay put and wait for a nurse to come he says. Everything is under control.

Then the alarm does sound, loud and ringing ringing, first in the dormie then in my head ringing it and ringing it till I have to cover my ears like Lights Out.

'Cough Cough,' squeals Lights Out. She is holding the edge of the table and it is trembling in her grasp.

Chicken Angel puts her hands to her mouth. What has Lolo seen?

Chicken A's eyes are wide with terror.

I go cold. Onion skinned.

What does Lolo know? All over my body – forehead, back, chest – I can feel my skin tighten. My fingers are being clawed inwards, my toes curled. My lips are near splitting. I daren't move in case I tear, in case I blood out.

Just relax Mrs Murdoe used to say when I went onion skin.

Suddenly the day-room door swings open and two nurses rush in and race past us into the dormie.

Chicken Angel half rises, then slumps back. She wants to see what's happened but daren't look.

Slowly I stand.

Chicken Angel puts a hand on my arm. She is shaking her head.

I walk stiffly towards the dormie.

I get to the door but before I can push it fully open it

is slammed in my face. I hear the key turn in the lock. I stumble back breathing hard and fast. Something dreadful's in the air. It wafts past me, the reek of vomit and pitch and pee.

'It's Cough Cough all right,' I say back at the table.

'Listen,' says Chicken Angel.

From beyond the dormie door we can hear banging and scraping and then thud and then the sound of something being dragged and then another thud and then the banging of the other door and then nothing.

Nothing at all.

5

Lights Out stands up and listens.

It's OK I say in my head. Cough Cough's done this before, fitted out and then come back. They've probably put him on the machine or they've hypo-ed him back to normal. He'll be OK soon.

I breathe more freely. My fingers straighten. I run them over my forehead. The wrinkles have come back.

'Maybe he's fitted out again,' I whisper to Chicken Angel. 'I think they're giving him oxygen right now, opening his air tubes and puffing up his pulmonaries. That must be it.'

Chicken Angel squeezes my hand. I can tell she doesn't believe me because she squeezes me too tight.

Then Lights Out sits down and starts morsing, but on the table.

Cough Cough's gone she says. They've taken him away.

Suddenly we hear footsteps in the dormie. We all sit up and straight at the table like we do when Tin Lid's around.

The key turns in the lock.

A figure stands there.

It's Doctor Dearly.

Lights Out raises her head, sniffs and whimpers.

Doctor Dearly takes one step into the room, stops and adjusts his glasses.

None of us dare move. We know now something terrible has happened.

'G1 is dead,' he says.

Chicken Angel shudders and I let out a cry.

Lights Out just nods. She knew. She knew soon as the door slammed. She smelt it, the little leftover of Cough Cough.

'This should make no difference to you,' Doctor Dearly is saying. 'The body will be disposed of hygienically. Health and safety and your security are our primary concerns and during the rest of your stay here you can be assured everything in our power will be done to make your lives as comfortable and as secure as possible. Meanwhile you will remain here in the day-room until your dormitory has been cleaned and sterilized. The day nurse will inform you when it is fully functional again so that you can return to your beds.'

He nods, turns on his heel and leaves, locking the door behind him.

Cough Cough dead! Gone takeaway.

6

We sit there moosed.

I look at Chicken Angel. 'Poor, poor X-Ray,' she whispers.

And I cry and cry and cry. The tears burn my skin.

And I know now that over the last few days these tears have been waiting and waiting for CC. In my heart of hearts, in my soul of souls, deep in the burrow of me I've known he was going, known and not known, known and closed my eyes to his dying.

Refused to see the leopard closing in.

Chicken Angel stands beside me, holds my head in her hands and I hug her round the waist like I am holding on to my last hope.

'CC.' I cry his name like thirst at an empty cup.

How long we stayed like Jesus Hands I don't know. Not long possibly but after a bit I realized she was stroking my hair. Doing gently gently for me.

Gradually I calm and then, like Chicken Angel, I become aware of a drumming noise, loud and louder.

It is Lights Out morsing morsing on the table again.

Chicken Angel loosens my arms and bends over her. She strokes her hair too and bit by bit Lights Out stops morsing.

Very quietly and oh so gently gently Chicken Angel starts humming to her, murmuring and quietening her soul.

Chicken Angel is Mrs Murdoe for us now I think.

I wipe my eyes.

But who will be Cough Cough for us? Who will know things for us? Who will tell us about the Outside and the stars and London and Scotland? Who will warn us about the leopard?

Cough Cough dead! Gone takeaway!

I lip the words, taste their poison. Tox in my heart.

Chicken Angel is watching me. She reaches out her arm, draws me in again. I clutch her and feel the whimpering of her finger wings.

'We should have stayed with him,' I say. 'We left him to go takeaway on his own.'

And for the first time I think about takeaway. How the room turns to dusk, how the eyes die to light, how the door closes, how there's a dark hole crouching in the corner waiting to drag you in and swallow you.

I shudder.

'At least we could have held him, taken his hand,' I say through tears.

Chicken Angel isn't answering.

'What was she morsing?' I say after a while.

'She says Cough Cough's gone to Mrs Murdoe's,' says Chicken Angel turning to Lights Out. She strokes her hair. 'Cough Cough's gone in the Sky Boat, Lolo,' she says quietly. 'It's flown away with him over the sea and up in the sky. Like Mrs Murdoe promised. One day the Sky Boat will come. Over the sea. Over the sea.'

Her voice trails away like the mew of a bird fading in the hills.

'It'll be cough cough for all of us now,' squeaks Lights Out.

We don't answer, Chicken Angel and I. We don't even notice she's spoken.

The only sound is the gurgle of the waterhole.

7

Then the day-room door opens and Tin Lid comes in.

'Not eating?' She looks at me.

I shake my head.

'G1 died of heart failure,' she says. 'With his lungs he was lucky to have survived so long.' She watches me wipe my eyes. 'He didn't feel anything, so no need to get all goo-eyed. Your flame doesn't last forever, you know. Even you should know that. Just get on with it I say. We're only waiting our turn.'

I stare at Tin Lid.

What does she know?

'And you won't be needing supplements either, not now,' she says.

'But . . .'

'Doctor Dearly's orders. Now get this litter to the hatch. The sooner we get back to normal in here the better it'll be for all of us.'

Lights Out starts mewling.

'What's wrong with her?' says Tin Lid.

Lights Out morses the table.

Tin Lid puts her hands on her hips and looks on impatiently.

'Well?' she says. 'What's the stupid girl saying?'

Chicken Angel listens and frowns.

She looks up at Tin Lid. There's no afraid in her face. No monkey in her eyes.

'She says that you and Doctor Dearly are bad bads. She says that you're the witch that keeps Maiden China in her prison. She says the princess will escape one day. She says that Jack the Cat is our friend and will catch you out. She says you can't put a spell on Jack. He is spell-proof one hundred per cent. She says watch out for his claws. They are sharper than you think.'

Tin Lid sniffs.

'Stupid girl,' she snaps. But instead of mouth mouthing Lights Out she turns on Chicken Angel. 'It's you set her up isn't it?' she says. 'Telling her stories. I've heard you. You put that witch in her head. She's stupid, just stupid, and from now on you're not to encourage her. She's not a baby, you know. Just because you're . . . you're different and in here doesn't mean that you can't grow up and behave like ordinary kids. Any more stories like this Jack Cat thing, and Mr Trank, the Nasty Wizard, will be giving you a dose you won't forget. Got it?'

Chicken Angel just stares at Tin Lid as if she's looking through her. I can see she's doing a Lights Out on Tin Lid and Tin Lid doesn't like it.

*

158

I decide to ask Cough Cough if he really thinks we could trank a nurse.

But then . . . What am I thinking of? We don't have a Cough Cough any more.

And it takes a big swallow to stop tears again. I don't want Tin Lid to see me crying.

Then the phone starts ringing in her office and she hurries over to answer it.

No. I'll never be able to ask CC anything ever again.

We're down to three now.

And on our own.

CHAPTER 15

Everything Sucks

1

'Who's the freak at the counter?' asked Nail as they sauntered back to the PO and the caravan.

'My aunt.'

'Not yer mum then?'

'Aunt, mum. I think I know the difference.'

A girl with edge thought Nail. Well, he didn't mind
some sharp knives in his drawer. He could wait. Take
yer time he told himself. The feisty ones always come
hottest in the end. Yeah, best wait.

They were passing a wooden bench and Nail edged
Natalie towards it. Clean out a caravan? No way. He'd
rather do a bit of getting-to-know-you.

In the centre of the back rest was a small brass plate.
Evidently the bench had been placed in the memory of
a Mrs Margaret Murdoe who was sadly missed by all.
Nail leant back and rested his arm hopefully along the
top of the bench behind Natalie's shoulders. She could
lean against him any time she liked.

They talked.

Nail said he was from London up for a holiday at his

161

uncle's stud farm where he bred racehorses for rich Arabs and where Kenno was just one of the stable hands, a mucker-out as he put it.

Turned out Natalie was from some posh boarding school in Yorkshire. She was a boarder playing at being a day pupil. She was always running away, bunking classes and hiding in the hockey store where she kept her fags hidden inside an old goalie helmet. She hated the place. Every time they closed the gate on her she climbed the wall.

'Why?' said Nail.

'Why?' Natalie snapped. 'You want to know why? I'll tell you why.'

Nail whistled quietly. He could hear steam coming. Too late to turn off the bleeder valve. This was angry.

'Because they wear straw hats. Because nail varnish is OK but studs are so yesterday. Because they talk about horses and Porsches and it sucks. Because if you're butch you play cricket and if you're not you play netball and that sucks. And because they're all trying to be so now, so boy, so same as, they play football and that sucks. And the teachers think it's so progressive and that sucks because they're all so jilly and jolly and hockey and horsy and Country Life and corsets and they don't realize sticking a load of girls together for three months in the middle of Wuthering Heights sucks, sucks so much it turns them all into bitches or battery hens and that sucks and sucks. And they bully you and that sucks and they lock you in lavatories and that sucks and they put curses on you and that sucks and they pick on just one and that sucks and they don't stop till they've pecked you to bits and that sucks and if you're plain you're a Joan or a Jane and that sucks and some are in and some are out and that sucks and if you're out you want to jump in the pool and that sucks because they've drowned you before you know it and that sucks and when you mobile for rescue they've left bad text messages and that sucks and when it rains in the middle of the moors there you feel you're the only one left on the planet and that sucks and if you ring home Dad's out and that sucks and your mum says to pull your socks up and that sucks and it costs a fortune to keep you there she says and that sucks because she's trying to make you feel bad and that sucks so you bolt out and they catch you and you lie awake at night and it's freezing in the dorm and you're wearing a cardie and your nightie and your gloves and that sucks and you can't talk to anybody about it because they'd just tell you to pull your socks up and that always sucks and it's just a girl phase and a hormone phase they say and that sucks because your mum thinks but doesn't actually say you're really old enough to sort it all out for yourself and that sucks because, Nail, I just can't sort it all out for myself and that sucks because I should be able to and can't and that sucks and the fact that my mummy can't even make a phone call and do it for me sucks the most of all.'

'What a nightmare,' said Nail at last trying to keep his head above the torrent of her words. 'That place sure sucks.'

'Yeah,' said Natalie. 'But that was yesterday. This is now. This is Garvie. This is better.'

'So why aren't you back home?'

'Because . . .'

'It sucks,' said Nail.

Natalie nodded. 'They sent me here. To stay with Aunty Jessie and Ben the dog. I can only stay if I promise not to keep on running away. Mummy says it's only a phase. That's her answer to everything. It's only a phase. I suppose Daddy's endless meetings are just phases. I suppose the au pair is just another Daddy phase. Anyway he's threatened to cut my allowance.'

'Allowance?' said Nail.

'Oh, it just means money.'

Nail nodded. 'It just means means, I'd say. So you're a loaded toff.'

'Yeah. So?'

'And yer always doing runners.'

'Yeah. Same as you.'

Nail looked at her, sitting there arms folded, blonde hair crimped. The smell of her sun-creamy skin came faintly to him. He was that close.

'What do yer mean?'

'You're on the run. Think you're hard as. But I think you try too hard at hard. Why? Because you want to hide something.'

'Hide what?' said Nail, beginning to feel irritated. What was the little tart getting at?

'What about your "soft as" side? Ever thought of that or is that what you're running from?'

'Soft ass to you, Nats.'

'Natalie or Nat but so definitely not Nats, thank you. Anyway think about soft.' She dug him in the ribs with an elbow. 'You shouldn't get pissy-faced with me. You're a toff as well you know, with your uncle owning horses. So you'd better behave like a toff and pay for the pub.'

'Yeah,' said Nail, beginning to wonder what he was buying into. He'd thought he was in the saddle. Now it looked like Nats was giving him a good ride for his allowance.

They agreed to meet down the Garvie Arms at seven.

'Bring yer allowance,' said Nail. 'I don't do toff.'

2

It is nap time in the afternoon before they let us back into the dormie.

All morning we have to wait and we huddle our time on the Big Chair, and drink water and cry. We are all peeing to go.

Second tuck-in comes and it's cold – flat ham and sliced eggs. I'm not hungry. None of us are.

'You won't grow up to be big and strong,' says the nurse. He takes hold of Lights Out and raises her arms in the air. 'Look at you, little tiddler.'

He isn't really a nurse because he doesn't carry a trank pack but he has the same uniform. 'I've just heard about your friend,' he says lowering his voice. 'That's bad. But, well, it was on cards, wasn't it? They should have kept a better eye on him.'

Chicken Angel looks up. 'Cameras keep an eye on us, all the time,' she says.

'Cameras! Are you going to bunk off? I think not,' he says. 'Hardly the bunking types are you?'

*

After he's gone Chicken Angel murmurs: 'What's bunking?'

I shake my head. Who cares if we're bunkers or not?

Then Lights Out reaches down behind the cushion and draws out Maiden China.

Chicken Angel looks startled.

'Cameras are red-off,' I say.

Lights Out just has no sense. If Tin Lid catches her with Maiden China she'll get trank, no question.

Lolo morses Chicken Angel.

We're like the princess she says. Locked up but one day we'll escape from the witch and fly away.

Just then the dormie door opens and Tin Lid says we can go in for our nap.

None of us move.

'Now,' she snaps. 'Come on, there's nothing to see.'

Slowly we shuffle into the dormie.

Lights Out pushes Maiden China under her top.

Cough Cough's bed is still there, no bedding just a sheet stretched over the mattress blank and white.

And his bedside cupboard.

I lean against my pillow. I'm not ready for naps. CC must have gone takeaway in the night. But for the nurse telling me not to I could have touched him.

I see in my mind Cough Cough's huddled body, lumped under his blankets.

What would it be like to touch a dead body I wonder. Does it go all soft like a jelly? Does it turn into bones like the ones we saw in the desert on *The Natural World*? Where does all the blood go? Where has Cough Cough gone?

I look at the white bed.

I think of CC wheezing. CC telling me all about London and the sea and the stars. All the things he'd read about in his books. I think of him doing his fizzio and his balloons and the ones with the funny udders and how you could see his fat face through the TRANS-PARENT skin when he blew them up and how he came out gasping and how one time he let go the balloon and it screeched across the dormie and how Lights Out squealed because she thought it was Jack the Cat doing a daftie on her.

And I remember him slumped in his wheelchair hardly able to breathe any more and hardly able to see any more and how we were going to do the eye thingie so we both had one good one and how he smelt because he couldn't get to the washes because the nurses never came in time whenever we called and how I wish, I wish I could smell that smell of him again, cola-puke and pitch.

Tears swell and fall, swell and fall.

3

Chicken Angel and Lights Out are asleep.

The camera is red-off.

I slip out of bed and tiptoe across to the dormie door. Slowly I open it a slit and see that Tin Lid is sitting in her office doing something at her desk.

I close the door and go over to Cough Cough's cupboard. I slide open the drawer and feel for the envelope underneath.

It's still there.

I untape it and draw it out.

It's empty! All the tabs are gone!

I sit there staring at the empty brown envelope.

Something's wrong here.

Where have all the tabs gone? Did the nurses find them? Take them away?

No I say aloud. Because they wouldn't then bother putting an empty envelope back in its hiding place. They'd have got in the Hyena Men and squealed us for an explanation.

Then I remember the hypo that CC gave me. It's hidden now under the mattress. I lie down on my front and reach for it. I can feel its hard tube. That's good. It's safe.

I sit up again.

Who took the tabs? That's the question.

And why put an empty envelope back? What's the point of that?

Then without warning Cough Cough's words come back to me. *I'm getting out*. That's what he had said. *I've got my own surprise*. He said that too. *Something they won't expect*.

'Surprise,' I murmur. For a long time I suck at the word SURPRISE. I suck and suck till I reach the centre and a sickly bitter taste spills on my tongue.

I want to vomit. I swallow it down. At last I know where the pills have gone.

I know what you did, Cough Cough, I say. I know your secret now.

You took them yourself didn't you, Cough Cough? Swallowed them all so they couldn't experiment on us, so they couldn't take our eyes. Take mine.

Yes, you over-dozied yourself so they couldn't operate me.

'Oh, Cough Cough,' I weep. 'You went takeaway for me.'

4

For a long time I sit there hardly able to move.

I am shock still.

All last night – and last night seemed so far away now – all last night I think, Cough Cough was dying as he lay next to me. Into coma, into the dark windowless room, into nothing.

No one there holding him. No one to gently gently him to sleep.

And he never said goodbye because if he had we'd have guessed what he was going to do.

And stopped him.

All I want to do, all I will ever want to do now is cosy cosy him. My friend. That's all. Take him in my arms and cosy cosy him.

Now he's gone.

'You all right, X-Ray?' a voice says quietly. It is Chicken Angel, her face close to mine, her breath warm and sweet and faintly pukey.

I look at her emptily.

'Cough Cough,' I whisper.

'Yes,' she nods. 'I know.' She slides her thin arm under my neck and hugs me gently.

'All that pain and going blind. Perhaps it's best,' she says. 'He felt nothing. Not with the tabs.'

I stare at Chicken Angel.

How does she know CC took tabs? Over-dozied?

She sees alarm on my face. 'We had to do it,' she says. She sits up.

I am dumbfounded.

'Cough Cough asked me,' she says. 'He hadn't got the strength. I said no never. Never. He said I had to. Soon he was going takeaway he said. He had to go before the operator came for him. He said it was easy with tabs, he had hundreds. But he couldn't reach them any more. I had to get them. I had to help him.'

She has her hands on my arm.

I move them aside.

Why didn't he ask me? I was thinking. I've always been his friend.

'Don't push me away,' says Chicken Angel. 'Lolo asked Mrs Murdoe and she said it was right.'

I swing around.

'Lights Out knew as well?' I say. 'All of you knew except me?'

'Just the two of us,' says Chicken Angel. 'It was terrible, X-Ray. It was. It was. Please believe me. Please. Cough Cough was gasping for breath,' she says crying again. 'Gasping for takeaway you might say. What could I do? I didn't know what. He said he couldn't ask you to help. He said you weren't strong enough. He said it had to be me. I said no. He said he was ready. He didn't want to fixy out as if a pillow was being held over his face. He wanted takeaway cosy cosy.'

Tears well up in Chicken Angel's eyes.

'So last night after we talked and you were asleep I got him the tabs and the water and . . . and . . . helped him.'

Chicken Angel is trembling my bed.

'He just went to sleep,' she whispers.

You took him from me, Chicken Angel, I am thinking. Took him from me and never asked or told. Kept me in the dark.

I stare into emptiness. Just for a moment I am takeaway with Cough Cough.

'He said for you not to worry,' Chicken Angel is saying. 'He said we've got to stick together. He said he was going to a place called heaven, the one Mrs Murdoe told us about. He said it was better than Scotland. It was like *The Natural World* but without the leopards. He said he expected to meet Jack the Cat there because he'd never seen him in the Bin. And to tell you he and Mrs Murdoe were going to give some squeal to Doctor Dearly.'

Despite myself I smile.

Cough Cough and Jack the Cat going for walks together and CC telling Jack about elephants and jungles and Jack telling Cough Cough about his bag of tricks, talking talking till the sun goes down and the cat's fur is smoulder red and CC is breathing in the clear night air.

'Don't fit at me,' says Chicken Angel. 'Please. Please, X-Ray.' She bites on her hand. 'I shouldn't have done

171

it. I shouldn't have. But he would have gone soo . . .
soo . . . soon. He would have fixied like some of the
others. I couldn't let that happen, could I. Was I right?
Could I . . .? Who else . . . was . . . oh . . .?'

The words gulp for air in her tears.

I say nothing.

Nothing's to be said.

Suddenly she goes and jumps on her bed, hunches up
her knees, wraps her arms round them and bows her
head.

She is weeping weeping.

CHAPTER 16

Disabled and Deleted

1

Inside the emptiness of me a dull fist of anger tightens.
I feel like fitting out hard shot, blasting Chicken Angel,
blowing Lights Out to bits and bits.

I close my eyes.

Try and catch up with CC.

But little by little he is already fading.

His face seems not here like a face behind a misted
mirror. His voice has gone, not a whisper of it can I hear
any more.

I am looking into blackness. I am tumbling and drifting
through the dark skies getting further away from Cough
Cough. My anger is getting smaller and smaller. I am too
moosed to care any more.

Gradually a sound breaks through to me. It's Lights Out.
She is mewling and crying and pointing up at the Weather
Eye.

I sit up and listen.

Something's going on in the Outside.

Lights Out has her arms stretched out in front of her pointing at me. No, not pointing, reaching for me.

I hesitate.

Then we hear doors slamming.

I stumble across to Lights Out.

She wraps her skinny white fingers round my wrists. Her lips are popping and bouncing like a fish gobbling air.

Cough Cough she is saying.

I climb up and clamber on the bed. I pull out the knot and look through the Weather Eye.

It doesn't matter whether Tin Lid comes or not. It doesn't matter at all.

The Outside is bright and I have to thin my eye to see.

What I see is a white van with a big red cross. Two people, they look like Hyena Men, are pushing a trolley towards the white van. The trolley is just like the ones we have to lie on in Recovery. On the trolley there's a small hump covered in a white sheet. The men reach the van and one of them takes off the white sheet. Underneath is a green bag like a big lumpy.

It's Cough Cough.

I watch them slide the top of the trolley into the van.

Cough Cough has gone.

I watch the doors close.

Then I realize Chicken Angel is standing next to me. I move and let her see.

I can just hear the engine start.

'It's going,' she says.

She steps back.

'He's gone.'

2

All afternoon we sit on beds like silent monkeys.

I know Chicken Angel wants me to talk to her.

When we got down from the Weather Eye she tried to hold my hand but I wouldn't let her. She killed Cough Cough. Cough Cough, my friend.

Lights Out is still and silent. What is she thinking? I look across at her. Her hair is thin and straggly. Every day Chicken Angel brushes it. Every day more and more hair comes out and goes in the incinerator or the soil tub. No brushing today. And she's getting thinner. You should see her wrists, all bone, and skin white as Doctor Dearly's stretchy gloves.

Then the buzzer goes for third tuck-in.

It's broth and dumplings.

We eat in silence. I notice Lights Out is spilling and messing her trackie top. For someone without eyes she's usually good at eating. But she doesn't like eating animals and she knows it's chicken in the broth. She only eats the dumpling and Tin Lid tells her she's stupid, broth is nourishing and good for skin and bones.

She sends her to bed.

Lights Out shuffles out looking over her shoulder at Tin Lid. Sometimes her no eyes make her look very very sad and lost and alone. Then I want to hug Lights Out, cosy cosy her.

But she killed Cough Cough too so I can't.

I sit for a long time looking at Moose.

Don't blame Chicken Angel he says. Pulmonaries don't last forever. None of us do. Cough Cough said we should get out of here I say. Moose snorts. What for? The Outside is no place for kids like you.

But Lights Out wants to go to the sea I say, and if we escaped out we could do that. She wants to swim like a seal, like a fish.

She wants to have her head examined says Moose. Take my advice stay where you are.

But Cough Cough said.

Moose interrupts. Cough Cough was off his trolley he says. Dozied up to the eyeballs. Didn't know what he was saying. But I do. And I say stay where you are. That's what I do. Nothing like staying where you are.

I'm thinking Moose is right when I hear shouting coming from the dormie.

I rush in.

3

Lights Out is crouched on her bed whimpering.

Tin Lid is standing in the middle of the room and holding up Lolo's book. She wants to know who's been hiding it and why we have ignored Doctor Dearly's orders. Had we forgotten books were banned? Or were we trying to defy Doctor Dearly and undermine everything he has been doing for us. I want to ask what DEFY means but of course I daren't do that.

No one says anything. I'm wondering whether to say it's mine so Lights Out doesn't get tranked for having a book when Tin Lid shouts again.

'And what is that?'

She is pointing at the Weather Eye.

I'd forgotten to close it up.

'What is it?' she repeats, biting on each word.

'The Weather Eye,' says Chicken Angel.

She turns on me. 'Don't just stand there. Get to your bed.'

Then she returns to Chicken Angel. 'Weather eye? What's that?'

'We look at the weather. If it's clouds we say –'

Tin Lid interrupts her. 'And how long's this been going on for? Explain. Explain.' She seems very angry about the Eye. If I was as strong as Moose I'd kick her hard.

Chicken Angel looks at me. Tin Lid sees this and turns round. She points a finger at me. 'Do you know about this?'

'Yes. Mrs Murdoe said we could look out. We would learn things she said.'

'Well, Mrs Murdoe's dead and gone. Forget her. I want to know why you've kept this secret. It's forbidden to look on the outside. Why have you been so underhand?'

UNDERHAND?

We've never heard of underhand. And I think of Cough Cough. My heart saddens. He knows what underhand means.

'It was just a game,' says Chicken Angel. 'That's all. Just a game.'

'It's dangerous looking outside,' says Tin Lid. 'It's going to be covered over. I'll tell Security. What is it with you lot?'

She waves *The Golden Treasury* at Chicken Angel. 'This is the last book you'll ever see.'

She stands there in the middle of the dormie for a moment, letting her words sink. 'If I ever have another piece of your . . .' She never finishes.

A strange sound stops her.

It's like a bell ringing and ringing.

'What's that?' she shouts.

She looks across at Lights Out.

It's coming from her bed.

My heart stops.

It's Maiden China, the princess crying to escape.

It's the clock, and it's ringing and ringing and Lights Out is fumbling to stop it.

Tin Lid runs over to her bed and rips back the sheets.

She grabs the clock.

'Where did you get this from? You stole it. You stole it.'

Lights Out shrinks from her, mewling and mewling.

'Right, that's it,' says Tin Lid. 'We don't want thieves in here. No wonder it costs so much to keep this place going. Now, you stupid girl, I'm going to teach you a lesson.'

She throws the book and the clock down on the bed and reaches inside her trouser pocket.

'No. No,' cries Chicken Angel. 'You can't trank her. No. Please. Please, nurse. No trank. No trank.'

178

I slide my hand down and under the mattress and reach for Cough Cough's hypo.

4

Back at Coddy's Nail found Kenno vibrating to AC/DC.

Kenno didn't believe Nail's story about the leak and the plumber but he didn't say anything. One day he'd get his own back. Nail wasn't that smart he couldn't be screwed.

Nail for his part was kicking himself.

Hadn't he agreed to meet Natalie and wasn't he due to pick up Kenno's mum about the same time?

Well, he'd have to leave early and pick up Nats on the way. They'd deliver Ma Kenno and cruise down the pub. Then he remembered he had to make another delivery to the Naz guy. Well, Nats would have to live with that. Now if he could persuade Kenno to plug himself into four hours of prime-time telly instead of going to the Bin place he'd be away.

Kenno wouldn't do it for less than a fiver.

'If I score tonight you're next in line,' said Nail trying to force a discount on the five quid.

'Up your bum,' said Kenno.

Which reminded Nail he hadn't had the money off Coddy for the previous night's drop.

5

Natalie was late.

'Let's move it,' he said as she got in the van.

'Funny smell. This the best you've got?'

'The Merc's in the garage. Paint job. Nice gear,' he said eyeing her red leather jacket.

'Thanks.'

Nail checked the road. 'We're going to the Bin,' he said.

'Better be good as the Garvie,' said Natalie.

'It's as good as it gets,' said Nail. 'It's full of dafties and NHS rip-offers and body-tights.'

'You mean the kooky kiddie place? Well, mister, you sure know how to entertain a girl.'

Nail bounced the van down a narrow lane. 'Exhaust's going. Another Coddy mess-up.'

He gave the engine a bit of a rev. It growled back.

'We've got to pick up Kenno's ma and do a delivery for Coddy. Ask no questions. And just remember you're Kenno's sister and you're training to be a nurse for handicapped kids.'

'Disabled,' said Natalie.

'Unabled,' said Nail.

'Destabled,' said Natalie.

'Bungled,' said Nail.

'Gargoyled,' said Natalie.

'Hunchbacked.'

'Notre Damned.'

'Defects.'

'Recalls.'

'Retards.'

'Freaks.'

'Mutants.'

'Muppets.'

'Morphs.'

'Mongs.'

'Deletes. The nurses call them deletes.'

'Why?'

Nail shrugged. 'Because they're mistakes?'

'That's cruel,' said Natalie.

Nail slewed the van round a tight corner.

'Are we late or something?' said Natalie. 'Only I don't want to go into a lorry and come out a vegetable.'

'Or unabled,' said Nail.

'Or lego-ed.'

'Lego-ed?'

'In bits,' said Natalie. 'I don't want to lose any bits.'

CHAPTER 17

Tin Lid Gets It

1

Lights Out is trying to get off the bed but Tin Lid has her by the wrist and is dragging her back. All the time she is trying to pull the hypo out of her pocket.

She'll break her little wrist like this.

I pull my hypo out, take off the cap.

Chicken Angel has seen me.

Tin Lid has hers out. It's a ready one. All she has to do is flip the cap off.

Chicken Angel is hitting Tin Lid.

The alarm is still ringing.

I'm trying to put the needle into the capsule.

I look up quickly.

Chicken Angel is standing on her bed swinging her note-book at Tin Lid.

Again and again.

Suddenly Tin Lid swings her arm and hits Chicken Angel. She crashes against the bed head and slides down.

The notebook drops to the floor.

Chicken Angel lies slumped on the pillow, not moving.

My hand is trembling. I push the needle in far as it will go and pull out the plunger.

I watch the plunger.

I watch Tin Lid.

She's bending over Lights Out holding her down with a hand on her chest. She's pulling the hypo cap off with her teeth.

I slide down and lurch across the dormie.

I ram my needle into Tin Lid. Right into her backside – up to the hilt – shove her hard and push all I can on the plunger.

She's off balance and screaming and I get most of it in before she throws me backwards.

I stagger away and she comes screaming at me.

I slide to one side and snake under Chicken Angel's bed.

I can see Tin Lid's on her knees and moaning.

She is searching for me. Her eyes are wild.

She's seen me.

She crawls beside the bed and grabs at me. I kick at her and escape out the other side.

Kneeling, I look over the bed.

Chicken Angel is very still.

The alarm rings and rings.

Tin Lid has staggered to her feet. She's got the hypo back. Her eyes keep opening and closing.

Behind her, standing on the bed, is Lights Out.

In one hand she has Maiden China, singing singing.

Slowly she raises an arm.

'I'm going to kill you for this,' says Tin Lid to me. Her voice is slow and the thin of her eyes is all white.

Lights Out reaches out and touches Tin Lid on her cap, very gently gently. Then she brings her arm down and smashes the clock right on the top of Tin Lid's head.

Tin Lid slumps to the floor.

The alarm stops.

'What's happened?'

It's Chicken Angel. Lights Out helps her get up.

Chicken Angel shakes her head. Then she sees Tin Lid on the floor, her white cap turning satin red.

She puts a fist to her mouth. 'She's moosed. What have you done?' she says staring at the floor.

Lights Out speaks. 'Broken the clock,' she says.

It's true. It's not ringing.

Chicken Angel smiles. 'Oh, I feel so funny.'

'It was Tin Lid,' I say, 'She hit you.'

'Then it serves her right,' says Chicken Angel.

We all look at each other.

'They'll kill us for this,' says Chicken Angel at last.

'What shall we do?' I say, knowing that there's only one thing left for us to do.

'Go and find the Sky Boat,' says Lights Out.

'Go to the sea. Yes, we must. Like Cough Cough said.'

At least we could do that for him I think.

Hypo Tin Lid then use the key card for the door CC had said.

I run to my bed. Pull the key card out from under the mattress.

We get trainers. Put trackies over our jamas. Suddenly we are thinking very cool, very Mrs Murdoe.

Then I hear a deep old voice in my head.

'Stay where you are. Say it was an accident.' It's Moose again.

No Moose. Not this time. Have to go.

'What about the cameras?' says Chicken Angel.

All three of us drag Tin Lid down between the two beds and push her out of sight under Lolo's.

It exhausts us.

We rest for a moment, all wheezing.

'We have to hurry,' says Chicken Angel. 'Someone might come in.'

'Don't forget the key,' she says.

'Don't forget your story book,' I say.

2

Next thing we are out in the corridor. Up the steps to the library like Cough Cough had said. We start to climb the stairs.

It takes a long time. Each step we have to wait for puff. We've never climbed stairs before so it's not surprising it's hard.

Chicken Angel is the slowest of us, which is strange because she's the best of us all at walking and standing. Even Lights Out is better than her on stairs.

*

The library is full of books, more than we've ever seen, but most of all it has a big window and the panelling is open and we can see the Outside. It's huge. Bigger than the Outside we can see through the Weather Eye. It stretches and stretches. We're bound to get lost there. It's so COLOSSAL.

'Come away,' hisses Chicken Angel. 'They'll see us.'

'Shall we wait till dark before going down the fire escape?' I say.

'If we stay here they will find us,' says Chicken Angel.

I sit down in a big red chair. Perhaps we should have stayed in the dormie, in bed, warm, cosy cosying ourselves.

Too right says Moose.

Too late he adds.

3

They drove up to the security barrier. Dougie stepped out and raised his arm. Nail wound the window down, said Nats was Kenno's sister. Dougie nodded OK.

He waved them on.

They were just entering the car park when the alarm went off. It screamed from the wall above them.

'Close the window,' shouted Nail.

From a distance came the sound of a police siren growing louder and louder by the second. For a minute Nail thought they'd been suckered.

But the siren faded and the night filled with silence again.

Nail eased the van up to the green door.

'What's going on here?' said Natalie.

'Deliveries,' said Nail. He got out and tapped on the green door.

Waited.

Tapped again.

Nothing.

He swore. Where the hell was Naz?

This time he knocked.

'Watch those noddy cameras,' he said to Natalie as she got out of the van.

'What we delivering?'

'Tights. And don't ask,' he said.

Still no Naz.

'Look, Nats.'

'It's Natalie. I've told you before.'

'Look, Natalie. Do us a favour. You're waiting for a guy called Naz. He knows we're coming. You don't have to do anything, just open the van, give him the white boxes.'

'What're you doing?'

'Going to Security. Picking up Kenno's ma. She goes mental if we're late. And I don't need attention like that at the moment.'

Nail left.

4

He waited outside the Security entrance.

No Kenno's ma, just the whine of an ambulance in the distance.

188

Nail decided to ask questions.

Inside he stood beside a high counter set in the corner of the dark panelled Lodge hallway, a space hung with huge paintings – grouse shoots and heather-rimmed waterfalls – and giant antlers and the heads of snarling wildcats and swords and shields and a sweeping staircase attended every step or two by a white marble figure of some ancient goddess holding up a torch for whose flame was substituted a large electric light bulb.

'What do you want, laddie?'

Security.

'Come to collect Mrs Moodie.' He nodded at the other jimmy sitting at a desk behind the counter. He'd been on duty the previous night. 'Kenno's ma, remember? I came last night.'

The man nodded but said nothing.

Then Nail noticed one of the monitors. A woman was lying down on a bed. She looked asleep. She looked like Kenno's loving ma.

He froze.

It *was* Kenno's ma.

'What's happened? What's going on?' said Nail.

'We're not sure. Some accident.'

Nail leant over the counter. 'That looks like her.'

'Who is this?' said a cold voice.

Nail turned round.

'Laddie come for Mrs Moodie, Doctor Dearly.'

'Get him out.'

'Hey, Mister Doctor. I want to know what's going on. That could be my friend's ma lying there looking like she needed a funeral.'

'Just who are you?' said Dearly.

'Nail, hard as. And I'm Mrs Moodie's taxi.'

'Well, Mister Nail, I'm Doctor Dearly, chief medical officer and senior administrator here at Bin Linnie. Now, you can just turn round and take your taxi with you. You are not needed. Mrs Moodie has had an accident. She's going to make a full recovery. She'll be home tomorrow. We'll call you if we need you. Now leave, please.'

Nail hesitated. The man had an unblinking way of looking that made you feel you were being scoped. It made Nail feel he had to apologize for himself.

Maybe it was because Dearly was tall and thin and had a scrubbed look to him. He seemed antiseptic, sterilized, as if he washed in disinfectant and not soap. His metal-framed glasses, his creaseless tie, his precise manner of talking, the way he sneered 'Mister Nail' like it was a virulent new bacteria, all said: I'm a doctor, you're a pusie.

'What sort of accident?' said Nail. 'I need to know. Everyone will need to know, Coddy and Kenno.'

'You will not need to know. No one will need to know, not until I say so. I will decide who to inform and when. Now either you leave or I get Security to remove you.'

Nail shot a last glance at the monitor. It was Kenno's ma all right. Bandaged round her head and drugged out by the look of her. Someone had bricked her he was sure of that.

'Make me,' he said.

Dearly's head jerked. His eyes swivelled and locked on to Nail, black and reptilian. Slowly Nail backed off instinctively.

*

190

'Get out,' hissed Dearly. 'Get out.'

Back at the van he said to Natalie as he slid behind the wheel: 'Someone has planked Kenno's ma.'

'Yer what?'

'And don't expect Coddy to weep cannies over it.'

'Planked?'

'Yeah, she's had some accident. Some creep of a doctor says she'll be right tomorrow.' He turned the ignition.

'What about Kenno?' said Natalie. 'Does he know?'

Nail shrugged.

'Hope she's going to be OK,' said Natalie.

'What about Naz?' said Nail.

'Sorted,' said Natalie winding up her window. 'Now let's get out of here. Go, go, go.'

'OK. OK, Nats,' said Nail. 'Natalie. Stay cool. Police can take this van down to nuggets now and they won't find booty anywhere.'

'Booty?'

'That was a bit of second-hand trading for Coddy, Kenno's dad. Say no more.'

'Oh, God,' said Natalie.

Nail turned out of the car park. He shot a glance at the girl. 'You did offload the stuff, didn't you?' he said.

Natalie nodded.

'Well, most of it,' she said.

'Most?' cried Nail. 'What happened?'

'It wasn't my fault. The cameras started so we had to stop. I was inside helping that Naz yip when they started. I just had to go.'

'Sod it.' Nail gritted his teeth. 'So we still got stuff on board?'

Natalie nodded. 'If you'd said earlier.'

'Christ, if we get nicked. Hell, Nats.'

'Hell, you,' said Natalie.

Too late now thought Nail as he swung the van down the central roadway towards the security barrier.

5

A man was standing in their path his hand up to halt them.

It wasn't Dougie.

'We're shot here,' Nail said. He wound the window down. 'Just play all over cooperative. They like you wagging tail.'

I'll give you cooperative thought Natalie. He could have warned her earlier about the dodgy gear. Was she crazy or what? Playing bandit queen in some criminal gang running bootleg hosiery with a nutter boy she hardly knew.

'Anything wrong, sir?'

'Out!' said the guard.

Slowly Nail opened the door.

'Over here. Legs apart.'

Just then Natalie got out and stood up facing them both with her arms resting on the top of the door. 'Officer, officer, it's my ma. There's been an accident. I've gotta go. Tell my dad.'

Officer? Officer? thought Nail. Natalie, he's a plod with a badge for God's sake. Then he lit up to what she

192

was doing. Officer! Nice one, Nats. Pat him with a bit of promotion and he'll bark us through.

'Looked like they attacked her,' said the guard.

'Attacked?' Natalie put hands over her mouth and smothered a scream.

'I'm sorry about that, I thought you'd know,' he apologized. 'I heard some of the kids were getting wobbly. They say they can be right maniacs if they miss their medication.' The guard paused. 'Have you seen the doctor?'

Just then the guard's radio crackled.

He walked a few steps away, ear down.

Nail breathed hard. He could hear the muted rasp of another voice.

That freaky doctor he thought.

'Yes, Doctor Dearly. Straight away. There's one here now.'

Could be trouble said Nail to himself.

He glanced across the roof of the van at Natalie. She was running her hand through her hair. She pulled a face at him. Nail frowned. She was up to something.

The guard was back.

'Sorry, miss, but . . .'

Natalie stopped him with a burst of sobbing.

'I'm sorry, we've got to do vehicle searches,' he said trying to be determined. 'Is the back locked?'

Suddenly Natalie turned it up. 'Attacked?' She screamed. 'Attacked?' She began crying gushes. 'Ring the doctor. Ask him. Ask him.'

Nail watched her amazed. Was she real or was she Oscar!

'OK, miss, OK. I'm sure she'll be all right soon.'

'I just want to go home,' Natalie blurted. 'I just want to go home.'

'It won't take a minute. I can assure you.'

'What if she's dead?' Natalie turned to Nail. 'What if she's dead?' She banged and banged on the roof of the van.

Nail gawped at her.

The guard took a step backwards.

She turned on him. 'You knew and you never told me,' she jabbed a wicked finger at his chest.

Don't overdo it, Nats, Nail was thinking. Don't overdo it.

Nail could see the guard calculating the odds, thinking that if he took another step forward the mad girl would deck him one, Bin style.

Then he'd be in for the needle and a stretch in the fog thought Nail.

Natalie was shrieking now, going hyper. She was right off the dial.

'For God's sake, get her out of here,' the guard said suddenly, turning to Nail. 'Give her a whisky workover and shut her up.'

Nail went round the front of the van and helped Natalie into her seat.

'Do the belt up,' she whispered. 'Show you care.'

He clipped her in safely.

Once back in the driving seat he juggled the lever into first and edged forward.

Not too quick. The jimmy might change his mind.

Neither of them said a word for a while.

'Phew,' whistled Nail. 'What were you on there?'

Natalie was doing deep breathing.

'Well anyway, good one, Nats.'

'Natalie.'

'Natalie. Come on. What bottle of stuff did you get all that heavy from?'

'That's called emoting and you get it at drama class, Toe Nail.'

'Nail. Now, let's find a pint.'

He turned off the main road on to a steep narrow lane. 'Back way,' he said. 'Forest trails and no police.' He glanced at Natalie. 'No licence,' he said.

She groaned.

They drove in silence for a while.

'Come on,' said Nail at last, 'we're out of it. I'm sorry I didn't tell you about the delivery to Naz. How was I to know those wacky cameras would roll?'

'You shouldn't have used me like that. If I'm going to be a part of some dodgy scam you and that Kenno are running I'd like to know,' she snorted. 'So I could tell you both to get stuffed.'

Nail said nothing, but swore quietly. What was such a big deal? They were out, weren't they? Nobody was arrested.

'And what would happen if I'd got caught, eh? Didn't think of that, did you? No, it was Nail, hard as, the big gob, keeping his head down and letting someone else take the rap.'

Nail closed his eyes. Was she a razor mouth or what?

'Look, it won't happen again,' he said.

'Too right,' she said. 'Now you can get me home.'

They'd just entered a heavily wooded area when suddenly they heard a strange moaning sound.

'What the hell was that?' Nail slowed. 'Was that us? Was that from the back?'

'Oh, no!' Natalie exclaimed.

'Now what?' said Nail.

'There's something you need to know,' she said. 'Stop the van.'

Nail braked, slowed down, stopped.

As he pulled on the handbrake there was a bang from the back.

'It's OK,' he said. 'Probably that naff door.'

He got out.

'Wait,' said Natalie.

Nail stopped.

'We've got somebody inside.' She was standing beside the van head hung down.

Nail leant on the roof and looked across at her.

'Not Naz, you mean?'

Natalie shook her head. She held up three fingers.

'Three?' he said. 'Three what?'

Then he ran round to the back and yanked open a door.

CHAPTER 18

Riding the Leopard

1

Nail gawped.

Three kids.

He stood up. 'Christ, Nats. There're three kids in here.'

Natalie didn't move.

'And one of them's got no . . . eyes.'

He swung round. 'They've got to be some of those freak kids, haven't they?' He stared disbelievingly at Natalie.

She stared back.

'Even half a brain could work that out,' she said.

Nail scowled.

'What were you thinking of? They're retards.'

'I couldn't just leave them, could I?' she said.

Nail made no sense of it. 'How did they get in there? How did they get out of the place?'

Natalie looked down. 'I just couldn't leave them,' she whispered.

2

Nail closed the doors and walked round the van and stood beside her

'Course you could,' he hissed. 'What do you think we are? Junior Oxfam?'

'OK. OK. They were there. Inside the van. I came out of Naz's place and they were there. In the van. I didn't have time to ask questions. I slammed the doors and got out. And then you came back, and there was all that stuff about Coddy's ma and then Security trying to boot search us. I just forgot about them till just now when we heard them.'

Nail slammed the roof. 'You forgot! Yeah! Sure, you forgot we had a van load of noddies on our backs.'

One of the kids wailed inside.

'Jeez, Nats. So that was why we got all that performance at the security gate. You were running a side bet of yer own, bootlegging kids.'

'Get stuffed, Nail. If it wasn't for me you'd be down the nick up to your ear in body stocking.'

'So who's not telling now, eh?'

Natalie said nothing. Be fair, she couldn't have just dumped them. She'd run out of Naz's place and only glimpsed them as she slammed the door. She'd checked the back window. They were sitting arms round each other stiff with fright like a nest of flightless chicks. No, she couldn't just throw them out. She'd had no time to think. Yes, if she'd had more time, well, she might have done something else. Got rid even.

'They were just there,' she said.

'Just there!' mocked Nail. 'Like every day you pick up a vanful of freaks and take them wheelchairing round bonny Scotland.' Nail turned away exasperated. 'God, Natalie. What were you thinking of?'

'They looked so lost. Anyway who said they were freaks?'

'Everybody says so. That's what Bin Linnie is. It's freak factory.'

'That's just newspapers and gossip for you.'

Nail threw his hands in the air. 'One of them has no eyes, Nats. No eyes. Another one has no hair and blood dribbling from his mouth. I've just seen it.'

He stepped into the road and looked at the van.

What the hell had she got them into?

'Anyway,' said Natalie after a few moments, 'they can't be that daft if they can get out of the Bin.'

'They only got out because you were stupid enough to help them. And do you really think they can survive out here?'

'Why not?' said Natalie. Nail was beginning to get up her nose. Only interested in his own little life. Piss on everybody else. 'Why not?' she challenged him. 'Blind people do.'

'At least they have eyes,' said Nail.

'What's that got to do with it?'

'Everything. Being blind's one thing, having no eyes is another. It's not right. Not normal. You can't go wandering round the place like that.'

'Why not? It doesn't hurt you.'

Nail frowned. 'Well, they're not staying here. Not in the van. They'll just have to . . .'

'Have to what?' said Natalie. 'Wander round the place? On their own? Come on.'

'Come on nothing. What did you think was going to happen letting out a load of seconds like that?'

'Stuff you, Nail, I didn't let them out. Like I said they were just there. I didn't think. I told you. I didn't have time to think.'

'So, little fairy godmother Natalie said, "In you get, children, and we'll taxi you to the end of the rainbow!"'

'Stuff you, Nail. Stuff you. What are you scared of here? They'll get up and bite? Suck your blood?' Natalie slapped the roof of the van.

Suddenly from inside came a strange howling noise.

Natalie ran round and looked through the rear door window. It was the little no-eyes mewling. She was clinging on to the blonde girl.

Jeez. How thin her arms were! Like candlesticks.

She pulled one of the doors open.

The three kids shrank back.

'It's OK,' said Natalie. 'It's OK. No one's going to hurt you.'

'Yes, yes,' said the bald one his lips gleaming red. 'Lights Out says the leopard's coming.'

'We've got to go now. Hurry before it's too late,' said the girl.

'Right,' said Natalie, backing off. 'Stay where you are. You'll be safe there.' She closed the door gently.

'Something's frightened them,' she said quietly to Nail. 'The little one's petrified. She's lost it. They all have.

They think there's a leopard after us.'

'A leopard?' said Nail. 'Sure. Big-cat-with-spotty-fur type, right?'

Then they heard a car coming.

'Could be Security.'

They dashed to the van.

Nail floored it. The exhaust snarling in response.

Up the road and then down a track into the forest.

'Hold on. Hold on,' cried Natalie. 'You'll kill them. You'll kill us all.'

From the back the howling got louder.

'Spotty cat's gaining on us,' laughed Nail bitterly.

'Slow down. Slow down,' Natalie screamed, gripping the safety belt but unable to buckle it in position.

Nail eased up a little.

All he'd wanted was to shoot a few pints with the girl and see if there was game on or not.

And now? Now, he was doing safari safari, hot-rodding Coddy's crappy van through the Garvie forest pursued by leopards and carting a backload of noddies from the funny farm.

'Stop will you. They'll fall to bits,' Natalie was shouting. 'They're delicate. You've probably broken one of them, that's why they're bawling.'

'I don't care if they're ping pong china dolls,' said Nail, 'we need to find some quiet and get this bleedin' mess sorted out.'

3

A few minutes later he pulled into a clearing and stopped under the shady awning of some massive conifers and beside a wall of sawn logs crudely roofed with sheets of corrugated aluminium.

He left the engine on and growling quietly. He wasn't staying long. Sort them out, take them back he was thinking.

'They need cleaning up,' said Natalie. 'It smells in there.'

'Yeah,' said Nail. 'You sort them out, then we take the little monkeys back. No messing.'

They got out and Natalie opened up the back again.

Nail stood to one side. He could see the bald one's lips were glossed with blood, and a fang of red ran from one corner of his mouth down the chin. The little eyeless one was trembling in the arms of the girl with the blonde hair.

Bloodsuckers thought Nail. Banged up for years probably screws you up big time.

'Don't let the leopard in. No leopard please,' said the blonde girl.

Natalie threw up her hands. 'There is no leopard.'

'But we can hear him. He's been after us all the time. Lolo hates leopard.'

'They are one hundred per cent bonkers,' said Nail. He peered in at the three kids. 'That's all we need, nutters.'

'Shush,' said Natalie.

'It's growling and snarling.' The girl was nodding and nodding.

'What is she jabbering on about?' said Nail.

'Something's scaring them,' said Natalie.

The little one called Lolo mewed.

'Turn the engine off, Nail,' said Natalie all of a sudden. Soon as it died the kids quietened.

'That's the leopard,' she said. 'They've never been in a van before. Leaping and roaring down the road the way you drive, not surprising they thought they had a leopard after them.'

'You were the one wanting to varoom varoom out of it. Leopards? They're bonkers, Nats. Like you.'

'You're not getting it, Nail, are you? It's just their way of saying they're scared. Think of it, these are kids banged up for most of their lives. They're not going to see things like you and me, are they? You just have to tune in and listen to their song. Right?' Natalie gave him a frown.

'Coddy's van a leopard, Natalie? Get real. Tune it much as you like it's still a mongy wheelie bin.'

Natalie closed her eyes. Why did boys have to be such planks?

Nail peered over her shoulder. The three kids were nudged up together and now had their backs turned towards them.

'They look like scabby monkeys in there,' he whispered.

'Better get them down,' said Natalie. 'Check them out.' Nail backed off.

No way was he touching them. Nats could do it. She was the one who opened the cage in the first place. Only right she should sort them.

'I'm out of it,' he said and wandered off in the direction

of a large tree. He leant back against the trunk and slowly slid down till he was sitting hunched on a bedding of soft pine needles. He stretched out his legs.

Natalie watched him. 'Selfish git,' she thought. Sitting there like some Saturday night loser wellied on the pavement.

She was angry at him, sure, but more annoyed with herself. He could at least have helped her clean the kids up. She thought she had him sussed. How annoying was that! She had him down as a good for a laugh type, a hot boy, neat cover. But a soft number underneath. Well, she was wrong, wasn't she? Inside were bad tracks, hard ego. Nothing else.

'It's OK,' she said to the kids. 'No one's going to hurt you.'

4

I lick my lips. They're warm because I've blooded out because we were monkey scared and I went onion skin. Chicken Angel is doing gently gently on my arms and back. 'You've forgotten your gloves,' she whispers.

Too late now as Moose would say.

Suddenly the girl is standing looking in at us.

We all look at her.

She hands us a bottle of water. I take some, wipe off the blood and hand it to Chicken Angel. She feeds Lolo and then she takes a drink herself.

The girl has got crinkly hair like Lolo but it's blonde like Chicken Angel's. She's has a red jacket and mammaries like Chicken Angel.

She says it's OK for us to come out. She's going to help us and we are in a big forest.

She reaches in and Chicken Angel takes her hand. Lolo holds on to us both and together we have to crawl towards the girl. We are like a three-headed animal. Once we saw a freak pig with two heads on *The Natural World*. But we are not freaks so that's not right to say we're like that pig. Not freaks, no. We're one-headed kids like everybody else.

The girl says her name is Natalie. She is smiling like Mrs Murdoe used to smile.

We slide out of the van and the air is cold but it smells strange. It's the air of trees.

'It's big,' whispers Chicken Angel. 'Where are the cameras?' Her voice is croaky. She needs more water.

Then we climb back into the van. The trees make us feel small. We are much bigger inside the wheelie thing.

Natalie says it's OK. It's safe to come out.

Lolo morses Chicken Angel. She says she can hear a Mrs Murdoe voice but who is the Hyena Man.

Natalie laughs when Chicken Angel tells her what Lolo says.

'That's Nail.'

'Is he going to send us back to Doctor Dearly?' says Chicken Angel. 'Is he going to hypo us?'

'No one's going to hurt you. What's hypo?'

Lights Out morses again.

'She says it's where Tin Lid puts on this sting and pushes it right through you. You moose out for hours after, days sometimes.'

The girl looks monkeys when she hears this. 'That's awful,' she says.

I lick my lips.

The girl climbs inside the van. She starts to clean my face with a paper towel. She is very gently.

I look at her watch. It is nearly ten. Time we were in bed.

I can see Chicken Angel is thinking like me. We've missed last tuck-in and dozie and Tin Lid. Moose will be wondering where we are and Doctor Dearly will be shouting in the voice-over and sending out the Hyena Men to catch us.

'If the Hyena Men catch us,' says Chicken Angel, 'they'll hypo you too.'

'Well, they're not going to catch us are they?' says Natalie.

Lights Out starts morsing.

'What's she doing?' says Natalie.

Chicken Angel explains. 'Her name's Lights Out and this is how she talks.'

Natalie looks at Lolo carefully. 'Uhhmm. Does she have . . . I mean . . .'

'A tongue?' I say. 'Yes, and sometimes she talks but she likes touch best. That's how she sees. Cough Cough said she can feel the warm of you.'

Chicken Angel interrupts.

'Yes, yes. Let me tell, X-Ray. Let me. She's my friend.'

I nod OK. But I'm going to tell the Natalie girl about Cough Cough. My turn's next.

'Lolo can hear the heart of you even after you've gone,' says Chicken Angel. 'We leave VAPOURS everywhere says Cough Cough and Lolo smells us. She can hear storms coming, the first hop hop of rain drops.'

'Why is she so thin? Why are you all so thin? Don't

they feed you in there? And who's Cough Cough? And why are you bleeding so much?'

By now Natalie is out of the van and standing and pointing to us to come out.

I'm the first and while Chicken Angel helps Lolo down I start telling Natalie about Cough Cough.

'He died,' I say. 'Went takeaway in an ambulance. He wasn't a lumpy like the others. He was my friend. And his eyes went yellow. But his pulmonaries were wee wee balloons like Mrs Murdoe said and he couldn't get enough air to keep himself up. But he gave us a hypo and we tranked Tin Lid and that's how we got out.'

'Tin Lid?'

'She's the nurse. Cough Cough called her a HYPO-MANIAC. They trank us with the hypo and then do tests.'

'And if we say no they get in Hyena Men and hold us down,' says Chicken Angel.

'And they took our books and all the pencils.'

'And the mirrors,' says Chicken Angel.

'And Pippi,' I say.

'And *The Natural World*.'

'And they closed the Weather Eye.'

'And they gave us more and more dozie.'

'And they took Cough Cough away.'

'They tried to take X-Ray's eyes.'

'And Doctor Dearly said it was for our own good.'

'So we ran away because Cough Cough said it wasn't for our good and that Doctor Dearly was going to delete us.'

'Then Moose said we were stupid to run away but we

207

couldn't help tranking Tin Lid because she was going to hypo little Lolo and take Maiden China away.'

'Wait, wait,' says Natalie girl. 'Takeaway? Lumpy? Mrs Murdoe? Maiden China? Losing eyes? What is all this?'

Chicken Angel and I look at each other. 'It's what happens, Natalie girl. People going takeaway, witches locking up princesses, Hyena Men coming. In the Bin. It's what happens in the Bin.'

'It's all in here,' says Chicken Angel, holding up her notebook.

I frown. 'But you said you wrote dreams in there,' I say to her.

'Bad dreams,' says Chicken Angel.

The girl has her hand in front of her mouth. She looks halfway moosed.

She thinks we're all dafties. I can tell.

I think we've said too much.

'What's wrong with your skin?' she says to me.

'It's photosensitive,' I say. 'Doesn't like light.'

'You can see his ribs in the shower,' says Chicken Angel. 'And he's always bleeding. That's why he's called X-Ray.' She smiles at the Natalie girl. 'I'm Chicken Angel because I've got wings and this is Lights Out.'

We all turn round. Lolo has got back in the van and is curled up asleep. She is hardly breathing. I hope it's not too cold for her. I'm beginning to feel the green air of the forest chilling my face.

'I'm hungry,' says Chicken Angel.

'Are there other kids in the Bin?' asks Natalie girl. 'Are you all orphans?'

ORPHANS?

We've never heard of orphans. We're children. Chicken Angel asks Natalie girl what orphans look like. Are they like spooks?

Natalie girl says nothing. She just looks sad. I think we're going to have to help her. Maybe she's one of these orphans. Maybe if we can find the Sky Boat she can come with us.

'We're the last,' I say. 'The others went lumpy a long time ago. '

'Lumpy?' says Natalie girl.

She closes her eyes.

'I don't think I want to know.'

5

Nail watched Natalie helping one of the noddies out. It was the blonde one.

She had something on her upper back, something under her tracksuit top, something squirming. He felt his stomach tighten.

What a freak show.

Retards. All that stuff about leopards. Troupe of nutters. How they'd escaped from that place he couldn't imagine. And just how they'd planked Kenno's ma was an all-time mystery. They didn't look like they could blow a candle out between them.

One pint, just one pint was all he wanted.

Now two of them were standing on the grass, thin and pale and holding hands like a pair of paper cut-outs. The girl had opened a cardboard box and was wiping the bald kid's mouth with a tissue. Then she took his hands.

'Jeez!' muttered Nail to himself. He could see the kid's trackie bottoms were smeared with red where he'd tried to wipe his hands. 'We need a half a hospital for this lot.'

They'd have to take them back. And soon. Otherwise it would look like abduction or something. You couldn't just pick up a bunch of kids in the middle of the night and disappear into the big nowhere he told himself. They'd have to hand them over sooner or later. It was no sweat. OK, the girl could give them a taste of what it was like to be free, to be in the great outside, to be cold and lost and not have so much as a choccy bar between you and starving hungry.

A few hours of Garvie Wood and some Scottie mountain pizzle and in no time they'd be grunting to get back to the batty farm.

Yeah, give it a bit and then they could just drive back to the Bin and dump them. Say it was all a big mistake, wave bye byes and get on with a life pulling girls and pushing pints.

Then he remembered the doctor at reception and his cold contempt and his thin lips, thin as worm skin. And how he'd threatened to throw him out. He could see that face in his mind now, those unblinking eyes, like they were glass, like they'd stalk you everywhere, like they'd never give up till they'd cornered you and sunk fangs in your throat and sucked you limp.

He shuddered.

Looked up.

*

Over the glade spread a black matrix of branches, and below, roots stretched along the ground, thin and knuckled, like the fingers of another malevolent being inching silently towards the huddle of retards.

Poor little noddies he thought. But what could he do? Eyes or no eyes every life was a lottery. Did he have a choice when his brother died? Did he ask for a drunken mother and a walk-out dad?

A pot luck life it was. Go with the flow, eh?

He looked at the flow of the last few days. The girl at the PO, Coddy's van and the Naz scam, and taxiing three freako kids through Garvie Wood by the light of the silvery moon.

What sort of flow was that? He could pull the plug on the kids and take them back to the Bin. Turn the clock back and start again from yesterday, but then Nats would tell him to get stuffed and did he want that? And Coddy would probably meatball him and parcel post him back to London if he didn't get the van back – pronto.

Either way he had to take a chance.

6

A creamy half moon was rising too, a boatless sail adrift in a limitless sky. Nail watched it seemingly caught in the wide-open black jaws of two giant branches. Crocodile carrying its egg he thought, as some old nature film from telly, *The Natural World* or something, suddenly started running in his head.

He looked over at the van. They were all back inside. Too cold probably.

The kids were in a tighter huddle now, arms intertwined. For warmth he wondered?

The blonde-haired girl was murmuring something and Natalie was leaning over them listening. Then the kid he'd seen first, the one with zero eyes, started finger tapping her arm.

'What is this?' exclaimed Nail. 'She's not going soft on them is she?'

Then he saw the kid without the eyes was holding a clock, a yellow alarm clock. What does she want with a noddy clock for God's sake? he asked himself.

He stared at the four of them. Get them back he told himself, before they catch their death. In the light of the rising moon they looked bleached out. He was surprised the bald kid had anything as bright as red in him.

CHAPTER 19

Not So Softly Nail

1

'Well, we can't take them back there,' said Natalie, coming over to where Nail sat. 'It sounds a nightmare that place.'

Nail was about to protest but saw the kids had followed Natalie. On her back the blonde one was carrying the thin no-eyes kid, who seemed to be asleep.

'This is X-Ray. He's got this special skin. Very delicate. This is Lights Out because she's . . . well . . . you can see why. Best to call her Lolo like Chicken Angel here, who's tall and got this lovely hair.'

Chicken Angel smiled. She gently lowered Lights Out, who mewed and tried huddling up to Nail. He quickly moved out of her reach.

'That's because she's got wings see,' said Natalie. 'Show Nail.'

Chicken Angel turned her back to Nail. He could see what looked like trapped fingers wriggling under the tracksuit top.

Christ he thought. It's enough to make you puke.

'And this is Nail,' said Natalie. 'He's my friend. He can get bad tempered and shout a lot. But don't worry.

He's OK inside but he doesn't know that yet.'

Chicken Angel smiled and held up her palms for Nail to see with all the fingers raying like the sun. X-Ray spread his hands too and bowed a little. Nail could see his skin was part see-through and open weaved with dark threads straying across the palm. Later on he realized that these were blood lines exposed by the tender thinness of his skin.

Lights Out had woken up. She sat up and faced Nail. Then she reached forward to touch him. Her bony hand moved very slowly like she was about to touch a spring-loaded frog.

Nail drew back. 'No,' he said. 'No. Don't let her do that.'

Natalie knelt down beside him and gave him an elbow in the ribs.

Nail grunted.

'At least smile,' she whispered in his ear.

'Hi,' he said.

The three kids just stared at him. Lights Out reached over to Chicken Angel and began tapping on her arm.

'They call that morsing,' said Natalie. 'It's how they communicate. At least that's how Lolo does.'

'For God's sake, Nats!' Nail burst out. 'You mean they can't talk properly either?'

'Course we can talk,' said Chicken Angel. 'What do you think we are, deletes or something?'

Nail backed off and raised his hands as if in apology.

'Just don't touch me, that's all. No one morses me, understand?'

Everyone looked at Nail.

'And don't just stare like that. It's bleedin' rude.'

'And who's rude?' said Natalie, giving him another elbow. She swung round and knelt upright in front of him. 'We've gotta help these kids,' she whispered between tightened lips. 'That place should have been closed down years ago. It's like a prison. It's a concentration camp. It really does suck. They feed them pills and pills and more pills. Dope them up with needles and stuff. If they get out of line they jab and jab them stupid so they're out for days on end.'

'Moosed out,' said X-Ray, who now stood right next to Natalie.

'Moosed out,' she repeated, not quite sure what she was saying. 'They don't have telly, or books or anything. It's disgusting.'

'We have pictures,' said Chicken Angel. 'We picture all the time. Mrs Murdoe's a picture. We have pictures for Jack the Cat and the Sky Boat and monkeys and Pippi and porridge and roses and suns and stars and the sea and the moon and parrots and angels, but not for Tin Lid or Doctor Dearly or onion skin or pee or pitch or Hyena Men.'

'Hyena Men?' said Nail.

'I think they mean Security,' said Natalie.

'Do you want to be a picture, Neil?' asked Chicken Angel. 'You've got bonny eyes.'

'OK. OK,' said Nail. 'That's enough. Thanks but no thanks. Forget the eyes. I don't think I'll bother.'

'It's easy to be a picture, Neil boy,' said X-Ray.

'Nail. My name's Nail.'

'Funny name,' said Chicken Angel.

'That's because he's hard and sharp,' said Natalie.

'Then he should be called hypo,' said Chicken Angel.

'We don't have a picture for that,' said X-Ray.

Nail turned to Natalie. 'If the Bin is so bad why doesn't someone complain? Everyone else does these days.'

'Because no one knows about the place and what really goes on there.'

'What about Kenno's ma?'

Natalie shrugged. 'They probably pay her to keep quiet.' She paused and turned to X-Ray. 'Tell him. Tell him about your friend . . . what's his name?'

'Cough Cough.'

'Yeah, tell Nail boy about Cough Cough and the eyes.'

Nail sat up. 'No. No,' he said. 'I don't want to hear any more. About eyes or anything.'

'What's wrong with you?' said Natalie, leaning backwards and staring at Nail like she wanted to slap him. 'It's all wrong. Someone's got to do something about it.'

'But it doesn't mean we have to,' Nail whispered fiercely.

Natalie stood up. 'So, you want to take them back? Is that it?'

Nail went silent.

No one said anything.

Suddenly they all stopped still, listening.

Owl hoot came woo-wooing through the trees.

Lights Out mewed. Natalie put her arms round her but she shrugged her off and pushed up against Chicken Angel. Then she started morsing.

'What's she saying?' said X-Ray.

Chicken Angel waited a moment. 'She's seen the Sky Boat and wants to sail away in her.'

Nail groaned. 'I told you, they're bonkers, Nats.'

'Shut it, Nail. Just listen.' She turned to the kids. 'What sky boat?' she said.

'It sails over the sea and into the sky,' said Chicken Angel.

'Ah, I see,' said Natalie. 'It's the moon, isn't it?'

Chicken Angel and X-Ray frowned.

'No, not the moon. Mrs Murdoe told us about the Sky Boat,' said X-Ray. 'She said one day we'd sail away in that bonny boat and never come back.'

'Well, I think that's bonny beautiful.'

2

By now Nail had stood up. He took hold of Natalie's arm and drew her a few steps to one side. 'OK, we can't just let them go,' he whispered. 'They'd never survive round here, obviously.' He paused. 'Look, what we could do, and it would get us off the hook, is leave them some-where safe like near a pub or something where they'd be found before they got run over or eaten by a big yellow leopard.'

'Don't be so unfeeling,' hissed Natalie. 'So hard as. Dump them and send them back there? No way. The only leopard round here is you. You're just washing your hands of them.'

'Of course I am. What's the point? They look like they're on their last wonky legs anyway.'

Natalie kicked him, hard as she could right on the shin. Nail shrieked, hopping and swearing and clutching his leg.

'Serves you right, you callous sod.'

'Look,' said Nail, leaning against a tree trunk and breathing hard, 'you're not thinking, you stupid mong. How can you look after kids who are bleeding and blind all over the place? What are you going to feed them on? Squirrel burgers?'

'No, because we won't stay here. We'll get in the van and drive somewhere.'

'Oh, yes. And get the sky ferry to the moon and back! And what happens when you hit the first police checkpoint. Eh? Not thought of that have you? Right now, the news will be out. The police will be crawling all over. You've got as much chance of escaping as . . .'

'As three disabled kids from a high-security unit in the middle of Scotland,' said Natalie.

'Ha, ha,' said Nail. 'And since when do you drive?'

Natalie breathed out deeply.

'OK. OK. It's not quite what I planned for this evening but think about it, Nail boy,' she grinned. 'It could be a right laugh. Taking a bunch of kids to the seaside.'

'Seaside!' exploded Nail. 'Are you crazy? Who said anything about the seaside?'

'Well, that's where you find the Sky Boat, don't you?'

'Christ, Nats. I've heard it all now. What's made you a freak head all of a sudden?'

Natalie paused. 'I remember seeing a film once. On TV. Mum and Dad were out, as per usual. It was in Poland somewhere in the war and these people were hiding in the sewers. They were resistance fighters trying to escape the Germans hunting them. They were in there for days and days. In the dark. No food, no sleep, nothing.

They'd given up hope. And then a miracle; they found a manhole the Germans had forgotten to seal.

'And there was this amazing scene where the leader emerges just head and shoulders above the street, above the cobbles. He lets the sun shine on his face. He's exhausted but they've made it. Then he turns round and the first thing he sees is the black jackbooted legs of a German officer pointing a pistol straight at his head.

'And I've never forgotten the look of despair in that man's eyes. To have come so far and have it end like that.'

Nail shrugged. 'It's a film, Nats. What's it got to do with us, stuck here in Garvie Wood with your noddy kids.'

'They're not mine,' said Natalie fiercely. 'They're nobody's and everybody's. And just for the moment they're ours. Yes ours. Yours and mine till it's all sorted and nobody gets jackbooted back into that Bin.'

Nail said nothing. Did she have a tongue on her! She was off on one, for sure. OK, so the place sucked, the kids were screwed up but that didn't mean he had to save them for the nation.

'Those kids,' Natalie was saying, 'have been locked away for all their lives; they've fought their way out. Just imagine after years of being trapped in there then making it past nurses and doctors and Security and into freedom someone turns round and takes you all the way back. This isn't snakes and ladders, Nail. This is their way out.'

'Great, then we'll take them to the nearest hospital. Let them deal with it. That's what they're there for. It's for their own good.'

'They don't want treatment. They've had years of treatment. A lifetime of being drugged and tranked, as they put it. This is their one and only chance of a bit of life. I mean, think of all the chances you've had and all the chances you've wasted. And me too. Just because you've done nothing with yours, just because your life's going nowhere doesn't mean they've got to miss out.'

Stupid noddy girl thought Nail. What did she know about his life? He still had plenty of time to take chances.

'So what's made you such a kiddieluvvie all of a sudden?' he said sourly. 'Not hours ago they were cartoon kids to you, first in line for the monkey house.'

'Well, I talked to them. Listened to what it's really like in that awful Bin place. And if you'd talk to them instead of blanking them you might change your mind as well. You can tell they don't have much time.'

'I don't know,' said Nail, 'my old gran looked like death all her life. Legs thin as roll-ups. Lasted into her nineties, the old biddy. Only went because she got bored.'

'Well, you only have to look at these kids to know they're on their last legs, as you put it.'

'Then we'd better get them back where they can get proper medical care and food and warm.'

'They're not going back to that place.' Natalie squared up to Nail, her lips trembling. 'No way.'

3

Just then her mobile rang.

They both stopped.

'Don't answer it,' said Nail.

'Could be Aunty Jessie,' said Natalie. 'I need to talk to her.'

Nail nodded.

'Natalie?'

Nail recognized the voice. It wasn't Aunt Jessie. It was Kenno.

Natalie looked at Nail. He shrugged.

'Yeah.'

'Where are you?'

'Who is this?'

'It's Kenno, remember me. Came to the Post Office a few days ago with a mate called Nail.'

Natalie ummed.

'What's up?'

There was a pause. 'Coddy's van's missing and he's steaming and Nail had it. He's not with you is he?'

'No. Should he be?'

Another pause. By now Nail had his ear to the phone as well.

'Only,' said Kenno speaking very slowly, 'my ma's had some kind of accident. Didn't they tell you when you went to Bin Linnie together to pick her up?'

Hold it thought Nail. How did Kenno know Natalie had gone to the Bin with him?

'I don't know anything about going to the Bin,' said Natalie.

'Because three inmates have escaped. You know the sad little kids they keep there. Know anything about that?'

Nail started thinking. '*Sad? Little? Kids?*' Didn't sound like boggie-mouth Kenno. He thought the specimens in the Bin were non-human, the sort of things you bottled and left to escape in horror films.

The phone had gone silent now as if the battery in Kenno's brain had run out of ideas.

Nail put the phone to his ear again. He could hear something in the background – telly or a radio chattering.

'Well, if you see that no-hoper Nail tell him from me,' said Kenno's distant voice, 'he's a . . . in fact, just put him on the line.'

Nail put his hand over the speaker. 'Say you're tired and going to bed. That you haven't seen me all day and that –'

'And that you really are a no-hoper,' mouthed Natalie.

Nail gave a thin smile.

Then it struck him – why Kenno was suddenly so schoolie polite, why he was talking nicey nicey about 'Bin Linnie' and 'kids' and why there was crackling talk in the background like a radio on a bad day. That wasn't station Garvie on 93 megahertz, the Voice of Lothian. That was walkie-talkie stuff. And it meant only one thing.

Police or Bin Security again. The Hyena Men were at Coddy's and checking up.

With either or both in his ear, Kenno wasn't going to foul-mouth freakie kids. But doing the boggie on his mate Nail, that was OK. He'd driven off with a load of bunking kids. In police eyes that had perv written all over it.

He snorted.

Now they'd be after them.

'Natalie? Are you still there?' Kenno sounded urgent.

'Switch it off. Switch it off,' Nail hissed. He drew a line across his throat.

Natalie understood. 'Piss off, Kenno,' she said and cut out.

'They've got somebody there,' said Nail nodding. 'That freaky doctor probably. Pusie Kenno. He was trying to shop us, Nats.'

He swore.

'That was a put-up job,' he spluttered, jabbing a finger at the mobile. He just couldn't believe it. Kenno, a mate, shopping them.

Natalie leant her forehead against the tree like she was counting for hide-and-seek. She was a bit shaken by the phone call. By the idea of the police. By Kenno trying it on.

Nail watched her.

Why not get her to go to the PO, to her aunt's? he began thinking. After all they'd need some clothes and food and stuff and where else were they going to get some? And she couldn't just disappear for a few days without explaining, could she! Otherwise thought Nail, he'd be a prime target for abduction, molestation and Police knows what else they'd dream up for a charge sheet. Vehicle theft. Driving without a licence. Driving without tax and MOT. Driving without insurance. Just driving. God, they wouldn't throw the book at him; they'd throw a whole library.

It was OK for Natalie to go all gooey over some short-changed plookie kids but he was the one in line for a right wrong verdict.

Yeah, get her to the aunt's place and then persuade her to give up the whole crazy seaside number.

'Do you think they were trying to trace us? Can they trace mobiles?' Natalie was asking.

'I don't know but we're getting out of here.'

'Not without the kids,' said Natalie, standing up again. She turned.

4

The kids were back in the van, sitting in line holding hands and staring at the two of them.

Natalie ran towards them. The kids immediately huddled.

'It's OK,' she said. 'It's OK.'

Then Chicken Angel separated from the others and climbed out of the van and approached Nail. 'If I let you read my story will you take us to the sea?'

'To the Sky Boat?' said X-Ray joining them.

'Or,' said Natalie, looking him straight in the eye, 'are you going to wear your jackboots, Herr Nail, and like you said, take them –'

'Before you finish, I never said that,' said Nail.

He shook his head. He felt like he'd walked into Oz land. Natalie would have him dancing up the yellow brick road next.

'I haven't a clue where the sea is,' he said in Natalie's ear.

By now they were standing beside the van.

'East, west. This is Scotland. Where does the sun rise?'

Just then Nail felt something touching his hand. It was zero eyes. He pulled it away.

'She just wants to feel you, smell you,' said Chicken Angel.

'Tell her I don't want to be felt. And I don't want someone smelling me. It makes me feel like I've puked myself.'

'She only wants to touch your face. It's her way of seeing you. She makes pictures with fingers.'

The thought of the little freakie feeling over his face quite turned Nail's stomach.

But Lights Out had read Nail's thought. She began morsing X-Ray who was nearest.

'Mumbo noddy jumbo,' muttered Nail.

He should have kept his big mouth shut and just said N.O. to Natalie. NO, they weren't sky boating. NO, they weren't following the rising sun. And YES, they were going back to the Bin. The whole thing could turn into a life-long nightmare. He wished he was back in Coddy's kitchen, necking down cannies and chewing chips.

'Nail boy, want to know what she's saying about you?' said X-Ray.

Nail said nothing. He was fiddling in his pocket for the van keys.

'She says you think you're a leopard but you're really a pippi inside like all the rest of us. She says your pippi wants to escape like the princess in the clock but a wicked witch has her locked up inside.'

'Rubbish,' said Nail.

Suddenly, like they had one mind, the three kids all went very still. They joined hands. 'Is Nail boy really going to take us?' asked Chicken Angel. 'Or is he going to send us back to the Doctor?'

'He's going to take us all. We're going to find somewhere safe and get some food and go to the sea like I said.'

'Let's do Jesus Hands,' said X-Ray.

The kids touched their fingertips together and made a tent. They left a space for Natalie.

'Your hands are frozen,' she said. 'Come on, Nail, join in.'

Nail refused. 'It'll be spells and broomsticks next,' he mumbled.

Lights Out turned to face him. She smiled.

'See,' said Natalie. 'She likes you.'

'It's because he's got a pippi inside, like Lolo,' said Chicken Angel.

Before Nail had time to tell her she was talking nonsense, Lights Out had started mewing.

'Now what's up with her?' he said.

Chicken Angel looked startled. Lolo was morsing, fingers working faster and faster.

'What is it?' said Natalie.

'She says there's a leopard. Two leopards, coming this way.'

'I can't hear anything,' said Nail.

The kids scrambled back into the van and Natalie closed the doors.

'Come on. She's psychic, that little no-eyes.'

Nail fumbled with the keys as the lights from the first car came bouncing through the far trees.

Swearing, he fired the engine.

5

He swung the van round and skidded it behind the wood pile and out of sight of the road.

Slowly he wound down the window.

226

The glow from the vehicle lights aurora-ed around them.

Then they heard a voice calling over a loudspeaker. 'Geminis, we know you are there.'

Inside the van the kids held each other tight in a Jesus Hug.

'Doctor Dearly,' whispered X-Ray. 'He's found us.'

Chicken Angel wailed.

'Geminis.' The harsh voice called. 'This is Doctor Dearly, your medical adviser. I am here to help you. I am your friend. You are in great danger. Without proper food and medication your lives will be jeopardized. Show yourselves. A safe environment and the specialist care you need await you in Bin Linnie Lodge. You will be looked after. Your nurses are on standby ready to help. Show yourselves. Geminis, this is Doctor Dearly. I am your friend.'

Moments later two vehicles slowly passed by, their revolving roof spots setting the road and the side darknesses ablaze with light for a few seconds.

'Geminis, this is Doctor Dearly. You are in great danger.'

The voice began to fade away.

'Hyenas,' said Nail.

Natalie smiled. Nail was beginning to get the idea.

6

Suddenly the light flickers on. I am trembling but that may be the flutters. Lights Out is cosy cosy up to Chicken Angel. Her head is lolling. She is still holding Maiden China.

Chicken Angel is humming her. 'Lolo is cold,' she says, frowning my way.

That's bad I think, but she can't blame me.

'It was Lolo who moosed out Tin Lid,' I say.

Chicken Angel nods. 'We should never have listened to Cough Cough,' she says.

I am thinking. Maybe the Bin is better. Our natural habitat. We all have our place. Monkeys in the jungle, lions on the plains, Geminis in the the Bin.

But Nail boy and Natalie girl will save us.

CHAPTER 20

The Hyenas are Coming

1

'Well, what are you going to do?' whispered Natalie.

'What am *I* going to do?' said Nail. 'Am I James Bond, Mister Martini, all of a sudden? I keep telling you, Nats. It's not going to work. Those kids are shivering back there and probably starving. I am. I'm gagging for a pint right now. And what's more they smell, smell bad, and they need cleaning up. We'd be doing them a favour handing them back. We'll go to your aunt's place, clean them up. Give them something to eat.'

'And then dump them back at the Bin. That's what you're thinking. Isn't it? I can tell. Get her back home and she'll change her mind. You are a hard case. Kenno was right. And you can add *two-faced* to that.'

'No way,' said Nail slowly, gripping the steering wheel like he was throttling Kenno. 'What does that dummy know? What do you know?'

Natalie stared through the windscreen. 'Why would they think we had the kids?' she said.

'Because they've put two and two together. Van arrives as kids disappear, van vanishes, security guard questioned and admits not searching back of van, says girl claimed assaulted nurse was her ma. This obviously false. Guard now says girl's hysterics all a put-up job, a cover-up. Police agree. Boy and girl now prime suspects. Got it? Girl lies over phone. This confirms suspicion. It's a case of child kidnap.'

'How do they know I lied?'

'Catch up, Nats. How did they get your mobile number? Did you give it Kenno?'

Natalie shook her head. 'Oh, God,' she said. 'It must have been Aunt Jessie. Yes, I see. She gave it to the police, which means they must have gone to the PO, which means they know I wasn't there.'

'Tucked up in bed and reading *Mizz*,' said Nail. 'And now they'll be waiting for us. Trained marksmen, body armour, road blocks, a cordon of steel.'

Natalie ignored him. 'And the police got Kenno to call.'

'Entrapment,' said Nail.

'Which means,' said Natalie.

'We're stuffed. We can't go back to the Post Office. We'll be arrested and done for false imprisonment, abduction, God knows what.'

2

Suddenly Nail froze. 'What's that?' he whispered.

Something was ring ringing.

'A mobile?' said Natalie.

Nail shook his head.

It was getting louder and louder.

'It's an alarm. It's that noddy clock,' he cried. 'It's that no-eyes one.' He turned to Natalie. 'Get her to shut it. It'll wake up the whole snoring forest.'

Natalie reached for the door handle but it was too late.

A spray of light washed over the log pile.

'They're coming back.' Natalie twisted in her seat. 'Coming this way,' she said hoarsely.

Nail fired the engine and reversed the van out and bounced into the ruts of the dirt track behind.

Then he palmed the lever into neutral and leapt out of the car.

Natalie screamed at him.

He was going to shop them.

She went silent as soon as she saw what he was doing.

From the top of the wood pile Nail pulled down two, three, four logs. He dragged them across the track and rolled them into a staggered formation.

A fan of light swept over him.

'Stop. This is Doctor Dearly. You have been seen. What you are doing is illegal. Stay where you are. Do not move. My security men will assist you. I repeat, stay where you are and no one will get hurt.'

But Nail wasn't waiting.

He'd heard the bark of dogs.

He leapt in the van, rammed into first and spun away hurtling down the track leaving the pursuit log-jammed and revving in helpless anger.

'They've got dogs,' said Nail. 'The bastards have got dogs. What are they thinking of. Dogs will tear them apart. They're animals.'

Animals? Natalie wasn't sure whether he meant the Hyena Men or Doctor Dearly or just the dogs.

'I told you,' she shouted, 'it's a nightmare that place. And the people who run it are ghouls.'

Nail said nothing. He thought about Kenno's ma who'd worked for years at the Bin. She didn't look like a ghoul. Or did she change to Bad Wolf once she got inside? Is that what places like the Bin did to you? He knew Coddy thought she was a circling shark but, well, Coddy was always dabbling in dangerous waters. Served him right if he got his arm bitten.

Nail was now bent forward, his chin almost resting on the steering wheel rim, trying to see beyond the limited search of his headlights. 'Full beam doesn't work. Typical cowboy Coddy,' he snarled.

Natalie was checking in the side mirror. 'We've lost them,' she said. 'Let's stop and I'll get in the back with the kids. Go on bouncing like this and they'll be juiced, kiddie smoothie.'

'Quick then,' said Nail and the van gravelled to a halt.

Nail knew Dearly and his dogs wouldn't take long to get rid of his log stinger. And a clapped-out wheelie bin couldn't outrun a pair of Land Rovers especially in rough terrain.

'They're holding on,' said Natalie, jumping back in the van.

Nail was hoping the track would divide and leave Dearly not knowing which way to go. He just needed a bit of luck and the Hyena Men to make one wrong turn.

But the track didn't divide. It just went on and on,

rubbled and rutted through endless plantations of firs all the same, all the same.

He was trying to go as fast as he could without banging up the kids in the back, checking all the time in the wing mirrors for any sign of telltale lights behind.

Nothing.

It was so dark under the endless canopies of fir that he didn't dare put out his lights. And once Dearly could see the red of his rear ones they were done for. He thought of pulling off track and bouncing into the darkness, killing the engine and waiting for them to pass so he could steal out and backtrack all the yards to real roads and escape. But there was no way he could get the van over the continuous ditch that ran alongside them.

He hit the steering wheel.

Smack. Smack. Smack.

They were stuffed.

Then his luck really ran out.

3

They came slithering round a bend and there, dead ahead, right across the track was a single-pole, red and white barrier.

Nail braked hard and leapt out.

A metal notice hung on wire from the centre of the pole. 'DANGER' it read,

'ENTRY PROHIBITED – WEAK BRIDGE'.

Christ, the pole looked a ton weight.

Natalie was by his side.

'What are we going to do?'

'Lean on the end,' said Nail putting his full weight on the pole. 'It's counterbalanced.'

He doubled himself over the bar and Natalie climbed astride.

It hardly budged.

'They're coming,' cried Natalie. 'I can see lights.'

Nail jumped down and raced across to the other end of the barrier. 'It's padlocked this end,' he shouted. 'Only one thing for it. Get the other side, Nats. Time to gate-crash. Get the kids out. And hurry.'

'But what about the bridge?' shouted Natalie as she opened the van doors.

'We'll cross that when we come to it.'

4

We watch Nail boy swing the wheelie round. Then it roars and charges the post where the pole is chained. It's like in *The Natural World* when we saw the elephant push over the temple wall.

The wheelie fits out and pushes and pushes and the wheels smoke and squeal like the monkeys squealed at the elephant.

Natalie girl is holding us tight. 'Come on, Nail. Come on, Nail,' we all pray.

Suddenly the post cracks and swings away and the pole jumps up in the air like a fishing stick pulling up a fish.

We all get back in the wheelie with Natalie girl.

*

Then we hear Doctor Dearly. His voice comes at us through the trees. 'Stop where you are. You cannot escape. It is dangerous to go on. You are putting young lives at risk. Stop before it is too late.'

But Nail boy doesn't stop. The wheelie jumps forward. Through the little back windows we can see the lights of the Hyena Men and Doctor Dearly behind us. They are getting nearer.

Chicken Angel is holding me tight.

Natalie girl is saying not to worry. She puts on the light to check us out. 'Oh, X-Ray,' she says, 'you are bleeding, look.'

My hands are wet and red. She wraps some soft tissue round them.

'What about the bridge?' says Chicken Angel.

'We'll cross it when we come to it,' I say.

Chicken Angel looks at me with monkey eyes.

'Well, Nail boy said we'd cross so we'll be OK. Won't we?' I say, turning to the Natalie girl.

But she doesn't answer because suddenly one of the back doors bursts open and Natalie girl has to kill the light.

5

Natalie girl lets go of us and starts to scramble towards the door. And all the time we are shaking and the wheelie is banging and bouncing and Natalie girl is trying to grab the door and close it properly.

And every time it swings wide open I can see the lights behind are bigger and brighter and dodging around and in and out of the trees.

Lolo is morsing Chicken Angel. The Hyenas are coming she is saying. The Hyenas are coming. Soon she will start mewling.

Now the girl is holding on to the locked door and trying to grab the free one. Careful, Natalie girl, you are not Jack the Cat with a lasso tail and clever paws and used to swinging and jumping all over.

Then the other door starts to open and Natalie girl is falling and screaming and I throw my arm at her and she clings on and Chicken Angel holds me and we all roll and slide as the wheelie skids and jumps some more and my skin burns and bleeds.

'Stop, Nail, stop!' shrieks Natalie girl.

And he does.

The wheelie bangs and slides and stops.

And we all tumble against the back. Chicken Angel has her arms round Lolo and is able to save her but she is thrown herself against the back of the van. I'm thrown over and slide into Chicken Angel. Natalie girl slides into me.

Then Nail boy appears and screams to us to get out.

We climb out and he pushes us towards a bridge.

It's the DANGER bridge and we're not sure. Is it strong enough?

'Get over, get over,' he cries and we stumble to the edge of the wooden planks.

'It's OK,' says Natalie girl. 'I'll take you over.'

We all hold hands.

Nail puts on the sidelights so we can see a little.

There is no rail, just logs and planks and the sound of water below crashing over rocks.

Lights Out is mewling and the planks are moving and we can't see the other side, only the bridge sinking into darkness.

Mrs Murdoe help us. Jack help us, I say in my head over and over.

Suddenly the floor fits and throws light all over us. Something crashes down below.

Chicken Angel shouts.

Nail boy has driven the wheelie on to the bridge.

'Wait,' shouts Natalie girl. 'Wait till we've crossed. It's not safe for all of us at once.'

But Nail boy doesn't listen because just behind and very close is one of the Land Rovers. Its lights blind us.

'Don't look,' shouts Natalie girl.

I stumble forward, all monkey fears.

Then we hear Doctor Dearly's voice again but not the words because they're lost in the gushing sound of waters and the wheelie revving behind us.

And then I hear a plank crack like a biscuit and suddenly we are on a gravel track again and Nail boy is halfway across the bridge and as we turn the first big wheelie reaches the other side and in its lights Nail boy's little wheelie looks like a black bug, like we get in the Bin sometimes.

'Come on. Come on,' Natalie girl is shrieking at Nail boy. 'Do it. Do it.'

'Nail. Nail. Nail,' we all cry.

But Nail boy is moving very slowly and the wheelie is bending over and he's just about halfway across and then we hear the growl of dogs as the second big wheelie arrives.

'You cannot escape.' Doctor Dearly's voice cracks through a voice-over. 'Do not make us release the dogs. Stay where you are. We will save you. You will be safe with us. Your welfare is our priority. Stay where you are. Do not continue this folly.'

Nail boy shouts at the wheelie.

'What's FOLLY?' asks Chicken Angel.

Natalie girl doesn't answer.

I can see her lips moving.

There are black patches in the bridge floor and Nail boy is wheeling round one of them. They look like paw prints. Big paws.

Leopard!

A giant leopard has gone ahead of us.

Nail boy is nearly across.

Doctor Dearly's voice cracks again. 'You have ignored all warnings. This is your final chance before I release the dogs.'

Suddenly from the other side of the bridge the dogs start shouting and we can see their heads and sharp ears and stiff tails in the headlights. Then we see the Hyena Men bending over them.

'Nail,' screams Natalie girl suddenly, 'they're letting the dogs go.'

We hear the engine fitting and fitting hard shot, we watch it shake, we watch the wheels spin, we hear the bridge go crack crack. We hear the dogs barking, we see the wheelie shake. Nail is shaking the wheelie. Then it leaps forward and stops next to us.

'Get in, get in,' shouts Natalie girl to us.

We climb up. Ba-bang the doors. We can hear the Hyena Men shouting and the dogs shouting back. They must have crossed the bridge.

Next thing the doors are being pulled open.

6

We fixy. All of us pushed into a corner.

I cover my eyes.

Then I hear Natalie girl gasp.

I look up.

It's Nail boy.

NAIL!

He's standing there and looking at us and showing monkey teeth all over.

We stare at him.

'What are you playing at?' says Natalie girl.

'Just look,' he says. 'Out here.'

Slowly we get out of the wheelie.

On the other side the dogs are crying, but they haven't crossed the bridge.

'They're afraid of the bridge,' says Nail boy. 'Look.'

Some of the dogs walk and then stop and go back showing their teeth. The Hyena Men shout but it's no good. The dogs don't like what they hear, what they smell. Dogs have very Lolo noses. The bridge smells bad to them.

Because the dogs won't cross, the Hyena Men won't

cross. What's bad for dogs is bad for them. And for big wheelies.

'Don't think you've got away,' calls Doctor Dearly.

We get back in Nail's wheelie.

We drive for a bit and then we stop.

Natalie opens the doors for us.

Nail boy is leaning against the front bit. Natalie girl goes up to him and hugs him.

Then Chicken Angel hugs him.

So I hug him.

Then Lights Out finds him and she just holds his sleeve and presses her face into his arm.

I think he likes Natalie hugging. But not us. I don't know why. We're just kids after all.

'You're trembling,' Natalie girl is saying to me.

I am.

'It's not like the Bin,' I say with a shiver. 'We couldn't run away from Doctor D then.'

'No,' she says wiping my face. 'But we've seen the last of him now.' She smiles.

7

Between them, Nail and Natalie managed to clean up the kids, wetting tissues in a nearby stream and washing away blood and mess.

They drank the cool sweet forest water.

Then, under the front seat, they found a stash of chocolate bars. A Kenno haul.

But the kids weren't sure about chocolate. They'd never

seen it before. X-Ray said it looked like monkey blood and the others decided eating monkey blood was not good.

'But you've got to eat something. Are you on a special diet?' asked Natalie.

'We eat porridge and chicken and toast and eggs.'

'Every day,' said Chicken Angel.

'Don't you get chips and stuff?' said Nail.

But there was no time for X-Ray to answer because out of the forest and not far away came the howling sound of a hunting dog.

CHAPTER 21

Angel Blood, Leopard Blood

1

They scrambled into the van and Nail turned the ignition.

The engine whirred but didn't fire.

He tried again.

Nothing.

He swore.

Tried again.

Nothing.

Nail smacked his fist into the dashboard.

Then a noise near his door made him look sideways. Moonlight suddenly washed over the van and paled his face. Out of the trees he saw a figure emerging. He was holding something at arm's length. As the figure closed in Nail saw the glint of steel barrels.

A shotgun was pointing straight at him.

He sat very still.

The figure was beside the van now and reaching forward to open his door.

Nail could see him clearly enough. He was a tall man,

bearded and dressed in wellies and jeans and a short quilted jacket.

Next thing he was being motioned out and made to stand against the van while the man checked in the front.

'Gun in the back?'

'I don't have a gun,' said Nail.

The man eyed him up and down. 'What's someone like you doing up here in the middle of the night, hiding on a prohibited road?'

'I got lost.'

The man spat. Didn't believe a word.

'Yer not on yer own. I heard voices. Come on, son, yer up to something, aren't yer? Was it sheep you were looking for? Round here we string out poachers with fencing wire. Now tell me a better story or I'll set the dog on you.'

Just then the back door opened and Natalie struggled out.

The man swung his gun round. His dog growled. 'OK, Bruce,' he said quietening the animal. He eyed Natalie and smirked.

'Oh, that's what it's about?' he said lowering the gun.

'No, it's not that at all,' said Natalie. 'We've got kids in here and we need to get out and get them home. Sick kids.'

'Let's see.'

After checking he came back.

'More than sick if yer ask me.' He looked puzzled. 'So how did you get over Craigie Bridge just back there? I wouldn't trust a rabbit on that.'

Nail shrugged. 'Just drove over.'

'So how did you spring them from the Bin?'

Nail looked blank.

'Don't try it on with me, laddie. I'm not one of those plookies back there. I listen in to their radio traffic. They're panicking all over because of the breakout.' He paused. 'Now, how bad are they?'

'One of them's blind. The others are OK really,' said Natalie.

'OK? Who told you that? They're goners all of them.'

'How?' said Natalie.

But the man didn't answer. 'You'd better get them back ASAP. They won't last long out here. Nor will you. The police are already on your case.'

'We know,' said Nail.

'That place is like a concentration camp,' Natalie blurted. 'It's a crime the way they treat them. We're not taking them back. We can't.'

The man shrugged. 'Suit yerself, lassie, but they'll catch you. They will. Anyway, I've done my bit. Told you. Warned you. It's up to you now.'

'We'll just drive into the forest,' said Natalie. 'They won't be able to find us there.'

'They will, believe me. They did last time.'

'Last time?' said Nail.

'Yeah. One got away a few years ago. Found it dead out here. No one ever knew. It was all hushed up. Like everything else in Bin Linnie.'

'How do you know all this?'

'Because my mum was working there at the time. It happened on her shift and they blamed her. Said she had encouraged them. Helped them. So they got rid of her.

245

Said they'd have her for maltreatment and neglect if she said anything about the place. That's the kind of criminals they are. It's not the kids are warped; it's the management there and that cold bastard, Dearly. Keep out of his way. That's why I'm saying yer better off taking them back. Evidently it gets them in the lungs in the end.'

'Your mother's name isn't Mrs Murdoe, is it?' said Natalie slowly.

'Yes, it was. Was,' he repeated quietly. 'She died a couple of years ago.'

'Oh, sorry. Only the kids talk about Mrs Murdoe like she's a kind of guardian angel.'

'Yeah, well, she's with her own kind now.' The man stood up. 'Take the next turn left and follow the track till it hits the Garvie Road and then you'll see Bin Linnie straight ahead.'

'Thanks,' said Natalie. 'But we're taking them to the seaside. We promised.'

'Seaside?' The man thought for a moment. 'OK. This is for my mum. You're kids and doing crazy comes with the territory, I guess. And if you're screwing up Dearly you've got my vote. What you need right now is to rest up. There's an old caravan up by Loch Inchie. It belongs to the Forestry. You can use that. Anyone asks, say Chief Ranger Murdoe gave you permission. It's a good hour from here. By then it'll be near dawn. Hide there during the day. Travel at night. Avoid the main roads. Keep to forest tracks.'

'Rest up? Why during the day?' said Nail. 'Surely we need to get moving now.'

'Look, laddie. This isn't Thunderbirds to the Rescue.

246

These plookies are serious. You've seen what they're like. They hunt with dogs. They'll drop you down a well shaft with rocks in yer pockets if they have to. You've got a white van here and that's as visible as it gets.'

Natalie slumped back. 'We'll never do it, will we?'

'Just which way to the sea?' said Nail.

'When you leave the caravan follow the track round. You'll reach a derelict bothie. Take a right there and just keep going. Eventually you'll come to signs for the Visitor's Centre. Ask there or get a map. You'd better go.'

And with that the man turned and he and dog were soon swallowed by the deep shadows of the forest.

2

The track looped down, gently in and out of the trees, through scrubland areas of fir stumps and fireweed, through bog patches tufted with spikes of marsh grass, over shallow forded streams till it settled into a long incline.

Nail let the van freewheel.

'You know they think we're angels,' said Natalie.

Nail smiled. Angels were not his bag, no way.

'That Mrs Murdoe told them one day they'd escape the Bin by the hand of angels.'

'She the one told them about the Sky Boat and flying to the stars?'

Natalie nodded.

'Then she's as batty as the kids.'

They were silent for a minute. 'Look, angel,' said Nail at last. 'We need stuff for these kids, blankets and food.' He paused. Then dropped his voice. 'Are we really going to take them to the sea? We don't even know where it is. I mean that doctor jimmy's right. We're not trained to cope with kids like this. If it were ordinary ones, well, that's a different tune.'

'You promised,' said Natalie. 'You promised.'

'No,' said Nail, 'you promised.'

Natalie swore. 'Well, you went along with it. And why have we raced like insanity up and down and all over, nearly savaged by dogs and hypo-ed by mad doctors?'

'Because . . . because . . .' Nail wasn't sure. Probably because it was a laugh skid-panning through the forest at night. Probably because Kenno had shopped him and he wasn't going to let that pusie-face take him. Possibly because he fancied a portion of those soft Natalie lips that brimmed so purple-black in the moonlight. Possibly, possibly. Thing was, just how much did he really want the girl? Was she worth it? Worth a drive halfway across Scotland? Worth long distancing a bunch of banana brains with them?

He rammed into second as the track took a sudden rise.

'You know what I think,' said Natalie at last.

'No.'

'I think inside you're like me. You can't stand kids with nothing going for them having their lives run by the likes of that Doctor D. Why else would you drive a van over a rotten bridge roaring torrents below?'

'Hang on,' said Nail. 'Hang on. You're pinning hero

on me, Nats. I don't do heroes. People expect too much. Heroes have a hard time.'

'Well, the kids like you . . . now. You can't let them down. Doesn't it weigh on your conscience, all the suffering, all around? You only have to look . . .' Natalie stopped. She didn't want to get too heavy.

Nail looked up through the windscreen.

Conscience? What was that? Something that got in the way of having a good time! What did she know? He'd done his suffering. His mum and dad had seen to that. Mum! How bad time the name sounded. He'd seen her wreck her life. Waited for hours, weeks, months, years for his dad to come home. Watched his baby brother die. Nothing you could do there. That was life. It happened. You went with the flow. Take on all the bad out there and you'll end up in the nut house with the freaks and the zombies.

The moon's sail billowed and floated on the deep calm of the night.

Then into his head drifted the face of a small baby, skin purpled, eyes big as moons.

Blind and helpless.

He tried to blink the apparition away but another came mewling into view.

It was the little thin one with the no eyes. She was morsing him, tapping in his blood. He could see her again leaning her head against him after the bridge bit. Later he'd found stray hairs on his jacket and quickly brushed them off.

He turned to Natalie. 'If I get you there will you give us a kiss?'

'If that's what it takes,' she said.

Right, yer on thought Nail.

The wheelie stops once more. Is it the Hyena Men again?

We hardly dare move.

Chicken Angel holds me tight to try and stop the shivering.

Now she is whispering in my ear. 'Soon we'll be in the Sky Boat,' she says, 'safe among the stars sailing with the angels.'

But my head is full of flutters. We heard all that talking, hard barking sometimes and horrible things. About guns, and Mrs Murdoe, our angel, all dead and takeaway, and about us going back to the Bin.

'We've got to do smiley with that Nail boy,' whispers Chicken Angel. 'I don't know if he's a leopard or a Murdoe.'

'Lights Out says he has a pippi side and a leopard side.'

'That's sounds like Cough Cough talk,' says Chicken Angel.

I think about my friend CC. He has angel blood now. Mrs Murdoe said we were angels. Maybe we all have angel blood. Angel blood and leopard blood.

I wish Cough Cough was coming to the sea. I wish Cough Cough could see the Sky Boat. He'll need angel eyes for that.

Maybe CC is in the Sky Boat waiting for us.

Yes, I can see him sitting in the front waving us to

come closer and get in. He's going to pull up the anchor and then we'll be off. Flying over the blue blue sea.

Then the door opens and the girl is there and the moonlight enters and Chicken Angel's face gleams and her hair shines.

She is very beautiful. I like Chicken Angel.

Natalie says we have a little way to go before we stop for a rest. We are going to sleep in real beds. No dozie. No cameras. No Moose. No Tin Lid. No Doctor Dearly. No hypo. No trank.

4

They reached the caravan as the dawn was lifting the lid on the world.

Natalie carried Lights Out and laid her on one of the bunks. She drew the curtain closed, found a blanket and draped it loosely round the frail huddle of the child.

The others curled up too and were soon asleep.

By the time Nail returned from hiding the van under a cover of trees Natalie had managed to light one burner on the stove.

'Keep the place warm,' she said.

'Well, cook my beans!' Nail suddenly exclaimed. 'We got Heinz and rice pudding.' He was checking out the tins in one of the overhead lockers. 'I'm starving. Lucky that jimmy turned up when he did,' he said, 'otherwise you and I would be in the slammer now.' He stretched into the back of the locker and brought out a rusted tin. 'Sausages as well, Nats. How about that?'

He looked around.

No Natalie.

'Natalie,' he called sing-song fashion.

No reply.

5

He found her outside sitting on a huge slab of rock.

'You all right?' he said. 'Not hungry?'

For a moment she didn't answer. And then staring across the water she said: 'Nail, tell me we're doing the right thing by these kids.'

'Come on, Nats, don't lay that on me too. Remember, me flip, you serious. You heard what our man said back there – time is short and they ain't got long.'

'Yeah, but suppose they get ill with us. Did you notice how thin and pale the little girl's gone? She's seems, well, floppy. I don't think she's very well.'

'She was OK screaming at those Hyena Men.'

'That was because she was frightened stupid.'

She paused and turned to face Nail. 'Suppose they . . . you know . . .'

'Die?' said Nail.

'Yeah, go takeaway while we've got them. Then you know what that means – we'll be up for manslaughter or something, won't we? I mean that is serious stuff.'

Nail shrugged. Wasn't this what he'd been saying all along?

252

'I look at it like this,' he said. 'They've seen a bit in the last few hours. They're probably just knackered, like me.' He picked up a stone, walked to edge of the loch and in a quick sure movement skimmed it across the water till it died in a run of splashes like a flapping fish.

Natalie watched him. He had a good shape. Strong shoulders. Beyond his silhouette she could see, either side of him, the ripples from the stone casting wider and wider circles.

They could be pulses of energy she thought, coming from some deep mysterious source inside his body, disturbing the loch, disturbing her life.

Then he turned to face her.

'Natalie, if it's screwing you up having them,' he said, 'then let's call it a day and just take them back. They've had an adventure. Time to go home. That's not just me saying. That Murdoe guy said the same.'

She didn't say anything.

In a way she knew he was making sense. Then suspicion entered her mind. Was he saying this because in his heart of hearts he just wanted out? She could understand that. She was the one pushing. Why should he take the risk of getting banged up in a young offender's camp or whatever they did to people like him? It had just seemed a bit of a joke back in the forest, a bit of charity the two of them taking kids to the sea for a day. But that was before the Hyena Men and that Dearly spook. It had all happened so suddenly. Only now had she started thinking straight.

'OK,' she said gazing out across the loch, whose waters were turning pink in the rising sun. 'This is my fault. I've pushed it. You go, I'll take the kids. It's not fair on you.'

Of course she didn't mean this. It just made her feel good saying it. OK! Made her feel generous and sacrificial. And yes, she didn't want him to take it at face value and actually, really walk out.

'Hours ago you said I had a mission to save the little freaks,' said Nail.

'I've had second thoughts,' said Natalie.

'Oh, so now you want me to bog off?'

'No,' she said startled. 'That wasn't what I meant at all. I didn't want you to feel you had to do this. I didn't want you to feel I'd talked you into it.'

'No one talks me into things,' said Nail. 'No one.'

'Because you're hard as,' said Natalie coldly, suddenly sensing he was actually going to walk out on her. Yeah, he was the sort she thought. Never gave for free. Always had his price. Took whatever came his way. Pulling cars and flogging dodgy stuff and stolen goods. No family stability, that was his problem. That's what her dad would have said.

He'd turned back to watch the lake and above the line of his T-shirt Natalie could see the bronzy colour of his neck. Nice! Probably got the tan lying in parks lagered out and legless.

'You can't do it on yer own,' he said, walking back and standing in front of her.

She brightened. He was coming after all. It was going to be OK. She stood up.

'I think,' continued Nail, 'for their own good, they're better off in hospital or back at what's-its-name. It might be fun for us but we've got to think of them.'

Natalie stared at him.

'You bastard,' she said.

Nail was taken aback. 'You asked me. You said you'd take them on yer own, which is a mega-stupid idea if you ask me.'

'You're a one-off hypocrite. You're not thinking of them. You're thinking of yourself.'

'And what about you, Miss Bleeding Heart? You can't just cart a bundle of sick kids around because it makes you feel good.'

Natalie reached into her jacket pocket. 'You smug, selfish little git. Here take this.' She handed him her mobile. 'Now, ring your mate Kenno and tell him to tell his friend Dearly where we are and to come and collect us. Tell him you're sending the kids back to the Bin, where no one cares, where they'll be tranked and toxed like laboratory rats, and where they'll die exhausted and alone and forgotten. Now ring him, Nail, hard as stone. It's your call.'

6

I can feel something walking over my face. I wake with a start. It's Lights Out and she is tapping my cheek. She is very pale. She takes my hand and starts morsing me. With my free arm I reach across to Chicken Angel and shake her.

Chicken Angel is slow to wake. We are all very moosed out.

Chicken Angel says Lolo has seen Doctor Dearly flying through the air. He is like a huge bat flying through the trees looking for us, she says.

'A bat. A giant bat!' I start to tremble and Chicken Angel gets up and gives me cosy cosy.

'What shall we do?'

We agree to ask Natalie girl but when we pull the curtain back there is no one there.

We look out of the window.

And we see something that is amazing.

We forget about Doctor D.

We go outside.

Water. Water full of sky.

We are standing on the edge of the sea.

We stand outside. It is very bright.

'It's the sea,' I say.

Chicken Angel is too amazed to say anything.

'And,' I whisper, 'look, the Sky Boat.'

Chicken Angel follows my pointing finger. A little wooden boat is tied to a boulder and lies in the blue water.

'The Sky Boat,' she says slowly as if not believing it. 'Mrs Murdoe knew what she was talking about.'

'She's always right,' I say.

We smile over each other and do Jesus Hands.

'Safe at last,' I say.

Then we see Natalie and Nail boy. Natalie girl is fitting.

Something's happened I say.

When we reach them they look surprised. Nail has a mobile in his hand. 'Are you taking us back?' I say.

Natalie looks at Nail boy.

'You are, aren't you?' says Chicken Angel.

'You came out here so we wouldn't hear,' I say.

Chicken Angel nods.

Then Nail boy does something daftie, very daftie. He turns towards the water and hurls the mobile into the sea. As it climbs higher and higher it starts to ring. We all watch the tumbling ringing phone till it falls back into the water and splashes away.

'No one's going to send you back,' says Nail boy.

Natalie girl looks a bit moosed out. I think it was her phone and I think she wanted to send us back but Nail boy didn't and that's why he threw the phone into the sea. So he's not a leopard after all.

Nail looks at Natalie and smiles.

'Nail is going to look after us, save us. Hold us tight,' she says and she starts to smile too.

And everybody is smiling.

Then Nail boy says to Natalie girl: 'Hold you tight? What is that? Don't put me down for daddy. I've got a life to live.'

Chicken Angel and I look at each other. We don't know this 'daddy' thing. Later Chicken Angel said it is probably their word for hugging.

Back in the henhouse, that's what the Nail boy calls our new home by the sea, we eat and go back to bed.

The girl draws the curtain and says we are to have sweet dreams.

After a bit I whisper to Chicken Angel and she lets me cosy cosy to her. It is colder here than in the Bin and the air is stiffer. It is harder to breathe it in. Chicken Angel agrees.

*

257

Later I wake up. It is very bright. Not like in the Bin. Cough Cough is next to me because I can hear his wheezing. I turn and stroke his back. Then I feel little fingers stirring against my palm. Wings. Angel's wings. It's not Cough Cough. It is Chicken Angel. I remember then. We did cosy cosy. Cough Cough is goodbye.

I've never heard Chicken Angel wheezing before.
    That shows the air is harder here.

CHAPTER 22

Stupid Little Noddies

1

Nail stirred awake, his shoulder aching and stiff. He turned. Natalie was lying next to him on the floor.

'What?' He rubbed his eyes.

Natalie grunted, disturbed by Nail's movement, but she didn't wake.

What? Hadn't he agreed to have his foam mattress on the floor while she took the bunk with hers?

He sat up. It was bright.

A few hours ago she was slagging him off, now they were spooning. OK, so she'd apologized for calling him names and he'd apologized for hand-grenading her mobile. So they were square except she didn't know it was only the kids turning up that stopped him phoning Kenno.

He sat up and looked at her. Close to she wasn't quite so top of the range as he'd first thought. Her nose was just a little too pointed he judged and the front two teeth, which he could just see through her parted lips, bent slightly backwards. He hadn't noticed that before. And her fingers were a bit plumpy. But her skin was good enough, girly smooth with downy hairs, only visible to the close eye, running from the ear along the jaw bone and into the soft neck.

He wanted to touch her. Just one stroke. But he was scared of waking her. Then he laughed at himself. What had he boasted to that plookie Kenno? He would score, whenever. Pulling girls was picking cherries. Well, he had the pick now. So why wasn't he taking his chance? After all, just how many was he going to get?

He moved his hand over her shoulder.

She stirred and turned over. He pulled back as she opened her eyes.

'What time is it?' she said. 'And what's this?' She sat up and spread her hands out to indicate the mattress and the blanket and Nail.

'You were all over me,' he said.

She raised her eyebrows. 'Better check the kids.'

'Oh, forget the kids,' he said and took her hand, trying to draw her down to him.

She pulled away.

'Piss off, Nail. These are little innocents, remember. Just like me. Now, be a good boy and see if they're OK. Then who knows, maybe, one day.'

Nail got up. 'Come on, Nats, we need some fun now, while we got the chance. This isn't exactly yer standard day trip is it, ice cream and candy floss and donkey rides.'

He reached for the curtain separating the kids' sleeping area from their own.

Pulled it back.

260

Nail yelled.

Natalie shot up. 'What is it?'

'They've gone,' he said. 'They've done a bunk. Come on. We've got to find them.'

Natalie didn't move.

'Before something happens to them,' said Nail pointedly.

Natalie nodded at the window above the kids' bunk.

Drawn in the condensation was a picture of a boat. The sail was full. Under the hull ripples sped the craft along. Three small figures were sitting in the centre. Beside the flying boat stood two more figures waving.

'The Sky Boat,' Natalie breathed. 'It's beautiful.'

'It's mind-bending bonkers,' said Nail and dashed out.

2

He ran down to the water's edge. Natalie joined him.

Out in the loch, about two hundred metres from shore, was a small rowing boat. Three little figures sat in the middle. It didn't seem to be moving.

'Sod it,' said Nail. 'Sod it, sod it.'

Natalie waved. 'Come back, come back,' she shouted.

Suddenly the boat started rocking.

'You scared them,' said Nail. 'They'll capsize, the nutters. What the hell do they think they're doing?'

'Sailing the Sky Boat,' said Natalie. 'They think they're going to heaven.'

'If they don't stop rocking the thing the only place they're going is the bottom.'

'That's how they got so far,' said Natalie, 'because they haven't taken those.' She pointed at two oars floating in the water. 'Didn't know what they were, poor things.'

'It's one big mess this,' said Nail. 'Now what?'

'Now you have to get them back.'

'Me?'

'You.'

'Why?'

'Why you?'

'Yes.'

'Because they'll die otherwise and I can't swim.'

'Swim!'

'Swim!'

'Get lost, Nats.'

Minutes later Nail was breasting it through the icy waters, an oar spearing his way towards the swaying boat.

Natalie had watched him strip off right there, right in front of her without another word, watched him topple over the gravel and rocks at the loch edge then push into the glassy water unbreezed in the midday stillness.

She smiled.

He was wearing Tasmanian Devil underpants! Taz undies. Back at school she and her mate Bethany would have had a giggle about that. Hardman Nail wearing Disney devils. But now, as she watched his clumsy strokes, it seemed to her something, well, more warming than nerdy. It made him look vulnerable. Almost defenceless.

'Come on, Nail. Come on, Nail,' she breathed.

He looked so small in the vastness of the loch. If he'd have staggered out of the water at that point she'd have run to him, put her arms round him, warmed his shivering body, held him tight like you would a small child.

'Oh, Nail. Please, please don't drown.' An image of Nail's white body floating just below the surface flitted through her mind.

'Stupid little noddies,' she murmured.

He was nearly halfway there now. She could see his head jerking through the splash of his breaststroke, and his shoulders, his broad white shoulders, were surging and rising then falling then rising gain.

She wrapped her arms round herself and pressed her fists into her ribs as if to hold in the tension growing inside. She felt shivers run through her, surge almost, one moment cold one moment hot. It was as if her body had begun to synchronize with Nail's, with the heave of his stroke and the drive of his body through the water.

'Yes, yes,' she cried. 'Nearly there, nearly there.'

She found herself trembling. He must be so cold she thought.

Then she realized the boat was rocking. The kids were rocking the blessed boat. Just how stupid were they?

Didn't they realize Nail was trying to save them?

'Stop it. Stop it,' she shrieked.

Moments later her voice echoed back.

God she thought. What happens if Dearly and his Hyena Men hear that?

She leant down and picked up Nail's clothes: shirt, jeans, socks. She bundled them under her right arm and turned to the loch again.

3

Bit by bit, stroke by stroke, Nail was closing in on the boat.

Yes, yes Natalie said to herself. Go. Go.

Then something caught her eye. A bright flash. Something on the far side of the loch.

Sun on glass was it?

She squinted into the distance. Something was moving there. A vehicle of some kind.

A forestry worker? she wondered.

But that didn't seem right. Because it was moving fast, very fast. Someone was in a racing hurry.

Now it was bearing round to the right and coming straight along the shoreline towards her.

Even though it was still a long way away she could see dust puffing out from behind as it bounced along.

Then a chill of fear ran over her back.

She dashed back to the caravan telling herself please no, please no. Moments later she was back at the loch edge scanning the water with binoculars and fumbling with the focus.

Yes, Nail had reached the boat. Thank God she breathed.

Then she swept the glasses along the shoreline to her right.

'Don't let it be,' she whispered. 'Don't let it be. Not them.'

And then she found the vehicle. What a blur. She'd lost it. No there it was.

And then her heart stalled.

It was a green Land Rover.

The Hyena Men were back.

'Nail. Nail,' she shouted. 'Hurry. Hurry.'

But Nail was too busy sorting the kids.

'Look. Look. It's them. Come on. Get back. Quick.'

She shrieked and she shrieked.

And the echo repeated her panic, loud and mocking.

But still Nail didn't hear her.

She began picking up bits of stone and pebbles and hurling them into the loch hoping the splashes would get his attention.

And all the time she watched the Land Rover bouncing and clambering over the rough track beside the loch. She didn't need binoculars now to see the spotlights on the roof. It was the same vehicle that Dearly had used earlier to track them in the forest.

Then she saw one of the kids shaking Nail's arm and pointing across at the Hyena Men. Nail turned, hesitated and then grabbed the oar and started rowing furiously.

In front of him the kids formed a huddle and Natalie watched them duck each time he swung the oar over their heads, left then right, then left again, pulling strokes one side of the boat, then the other.

Slowly they zigzagged towards the shore.

Now that they'd seen the danger Natalie could run back to the caravan. She grabbed blankets, a couple of towels and van keys, slammed the door and dashed back to the water's edge.

Fifty metres to go.

'That's it, Nail. Come on. Come on. You can do it. You can do,' she shouted, leaping up and down.

Nail heaved and heaved.

Thirty metres.

She could see a figure leaning out of the back window of the Land Rover.

Twenty metres.

She splashed into the water, ready to grab the boat

Ten metres.

'Yes, yes, yes.'

Nail leapt out. 'I'll get the van,' he shouted. And he raced towards the edge of the forest.

Natalie pulled the boat in till it grated to a halt.

She leant over the side, reached for Lights Out and hauled her up. Chicken Angel was able to clamber out herself but X-Ray needed help. His hands were slippery with blood and to help him Natalie had to lift him out, hands under armpits, and stagger to the grass bank, trying all the time not to friction his skin.

Chicken Angel began dragging the bundle of blankets and clothes towards the van now racing towards them across the wide grass apron.

Natalie lifted Lights Out.

Nail braked and swivelled to a halt. He leapt out and wrenched open the back doors. He took the bundle of blankets, tossed them in the van and Chicken Angel struggled after. She spread out some blanket and Natalie lowered Lolo as gently and as quickly as she dared.

Chicken Angel stroked her face. 'Look, X-Ray's moosed out. Look.'

266

Natalie swung round.

X Ray was still lying exhausted on the loch bank.

'Come on. Get him in. Get him in,' bellowed Nail, rushing down to the water's edge.

He lifted him. 'Easy,' said Natalie. 'He's in a bad way.'

'Just tired. Tired,' the boy said, his head lolling against Nail's shoulder, blood crusted at the corners of his lips. 'You're all wet,' he murmured.

Nail shivered. 'Too right, kid.'

He staggered back to the van.

'Leopard. The leopard's coming, Nail boy,' whispered Lights Out as he laid X-Ray down.

'Bloody well is,' gasped Nail.

They slammed all doors and Nail hit the accelerator.

4

The van bucked forwards.

'STOP! STOP!'

It was the loud hailer again.

A giant voice calling through the tall firs.

'Get lost,' muttered Nail, his eyes fixed on a gap in the trees ahead.

Just beyond was the logging track. He knew any moment now the Land Rover could leap out from the loch road to their left and block the way. They just needed to get beyond that left turn.

*

They lurched on to the track.

'What happens if this is the road round the loch and we meet them head-on?' said Natalie.

'It isn't and we won't,' said Nail. 'Look.' He pointed ahead.

Natalie could see a fork in the road. The right-hand track turned on itself and seemed to slope downwards. The left hand rose steeply. This was the loch road, and blocking the way twenty metres from the junction was a large wooden gate.

Natalie laughed. 'Chained and padlocked,' she said.

'Yes?' said Nail.

Natalie nodded. 'Sure is.'

Nail slapped the steering wheel. 'That'll stop them.'

And as he spoke the Land Rover suddenly appeared skidding to a halt the other side of the gate.

'Yahooh,' roared Natalie as they shot past, turning down to the right and out of sight of the Hyena Men.

Minutes later she was urging Nail to pull over.

'What for?'

'Because you're dripping and you'll catch your death,' she said.

Nail grinned.

'It's not funny,' said Natalie. 'What if we get stopped?'

'Tough!'

'Well, I'm not riding with a half-naked person.'

'Oohh!' mocked Nail. 'What about a whole naked person?' He put his thumb inside the elastic top of his Taz trunks as if to lower them.

'Come on. Be serious. Stop. Get some clothes on. This isn't funny.'

'Oh, it is, Natalie girl. You, sitting there getting all eager, not knowing where to look.'

'In yer dreams.' She stared ahead, occasionally blinking when the low sun flashed them through a break in the trees.

Why did he have to be so . . . so . . . boy all the time she sighed to herself.

She'd side-glanced him as they'd slammed down the track away from the Land Rover. Yes, he did have touchable skin. And the thought of running her fingers across his chest made her throat tighten a little but . . . but, well, maybe he needed to grow out of kiddie kecks first. At least they weren't covered in Daffy Ducks.

And she was glad he wasn't pobby like some of the lads Bethany had fancied. She seemed to go for bouncy boys. And Beth liked chest hair. Chest hair! I ask you. How common was that?

Suddenly her thoughts were interrupted by a loud banging from the back of the van.

'Sort them, Nats,' said Nail. 'I need to get decent.'

When she opened the doors she found X-Ray asleep, head resting on Chicken Angel's lap, and Lights Out frantically morsing her.

'He's just tired,' she said.

'What's Lolo saying?'

'A leopard. Coming. Growling and growling. Mouth smoking.'

'It's OK. He's smoking because he's stuck, trapped. We're safe for now.'

But Lolo wasn't calmed. She morsed faster and faster.

'OK,' said Natalie. 'I'll tell Nail. Wrap her up. Use the blankets. Just in case it gets bouncy again.'

She closed the door and ran round to Nail.

'Everything OK?'

Natalie nodded. 'Lights Out says the leopard's coming, mouth smoking.'

'What does that mean, mouth smoking?'

Natalie shrugged. 'That's what the little one said.'

'Smoke?' Nail frowned. 'Exhaust fumes. Diesel maybe.'

CHAPTER 23

Doing Gently Gently

1

Natalie glanced in her wing mirror. 'Jeez, they're right behind us.'

Nail swore and slammed his foot down. The van leapt like a leopard.

'Must have crashed the gate,' he shouted.

'It's gaining, Nail. Hurry. Hurry. Smoke's pouring out of their engine.'

Nail shot a glance in his mirror.

A big grin spread over his face. 'Not smoke, Natalie baby. That's steam. The cretins must have punctured the radiator crashing the gate. Yeeess.'

'But they're still catching up,' said Natalie uneasily.

'Just got to hold them off for a while,' said Nail. 'They can't overtake us.'

'They could ram us,' said Natalie. 'I've seen a film where this lorry rammed this car. Sent it diving down a ravine.'

'You've seen too many films. They're probably free-wheeling now trying to save the engine from blowing. What we want is a hill, Nats. A climb, a steep one. Make

271

that engine work, make them blow a gasket, make them cylinders go boom.'

'They're right up close now. Oh God! Nail. We've had it. They'll kill us.'

Through the screaming of the engine and the rumble and thudding of tyres Natalie could hear the terrified moaning of the kids in the back.

'God help them. God help them,' she whispered.

Suddenly they went crashing through a stream crossing the track. Ahead of them the ground began to ascend. Nail rammed the van into third and roared up the incline.

'They're going to hit us,' cried Natalie.

The Land Rover was right on them revving and revving. Natalie could see a huge gash in its radiator. It looked like some one-eyed animal was charging and threatening to crush them.

'Faster, Nail, faster,' she shrieked.

Suddenly there was a dull thud from the back and the van lurched from one side then the other.

Natalie screamed. 'They've rammed us!' Her eyes were wide with terror.

'Bastards,' shouted Nail, desperately tugging at the steering, trying to counter the van's sudden tail wag.

'The kids are going to die. You've got to stop,' cried Natalie. 'It's not worth it.' She checked the mirror. 'Watch out, they're coming again.'

'Hold on.' Nail braced himself. The road was much steeper now and fell sharply away on either side. One more ram and the Hyena Men could have them off the road, over the edge and tumbling down the side.

Suddenly the track took a sharp left and Nail skidded the van round, tail spinning out of the turn, screeching gravel and dust.

The Range Rover couldn't make it and broad-sided in a flurry of stones and leaves. But it hardly stopped. The nose swung round, the vehicle lurched forward, engine furious, wheels spinning, as it careered back on track.

Natalie crouched down, watching in the mirror once more.

'They're coming again. Lots of smoke. You OK?'

Nail nodded, grim. 'I'm not giving up, Natalie. They tried to kill us back there. They didn't need to ram us. They could have just waited till we ran out of petrol or something.'

Natalie closed her eyes.

A sudden explosion from behind jerked her upright.

2

'They've blown up,' she cried. 'Look,' she said jabbing a finger at Nail's wing mirror.

Nail checked.

He just had time to glimpse three Hyena Men leaping out of the vehicle and steam geysering from either side of the engine compartment.

'Gotcha.' He slapped the dashboard.

Natalie leant back. 'No. Don't slow down yet.'

'It's OK. The Hyenas are going nowhere. They're

extinct. Deleted. They're out of it.' He grinned and eased up on the accelerator.

'Give it ten minutes,' said Natalie, 'to be sure. Put a couple of miles between them and us. After that we'll stop and check the kids.'

'I tell you that motor back there's scrap. Those guys are dead meat. I nailed them. Nailed them, Nats. Nailed them.' He heeled his hand into the centre of the steering wheel and set the horn blaring. 'Wheee.'

'Stop. Stop it,' shouted Natalie pulling at his arm. 'You'll frighten the kids. What's wrong with you?'

Nail let go the horn.

'No need to throw a fit.'

'Hey, come on,' said Nail. 'We could have died back there. But guess what – we survived. Did the biz.'

He eased the van down a steep turn and came to a stop.

'Can't be too careful with a crate of eggs,' he grinned. 'But did we leopardize those Hyenas? We did!'

He started to chant.

'We nailed them. We nailed them. We nailed them.'

Jeez thought Natalie, his voice suddenly grating on her. Why did he have to start yelling like some yobbo football fan? She could see why he was called Hard As. Thick As more like. 'Why don't you go back and van ram them all?' she said sarcastically. 'Really wipe them.'

'Oohh, listen to her,' said Nail.

Natalie fell silent. Why was she so pissed off with him all of a sudden? Hadn't he saved them from the Hyena Men, not once but twice? Yes, he had. She should be all over him now. So why was she wanting to give him such a hard time? Because . . . because she didn't want h-a-r-d.

That was it, yeah.

Not HARD.

She wanted SOFT. Why couldn't he do SOFT? Why couldn't he be called Ben or Sean or something? Anything would be better than Nail. He seemed so proud of the name. It wasn't exactly stars in your eyes. He might just as well be called spanner or boot. Boot would be good. She could see him putting it in. What she couldn't see him doing was mess, the soft and the squelchy, the bit in your life you couldn't really control, like blood and smell and dribble and puke breath and huddling and rubbery wings.

'I suppose it's the way you've been brought up,' she said suddenly as if making an excuse for him.

'What is?'

'This Hard As. This Nail thing.'

'What Nail thing? It's my name, isn't it?'

Natalie snorted.

'Where'd you get it from, a name like that?'

'What's wrong with it?'

'It's a bit DIY, that's all.'

'Well, Natalie isn't exactly five star.'

'At least it's a proper name. You'd never call a baby Nail, now would you? I baptize thee Nail. Come on. Natalie, yes, but Nail, no. I mean what did your mum and dad actually call you? What's on your birth certificate?'

Nail stared ahead. 'My real name's James,' he said slowly.

Natalie smiled. 'Really? James. Oh, I like James. That's what I call a real name.'

'Bond. James Bond,' said Nail grinning.

'Oh bog off,' said Natalie turning to face him.

Then she screamed.

3

Nail spun round. There at his window, mouthing mouthing, was the bloodied face of X-Ray.

He tapped on the window and disappeared round the back.

Natalie jumped out.

Nail saw a fingerprint of blood on the glass. He got out and started to walk, off the track and into the firs. 'No. No,' he kept saying to himself. 'No. No. No.'

In his mind he was standing behind an observation window looking at a tiny baby fed with tubes and drips slowly turning purple. Gradually he realized the baby's head was turning towards him, its eyes pleading.

But he couldn't help. He didn't know what to do.

In his panic he pushed against the glass so it wobbled and then his mother grabbed him, and took him away.

And the baby's face had X-Ray's eyes.

4

Natalie found him minutes later sitting on a fallen tree trunk head in hands.

'They're OK,' she said. 'I've cleaned them up again. But Lights Out doesn't look good.'

Nail said nothing.

'What's up?' she said.

No reply.

'OK. OK. It's my fault. I'm sorry about just now. I think what you did back there, I mean getting us away from those security people, was amazing, just amazing. Absolutely nailsome.'

She waited.

Nail looked up.

'Does that do it? I've apologized. Now it's over to you.'

Nail was puzzled.

'Jeez,' cried Natalie exasperated. All she wanted was for him to get up, put his arms round her and give her a hug. A big soft bear hug. She didn't know why but that's what she wanted. More than anything, in the whole of Scotland, the world, the universe.

Instead she got a real surprise.

'I saw the baby dying,' said Nail. 'He had that look in his eyes, like X-Ray has sometimes. Like the one with those wingy things has.'

'Chicken Angel,' said Natalie.

Nail nodded. 'Like X-Ray had just now when he looked through the window.'

'What baby?' said Natalie uneasily.

'The baby my mother took me to visit. I was five or six.'

'Her baby?'

Nail nodded.

'Your sister? Brother?'

'Brother.'

'And he died?'

Nail nodded. 'He went purple and I couldn't help him. I couldn't stop it.'

Natalie could see the tears in his eyes.

'He turned over and died.'

Natalie took Nail's hand. He drew it away. 'He bloody died, girl. And we did nothing. We used to visit the grave. Talk about closing the door. We took marmite sandwiches and my mum cried for a bit and then we went home on the bus. Then we stopped going and my father left and my mother gave up. Maybe she blamed me because I survived. That's what they say isn't it. The one surviving gets the blame.'

'So you feel bad about your brother and guilty.'

'No, it wasn't my fault, was it?'

'No. No, of course it wasn't but deep down you probably feel guilty. And that's what's making you . . . you . . .'

'What?' said Nail.

'Uhhmm. Hard maybe. Hard so you can control all the emotion. Hard because deep down in your heart of hearts you're blaming yourself and punishing yourself for letting your little brother die.'

Nail stared at Natalie, mouth open. 'How do you know all this?'

'Psychology is one of my GCSEs. And anyway women understand these sorts of things.'

'My mother didn't.'

'And that makes you angry and that's why you enjoy violence because it's a safety valve for all your anger and that's why you don't trust women. They frighten you because they might betray you and hurt you like your mother did.'

Nail shook his head and started to laugh.

'Frightened? Me?' he said. 'I'll show you frightened.'

He stood up, drew Natalie to him, put his arms round her and kissed her.

'Now,' he said, drawing away. 'How frightened was that?'

'I'm not sure,' said Natalie. 'Better try again.'

5

Chicken Angel and I are standing watching them.

'Are they fitting?' asks Chicken Angel holding on to my arm. I notice her voice is husky like it goes when you wake up after too much dozie and she is leaning on me like her legs are a bit watery.

Nail and Natalie are grabbing each other.

Chicken Angel grips me tighter. 'He's going to Hyena her,' she says, terrified.

Natalie girl goes very mouse, quiet as a book.

Nail boy does gently gently on her face.

She puts her arms round his neck.

They gently gently lips.

'Good picture,' says Chicken Angel. I put her arms round my neck and we gently gently lips as well.

Then we stop and Chicken Angel has my blood on her lips.

Nail boy and Natalie girl are still doing gently.

So we do some more too.

Then Nail boy sees us and comes over and says it's time to go.

So we all pee pee and get back in the wheelie.

I'm sitting in the front with Nail boy. The sun's behind us so it won't squeal me much.

I'm holding on to the sides of the seat.

The girl is in the back looking after Lights Out.

'Why did you run away?' I ask. 'Is it because you don't like blood? Doctor Dearly doesn't like blood. That's why he wears skin gloves.'

'Yeah, well, blood's not my favourite thing,' says Nail boy.

The van slows down suddenly because of an animal and I fall forwards and bang my head a bit.

The skin on the top of my face splits and blood comes out. Just a bit.

Nail boy wants to stop but I say no.

'Where's the eyes?' I ask.

Nail says, what eyes?

I say the wheelie's eyes. It must have eyes to see the animal and stop from killing and eating it.

Vans don't eat things he says.

One ate the princess I say.

Nail boy smiles.

I don't think he understands about princesses.

'Gently gently the wheelie,' I say to the Nail boy. 'Lights Out is . . .' I feel my eyes fill with tears. 'Lolo is . . . Lolo wants to ride on the Sky Boat.'

'She will,' he says. 'Trust me.'

'What's trust?' I say.

Nail boy says nothing.

'Don't you know?' I say.

'Course. It's what friends have. It doesn't let you down. Trust is when you don't tell lies.'

'What are lies?'

'You don't know what a lie is? Come on, kid. Everyone knows what a lie is.'

'Not me,' I say. 'We never had them in the Bin.'

'Don't kid yerself. The Bin is one great big lie. You were right in the middle of the biggest lie in Garvie Town. For all I know, the biggest lie in Scotland.'

'No one told us that,' I say.

'Well, that's the thing about lies. No one tells you. Lies always look all innocent. They never look like lies.'

'So,' I say, 'lies are bad?'

Nail boy nods. 'Double dearly bad, X-Ray. If you nick an apple and then say you didn't, that's lying, that is.'

'What's nick?' I say.

'Steal, lift, snatch, borrow. Got it?' he says sounding a bit like Doctor Dearly.

'What's steal?'

Nail groans. 'Were you born yesterday?' he asks.

I don't know when I was born. I shake my head. I know we were littles once.

'If a lie doesn't look like a lie, Nail boy, how do you know it's there in the first place?' I say to him.

Nail slaps the steering thing. He looks like Tin Lid when she gets annoyed and slaps the table in the day-room.

'You just do sometimes,' he says. 'Trust me, X-Ray. Not always. Some you see, some you can't. It's a matter of practice. If you tell a lot of lies you soon learn to see them around, I suppose.'

'So everybody tells lies to see if everyone else is telling them.'

'You know, you're a right pest, X-Ray. Did anyone ever tell you that? And I'm not lying.'

I cough up some chesty stuff, wind down the window and spit it out.

'You don't like us, do you, Nail boy?' I say.

'Yes, I do.'

'No. That's a lie. You call us retards. And Natalie says that's another one of those lie things. We are not retards. Or deletes like Tin Lid says.'

'What are you then?' he says.

'Kids like you and Natalie.' Then I say, 'You know, we didn't like you at first. Chicken Angel said you were like Doctor Dearly. Lights Out said no, you were pippi inside.'

Nail boy does another groan. The wheel thingie spins in his hands and we skid round a bend.

'Now you've saved us from the Hyena Men again we think Lights Out is right, you do have pippi inside. Now we like you.'

'You're only saying that because you want me to take you to the sea and the Sky Boat.'

'No.'

'Why?'

'Because that would be a lie.'

'Of course,' he says. 'Stupid me.'

We're jumping along under the trees like those daftie RODENTS we saw on *The Natural World* and I start to feel moosed. Next thing I know Nail boy is lifting me out and taking me round to the back of the van. He lays me down on a blanket and I hear him talking to Natalie girl.

I don't think they know how to get to the sea.

Lights Out knows. She can smell it. But she's dozied out. In deep moose-time.

6

Natalie was looking through the windscreen at the black spars of the fir branches. Ship's rigging, she was thinking.

She pressed her fingers softly to her lips.

'I liked that kissing, that gently gently,' she said quietly to Nail. 'Did you?'

He did. Yes, he definitely liked doing gently gently. Lips, yes. Hands, yes. And elsewhere? Everywhere? Yes, yes, yes.

Natalie gave him a look.

She could see what he was thinking.

'No way,' she said aloud.

But there was maybe in her mind.

'What?' said Nail all innocent. 'I was only wondering! Not asking.'

He had more than maybe in mind.

Then it struck him. They were motoring through Scotland and he hadn't a clue where they were going. 'We need a map,' he said.

'Oh,' said Natalie a little disappointed. He seemed in a hurry to change the subject. But he was right of course.

Why hadn't they thought of that before? Too much Hyena and Dearly and sick kids and jumping the jaws of dogs for starters.

'We could be going in any direction,' she said. 'Back to Bin Linnie even. We've been up and down round and round. And . . . and we've hardly had any sleep.' Suddenly a night in a warm bed back at her aunt's felt worth turning round for.

'Yeah,' said Nail. 'If we don't make the coast soon the Sky Boat will have gone without us.'

'Didn't that Murdoe warden guy say something about a Visitor Centre?'

Nail grunted. 'We're in the middle of nowhere at all.'

Suddenly he braked.

'What's up?'

Nail nodded ahead.

CHAPTER 24

Blackmail

1

Across the road was a gate. Parked on the far side was a green Land Rover. Standing beside the vehicle watching their approach was a man.

'Go back. Go back,' shouted Natalie.

Nail stopped.

She looked at him. 'Well, what are you waiting for? It's them, isn't it?'

Nail shook his head. 'No. It says Forestry Commission on the door. The guy's a warden.'

Natalie swallowed hard. 'He's coming over.'

Nail wound his window down.

The warden said nothing. He glanced at Natalie then walked round the van and returned to stand beside the driver's window.

'You're trespassing, laddie. This is forestry land. No public right of way.' He leant closer peering in, scanning the interior and frowning at Natalie.

'We were just going to the sea,' she said weakly.

'And got lost,' added Nail.

The warden stood up.

'Where you from?'

'Garvie.'

'Funny way to go to the sea. Took the scenic route, did you?'

Nail nodded slowly. He knew the warden was after something.

'Thought you'd see a bit of nature?'

Neither Nail nor Natalie answered.

'See any deer?' the warden said casually.

'Saw a heron,' said Natalie.

'Look, let's stop beating about the bush.' The warden's expression hardened. 'We get townies like you up here without a clue, after deer.'

Nail raised his hands. 'Not us.'

'I can report you to the police, you understand that don't you? Now, mind if I see what you got in the back, just to be sure?'

'Sure?'

'Sure you're not lying.'

Nail looked at Natalie.

'We've a right to search suspected vehicles.'

'Suspected?' said Nail. 'Suspected of what?'

'Poaching! Now please, the keys.'

'It's not locked. There's nothing in there. It's only –'

Suddenly a loud ringing interrupted him.

Maiden gobby China again thought Nail. Every time.

'What's that?'

By now Natalie was out. 'It's the kids,' she said.

'You got kids in there?'

'We're taking them on holiday. To the seaside for the day.'

'For the day? It's nearly four in the afternoon.'

Just then they heard the back door of the van open. The warden stepped back and Nail got out.

2

From round the back of Nail's wheelie bin a small figure appeared. It was X-Ray, his lips and chin smeared with blood.

'Oh, my God!' said the warden. 'What's wrong with him?'

'Nothing,' said X-Ray. 'I've got this special skin. Doctor Dearly says it's photosensitive. It's very thin. I'm not allowed to go out in daylight.'

'But why's he bleeding?' the warden whispered to Nail. 'Why's he no hair?'

'Ask him,' said Nail.

The warden bent down face to face with X-Ray and noticed the scabbing on the kid's head and the wormy veins running under the shiny skin.

'No need to be afraid, kid, I'm a forest warden.'

'A Hyena?'

'No.' He looked up at Nail.

'It's just a word he uses,' said Nail. He turned to X-Ray. 'It's OK. He's one of us.'

'Now where are they taking you?' said the warden.

'To find the Sky Boat.'

The warden looked at Nail again.

Nail threw up his hands.

'Is it one of these rides you get in a fun fair?' said the warden to Nail.

X-Ray looked puzzled.

'He doesn't know what fun fairs are,' said Natalie joining them.

'It takes us to heaven,' said X-Ray.

'We're all family,' said Natalie. 'This is my little brother's birthday and it was going to be a special treat, going to the sea. He doesn't get out much because of the sun. And now it's all ruined.'

Nail looked at her. Was this another Oscar coming on?

The warden turned to X-Ray. 'Is this true? This your big sister? Is he your brother?'

Say yes. Say yes. Say yes thought Nail. It's just a little lie.

X-Ray licked his lips and slowly nodded. 'Yes, but the Hyenas in the big wheelie tried to hit us and we all went bang bang and I started bleeding and Lights Out cried and Chicken Angel and I cosy cosied.'

Just then a phone rang in the warden's vehicle and he ran to take the call.

Natalie turned to X-Ray. 'Well done, kiddo,' she said hugging him. He pulled away. 'Sorry, I forgot. Your skin. Sorry. Sorry.' She took out a tissue and wiped his lips.

X-Ray looked up at Nail. 'That was a lie, wasn't it?' he said. 'About me being your brother.'

Nail smiled. 'Put it this way, X-Ray, it wasn't your lie, it was Natalie's. Let's say you just borrowed it. And it means we can now go and find the Sky Boat. No wardens. No Hyenas. Get that.'

'It was still a lie. And I've never told a lie before.'

Just then the warden came back.

'That was a call from my colleague. He's bringing some people in. Their vehicle's broken down. Punctured radiator, blown gasket. Forced off the road they said.' He stared at Nail. 'Were you involved in this in anyway?'

Nail shook his head. But he was thinking fast. The Hyena Men again! They needed to get out.

'It's just with your little brother saying that stuff about a big thingy trying to hit you and going bang bang,' said the warden.

'He's got a great imagination,' said Natalie hurriedly. She too realized that the Hyenas were coming. 'He tells stories all the time.'

The warden waited a moment. 'Well, just to be sure we'll wait till they get back here and then we can clear it all up, eh?'

Natalie let out an involuntary gasp.

Nail swallowed hard. Get the Hyena pack back on the scene and they were dead meat.

'And someone's broken into the caravan up by Loch Inchie. And that's nothing to do with you either, I suppose?' There was an unmistakable edge in the warden's voice now.

Nail thought quickly. The caravan reminded him of Murdoe. Did he say he was Chief Ranger? Maybe he could help.

'Yes,' he said. 'Chief Ranger Mr Murdoe said we could use it for the kids to rest up.'

'Mr Murdoe said that. You know the Chief Ranger?'

Nail nodded. 'Phone him, check it out.'

'I will.'

The warden went back to his vehicle.

Hurry, hurry said Nail to himself.

'We'll never make it now,' said Natalie. 'They could be here any minute.' She looked back up the log track.

No sign yet though.

Nail watched the warden talking into his phone.

'Come on. Come on.'

Eventually he returned.

'Well?' said Natalie. 'Please, please, the little boy's really sick now.'

'He says you're just about the stupidest kids he's ever met. And to get shot of you ASAP.'

Natalie beamed. Stupidest! That's just what they needed.

The warden opened the gate. 'Here, take this map. It's a mite tatty but it'll get you to the sky boat, whatever it is. Main A259's best.'

Nail nodded. 'Thanks. It's the A259 then.'

'And your tax is out of date,' the warden shouted after them.

3

Natalie was clapping and singing to herself. 'We're off to the sea. We're off to the sea.'

Nail stayed silent.

He was thinking about X-Ray. No matter how much he tried to push them aside he couldn't forget his words. I've never told a lie before he'd said. His voice sounded so hollow. And the look of emptiness and sadness on his face. Wow, he didn't need that. So, what was one little lie? he told himself. Hardly a visible grain in the world's daily accumulation of deceit. And strictly speaking it wasn't really a lie. X-Ray was a kind of brother, now. And also it was more of a story than a lie. And they only said that stuff about family to get them to the Sky Boat and away from the Hyena Men. So what had the little kid to complain about? It wasn't like a cover-up because they'd nicked some stuff.

And so on and so on. But it didn't make X-Ray go away. Instead Nail had to drive with the accusation drumming in his head – I've never told a lie before, I've never told a lie before.

Then Natalie suggested they stop. Nail to check the map, she to check the kids.

He pulled into a rest area.

He opened the map and found Loch Inchie. He slid his finger along the track, round past the turning where the Hyena Men gate crashed and down to McKinnon Wood where a small image of a picnic table marked the site where they were parked.

They were closer to the sea than he thought.

Then Natalie reappeared. 'You'd better come and look at this,' she said.

Nail joined her at the back of the van. The doors were open. Chicken Angel and X-Ray were kneeling either side of Lights Out.

4

Lolo's heart is ticking faintly. She smiles.

We kneel next to her. I hold one hand, Chicken Angel holds the other. Maiden China is ticking too.

Lights Out morses Chicken Angel. Tell me a story she says. Tell me about how Jack the Cat caught the Sky Boat.

Chicken Angel smiles.

'One day,' she says, 'Jack the Cat was out walking by the sea looking for fallen stars . . .'

Lights Out is already asleep.

I can see a lumpy on her neck now.

Nail boy and the girl are watching us.

'What's that?' Nail boy says.

Natalie girl leans in and gently rolls up Lolo's sleeve. Nail boy does a dearly.

'It's what they call a lumpy,' says Natalie girl.

'She's covered in them,' says Nail boy. 'What is it?'

Natalie girl draws him away. She turns to us and says to get some sleep. Soon we'll be at the sea.

She closes the door. Outside I can hear them talking.

5

'Lumpy?' said Nail. 'What the hell is it?'

Natalie shrugged. 'It's something that happens to them. They go lumpy and die.'

'Die! You just pop out all over and then die? I don't believe how matter of fact you can be, Nats. You're like, tomorrow it's going to rain. This is IT we're talking about. Big D.'

'They don't see it like that, Nail. They're off in the Sky Boat, star spray forever. Day trip to heaven. Single only. It's us down here have the hard time.'

. 'That Sky Boat stuff is nothing but candy floss, Natalie. The last big lie. Nats, listen to me. They'll throw the book at us for this. This is abduction, assault, the lot. We'll be banged up for life.'

'Like them you mean!'

Nail snorted.

'Now shush,' said Natalie. 'Or they'll hear us.' She drew Nail away from the van and they sat at a nearby picnic table.

'A kid dying,' said Nail. 'Look, now we really should try getting her to hospital. And the others too. They all look like they need some treatment. Wheezing and wheezing. Have you noticed that? How they wheeze and cough and spit now?'

Natalie nodded. She'd talked to the kids in the van while Nail drove to the loch. They weren't scared or anything. They just didn't want to be bagged up and dumped down an incinerator. They wanted to go on a ride instead.

'So these lumpy things are just swellings?' said Nail.

Natalie nodded. 'They get them all over. That's what Chicken Angel says. They last about twenty-four, forty-eight hours maybe and then . . . it's takeaway. That's their word for . . .'

'Yeah, yeah. I know. I know.'

'Once, there were lots of these kids in the Bin,' said Natalie. 'They all got lumpy. These three are the last.'

'They might have a chance in a hospital.'

'Well, the Bin's a hospital. A specialist unit. They've got nurses and stuff. They still died.'

'I say we take them to hospital. I don't want them on my conscience, Nats. Do you?'

Natalie sighed. Lolo might die but the other two didn't deserve to be back in moose-time dozied up to the eyeballs.

Neither of them spoke for a bit. Nail tried to imagine the look on X-Ray's face as they opened the door and he saw a siding of ambulances and trolleys instead of the Sky Boat. It didn't bear thinking about – those hurt eyes turned on him accusing, accusing. But what else could they do? They couldn't let them just . . . die without trying something.

'OK, here's what we do,' he said suddenly. 'We get to the main road and we take the Garvie turn. The kids won't notice. They're asleep. We go straight to the hospital. The kids get treatment and we're off the hook. We'll work out some story about how they came to be in the back of a van. Then –'

'No,' said a voice behind.

They swung round.

Standing a few metres away was X-Ray and leaning on his shoulder was Chicken Angel.

Well, are they psychic or what, Nail was thinking.

Natalie stepped towards them.

X-Ray put his hand to his mouth.

'It's for the best,' she said. 'We'd love to take you to the sea but –'

'We're not going to hospital,' Chicken Angel interrupted. 'We don't need medication.'

'We've got some pills,' said X-Ray.

'Why didn't you say?' said Natalie.

He opened his hand. She could see he was holding dozens of small green capsules. 'Cough Cough gave them to us,' said Chicken Angel.

'It's special dozie dozie,' said X-Ray very slowly.

'We could swallow them all,' said Chicken Angel. 'Easily.'

Nail and Natalie stared at the two kids. Slowly it dawned on them.

'You mean, if we don't take you to the Sky Boat you'll . . .'

The two kids nodded.

'Here's what we'll do,' said X-Ray. 'Chicken Angel goes in the front. Natalie girl with us in the back.'

'Stupid noddies,' muttered Nail. 'They don't trust us. After all we've done.'

Natalie smiled ruefully. 'So much for morality,' she said.

'Give me a good down-to-earth liar any day. At least you know where you are with them,' said Nail. 'Well, choice over, decision made. And when the police catch up with us just tell the truth – it wasn't us stopping you getting to hospital, right?'

'Police?' said Chicken Angel.

Nail waved his hands. 'Don't ask. Just don't ask!'

Then he looked directly at X-Ray. 'This is called blackmail.'

'What's that?' said Chicken Angel.

'It's worse than lying, that's for sure. Now get in and let's go before any Hyenas find us.'

Some time later they had passed out of forest and into high moorland travelling along a narrow winding hilltop road.

From the back of the van Nail was aware of a quiet singing, sometimes it fell to a low humming, other times it rose into a gentle lullabying.

He tried to catch the words. It was folky stuff.

> Speed bonny boat
> like a bird on the wing
> over the sea to Skye . . .

Well, they'd got the wrong boat. It was the bonny east coast for them.

CHAPTER 25

No More Lies, Little Brother

1

The blonde girl at his side wasn't saying very much.

He'd tried to get her to follow the map but she hadn't got a clue.

'Maps show you roads and how to get to where you want to go,' explained Nail.

Was there a map to get you to the moon? asked Chicken Angel.

No said Nail.

A map to get you to the stars?

No.

How big was the Sky Boat?

Dunno.

Was it on the map?

Nail shook his head.

'How will you find it then?'

Nail hadn't a clue. He left that sort of thing to dafties and people like Natalie. She could answer that one.

And when she asked him where the jungle was he gave up altogether. He just didn't have the geography for it.

'This is Scotland, sweetie. Now get some sleep.'

'We need dozie for that. We're saving them just in case.'

Nail raised his eyebrows. Just in case? he said to himself. He guessed what that meant.

'How long have you been in the Bin?' he asked.

'We don't know. Mrs Murdoe said we used to be grubs and then we went wrong and then we went to the Bin.'

'Went wrong?' said Nail.

'That's why the nurses used to call us spookies. We spooked them. Doctor Dearly said that was wrong. He didn't like that. He said we had to be called Geminis. Mrs Murdoe said that was because we came in twos. Somewhere she said there was another Chicken Angel. My sister.' The girl took a deep breath. 'Lights Out is my sister really.'

Nail said nothing.

'There were lots of us in the Bin,' Chicken Angel continued. 'Lots till they all went takeaway.' She turned to Nail. 'Will you go takeaway?'

'Yeah,' said Nail slowly. 'Everybody does, eventually.'

'It's not just Geminis, then?'

'No.'

'And will you get the Sky Boat as well?'

Not if I can help it thought Nail. With a bit of luck, I'll get the free-booze ferry.

He nodded.

'Then we'll meet again,' said Chicken Angel brightening.

To Nail's relief she suddenly changed the conversation. 'X-Ray says you're not as bad as you look.'

'He's a one to talk. What's wrong with the way I look?'

'You got spots on your face.'

'Those spots are what we call freckles.'

'Leopards have freckles. We thought you were a leopard at first. We thought you were going to eat us. We thought you were going to eat Natalie.'

Eat her? No, just having a nibble now thought Nail. Main course later.

The girl fell silent. She pulled at her tracksuit top. 'It's getting cold.' After a moment she said very quietly, 'Will you look after X-Ray after I've gone takeaway?'

'You're not going takeaway,' said Nail alarmed.

Chicken Angel smiled.

'It doesn't squeal,' she said. 'It's not like having hypo and hard trank. We just lie in the Sky Boat and it takes us away.'

Nail breathed in hard.

'Will you?'

'Uhhmm?'

'Look after X-Ray?'

Nail nodded. 'But it won't come to . . .'

He stopped. Chicken Angel had her arm stretched out and was rolling up the sleeve of her grey top.

The skin was covered in lumpies.

Nail put his foot down.

2

As they entered the dunes down a sandy trail sprouting with marram grass Nail noticed a building with a sloping wooden roof a little way ahead.

They pulled up outside.

What stood before them was an all-wood circular structure with a conical roof thatched with fir branches and decorated all over with shells and cones.

'What is it?' said Nail. 'A shelter?'

Natalie read the notice outside. 'St Otald's Dune Chapel.'

'Who's Otald?'

But Natalie was looking inside.

There was no door so she stepped through the opening into the gloomy interior. The others followed, Nail and X-Ray and Chicken Angel.

Wooden benches covered half the floor and in the far wall a small stained-glass window glowed faintly in the little light of the moon, displaying in greens and yellows the image of a woman with stars round her bowed head. She was holding a baby.

'It's Mary, the Madonna,' whispered Natalie. 'There's one like that in our chapel. At school.' She looked around. 'We could all sleep in here for a while,' she said. 'It could be warmer than the van. Lights Out will be better in here too.'

They brought the blankets and made makeshift beds.

Natalie carried Lights Out.

Kneeling, she and Nail laid her down gently.

A slow smile lit up her face.

Holding Nail's arm she pulled herself upright and pointed at the stained-glass Madonna.

Then she began morsing on his palm.

'It tickles,' he said. 'What's she saying?'

Chicken Angel took Lolo's hand. Lights Out started again.

'It's Maiden China, she says. She says she's free at last. The witch is dead. Now she can fly away.'

'That's daftie,' whispered X-Ray. 'It's not Maiden China. Can't be. She's got a pippi in her arms.'

Natalie put a finger on his lips to shush him.

Chicken Angel turned to Nail. 'She says you saved Maiden China from the witch. You set her free. Now she's shining on us and saying thank you.'

Lights Out turned to Nail. She touched his face. Then slowly she raised herself and leant against him.

He stiffened.

She put her hands round his neck.

He could feel the dry papery cheek, the warty skin of her arms.

She kissed him.

Then she slid slowly down his chest.

No one spoke.

Natalie bent over her and lifted her like you would a sleeping child. She held her in her arms slowly rocking her. 'Shussh,' she crooned. 'Shussh little baby.'

Then she laid her on one of the blankets.

Chicken Angel came over to where Nail was sitting and handed him a notebook.

Nail looked puzzled.

'Her diary,' explained Natalie, getting up. 'She's letting you read it.'

'She's never let anyone do that before,' said X-Ray.

Chicken Angel shook her head. 'I want you to have it.'

'But it's your special book,' said Natalie.

Chicken Angel hadn't taken her eye off Nail.

'It's for you. You've got to have it. It's about the Bin. All of it. About the Geminis and everything. I won't be needing it now.'

Nail nodded.

Natalie nudged him.

'Say thank you.'

'Thanks.'

Chicken Angel and X-Ray went to lie on a blanket.

3

Nail looked over at the still huddle of Lights Out.

'She . . .? You know what?' said Nail as Natalie knelt beside him. He could see her hair hanging down silhouetted in the faint light of the chapel doorway.

Natalie said nothing. Instead she curled up against Nail.

He tucked the diary under the blanket.

Poor little kid!

Then he noticed X-Ray wasn't asleep. He was looking at him, his eyes large and bright. He was shivering.

Nail got up, lay down next to him, drew him to his chest and closed his arms round the thin body. Gradually the shivering stopped.

'Go to sleep, little brother,' he whispered.

'No more lies, Nail boy?'

'No more lies,' said Nail.

'Tomorrow we find the Sky Boat.'

'Tomorrow we find the Sky Boat.'

'For Lolo.'

'For Lolo.'

Silence.

Now thought Nail, where the hell was he going to find a Sky Boat? Surely they weren't expecting to go out on the sea.

He could feel the little kid quietly wheezing and relaxing into sleep.

He got up carefully, took his blanket and draped it in a double layer over X-Ray.

Then he bent down and kissed the child's head.

It smelt of puke.

I just hope we find the freaky thing said Nail to himself.

4

Carefully Chicken Angel bends over Nail boy.

He's snoring a bit and has his arm round Natalie girl.

We wrap Lolo in a blanket. We don't want her to get cold in the sea.

Chicken Angel keeps stroking her hair.

I kiss her forehead.

Chicken Angel morses her. 'Goodbye, little sister,' she says.

We lift her together.

Carefully we edge out so we don't wake Nail boy and Natalie girl.

*

Chicken Angel says she knows where the Sky Boat is.

I know her secret.

When we did cosy cosy last night I felt things on her. Not her wings. I know how they feel, soft and squeezy. Not her mammaries either. These were hard and all over.

These were lumpies.

I know.

I've got them as well.

Just the two.

On my arm.

It won't be long now.

Not to worry said Mrs Murdoe, Jesus will be waiting for you.

As we leave Chicken Angel picks up a fir stick. It's fallen from the roof. She pulls off the side shoots.

'For the pictures,' she says.

5

The early sun strays through the doorway and stretches like bright gold cloth along the floor, over the sleeping forms of Natalie and Nail and up to the smooth wooden wall, where it hangs, a gleaming drapery.

Outside gulls wail and a breeze sings through the marram.

The tide is coming in. The sea is boisterous and even far out the waves are fringed with white.

The tide is coming in.

Over the unblemished sand it pushes irresistibly.

Natalie is the first to wake.

She edges out of Nail's slack hold and sits up.

The Madonna glints.

They are the only ones in the chapel.

The kids!

Natalie gets up.

Runs out. Checks the van.

They're gone.

The sea rolls in imperturbably.

She looks across the beach. Searches the tumble of rock to the west, follows the line all the way to end, to the very last boulder, which as she looks is slowly sliding under the swirling green waters.

She scans the beds of rock to the west, backwards and forwards over the pools and the floating bladderwrack, over the rubble of pebble and scree and to the far arm of land hugging the bay. Nowhere can she see the three children.

7

'What's up, Nats? Where are the kids?' says Nail, stumbling out of the chapel.

Natalie shakes her head. 'Gone,' she says, her voice hollow as the wind. 'Can't see them on the beach.'

'They must be in the dunes.'

Nail climbs to the top of the nearest hillock and looks all round.

Suddenly he stops, peers towards the beach and shouts. 'Something down there.'

They race through the last of the dune paths and stop at a line of broken shells and dried bladderwrack.

Ahead of them, where the white sand is wet, two lines of footprints are leading all the way across the beach towards the sea.

'Why's there only two?' asks Natalie. But she knows the answer.

They follow the tracks almost to the sea's riffled edge; to where sketched in the sand is the picture of an animal. It has terrible eyes. Its body is covered in spots.

'It's the leopard,' says Natalie.

Resting on the drawing as if crushing the back is a round stone.

'They've killed it. The little monkeys have killed the leopard,' says Natalie quietly.

Nail tries to puzzle this out but gives up.

He is staring at the wave ripples already erasing the tip of the leopard's long tail.

8

The footprints disappear into the sea.

Of the children there is no sign whatsoever.

'They can't have just walked in and . . .' says Natalie horrified.

Nail too can't believe the kids would just walk into the sea and drown. 'Maybe they thought they were fishes,' he says. 'They're daftie enough.'

Nail has drawn this picture in his head – kids wriggling into scaly silver bodies and gliding freely back into the ocean – because he knows another terrible picture is lurking there and he doesn't want that surfacing in his head.

Natalie has walked into the sea and the water is swilling into her trainers.

'Lolo.' She wails and cries the name. 'Poor Lolo.'

Nail is looking at the tumble of rock to his left.

'I know what's happened,' he cries. 'I bet they've gone round to the next bay when the tide was out.'

Natalie turns.

Without a word they race to the rocks and begin scrambling up.

Nail hauls Natalie over the topmost boulder.

The bay below is small, the sand is salt-white.

CHAPTER 26

The Sky Boat

1

What they see astonishes and terrifies them.

Drawn in the sand below is the shape of an open boat. It has a sail that looks like it's billowing in the wind. And benches. It seems to be pulling at an anchor firmly bedded in the sand.

They can see, drawn in the bottom of the boat, stacks of boxes and sacks. And a parrot and two monkeys sit in the stern. The sides of the boat are decorated with bunches of something. They look like flowers trailing in rippling water.

In the bow, on a triangle of raised decking, lies a small bundle wrapped in a white blanket.

'Lolo,' gasps Natalie.

Two oars lie across the sides of the boat ready for rowing.

Drawn in the sand all around are giant stars twinkling.

'The Sky Boat,' whispers Nail.

2

Beside the boat, looking out to sea, stand two small still figures.

'Chicken Angel and X-Ray,' says Nail.

Chicken Angel is leaning on X-Ray.

Their trousers are rolled up.

3

Suddenly from beyond the dunes they hear the chug chug of a helicopter.

It comes swinging into view.

As it does so, sirens sound in the dunes.

The chopper seems to hang in mid-air.

Police are running across St Otald's beach.

4

Chicken Angel and X-Ray have got into the boat and are sitting on the central bench.

The oars seem to rest in their laps.

They look far too frail for oars that size.

5

X-Ray looks up, slowly.

Can he see them?

Natalie waves.

<h1 style="text-align:center">6</h1>

X-Ray just stares.
Chicken Angel's hair rises in the breeze.
X-Ray turns, puts his arm round her shoulders.
Her head lolls on his chest.
There they sit.
Neither of them moving.

<h1 style="text-align:center">7</h1>

The first policeman arrives. Looks down, turns to Nail.
'Did you call us?'
Natalie shakes her head.
'What's this?' The policeman points below.
'The Sky Boat,' she says.
'Yeah, and that helicopter was Batman? Not funny, miss.'
'It is the Sky Boat.'
The ambulance men are at the bottom of the rocks.
'Up here,' shouts the policeman. 'It's just kids playing silly beggars. In the sand.'

<h1 style="text-align:center">8</h1>

Natalie and Nail have to climb back down.
A policeman walks them to the dunes.

Halfway there Natalie stops. Her hand closes over her mouth.

'Nail, look, look.'
She points to a drawing in the sand.

9

There are two figures, a girl and a boy.
  In the blazing white.
  Each has been given angel wings.

They are holding hands.